Before I
Knew
Him

Anna Ralph was born in Thornaby-on-Tees in 1974. She worked as a bookseller, in public relations and in journalism before writing full-time. *Before I Knew Him* is her second novel. Her first, *The Floating Island*, won a Betty Trask Award in 2008. She lives in Durham.

Praise for Anna Ralph

'Compassionate and beautifully written'
Woman & Home

'A remarkably well crafted book . . . Through an assortment of well drawn characters, the author displays her considerable knowledge of human nature and her sensitive insight into the human condition'
Living North

'Strongly evocative of childhood . . . Ralph draws wholly believable characters, tackling some painfully honest situations . . . This new novel adds to the reputation earned with her first work'
Journal (Newcastle Upon Tyne)

Also by Anna Ralph

The Floating Island

Before I Knew Him

Anna Ralph

arrow books

Published by Arrow in 2009

1 3 5 7 9 10 8 6 4 2

First published in Great Britain in 2008 by Hutchinson
The Random House Group Limited
20 Vauxhall Bridge Road, London SW1V 2SA

www.rbooks.co.uk

Addresses for companies within The Random House Group Limited
can be found at: www.randomhouse.co.uk/offices.htm

The Random House Group Limited Reg. No. 954009

A CIP catalogue record for this book
is available from the British Library

ISBN 9780099505365

The Random House Group Limited supports The Forest Stewardship
Council (FSC), the leading international forest certification organisation.
All our titles that are printed on Greenpeace approved FSC certified
paper carry the FSC logo. Our paper procurement policy can be found at:
www.rbooks.co.uk/environment

Typeset by Palimpsest Book Production Limited,
Grangemouth, Stirlingshire

Printed in the UK by CPI Bookmarque, Croydon, CR0 4TD

For Dad, with much love

1

Before I knew him, when he was still just a collection of movements and mannerisms I observed from a distance, when he had no history, no future I could guess, that is the time I'd have back. Then, he was a boy, like me, though nothing like me. Perhaps it was that, the difference, which drew me to him. But something else, too, more powerful, like the pull of the tide that sucks pebbles back to the sea.

I raised the collar of my jacket and walked the half-mile or so to the train station where we'd agreed to meet. The forecast had promised snow, but it felt too cold. A few lazy flakes tried their luck, shivering on the air before giving up.

Eight years.

Would I even recognise him? It would've made

more sense to wait for him at the flat, but he'd asked to be met. I'd thought we'd go straight down to one of the pubs on North Road then, but now I realised how impossible that would be; most of what he might want to talk about couldn't be mentioned in a bar. One quick drink perhaps, then home.

I passed underneath the arches of the viaduct and headed towards the steep, narrow road that leads to the station. Durham was bracing itself for Thursday night, pay day, and although the town didn't have the hectic quality of a weekend, the pubs would be filling up. Ahead of me, two girls teetered across the icy pavement on high heels, the one on the right with a skirt so tight it showed the cleft in her arse. Further on, a group of men, bare-armed in spite of the weather, caught sight of them and jeered, that braying laugh that tries to hide lust and always fails.

A few minutes later, breathless from the climb, I reached the northbound platform as a train was pulling out. His wasn't due yet, but all the same I scanned the face of every man who passed, trying to summon an image that worked. No use. My memories were too varied, too confused. I'd nothing to build on. I'd written to him a few times, care of his aunt's address, and he'd replied, once. He'd joined the army and was happier than he'd ever been. I still had that letter. Not that I hadn't for days, weeks, sometimes months at a time, been able to forget, but there'd always been something to draw me back: a voice, a smell, the shape of his head and shoulders vanishing into a crowd. Not him, of course.

And then, from nowhere, contact. He'd written to tell me he was coming to Durham, no more than a few lines, the date he'd be arriving and the time of his train. I'd sat with his letter in my hands for hours, stared at his handwriting until the words blurred in front of me. What did he want? Why now? Perhaps it was nothing more than curiosity; a moment of wondering he'd felt compelled to act on, posted the letter and then forgotten it. But if he didn't show . . .

I'd been waiting for him; I'd not realised it fully until now, but yes, I had been waiting. And not for a few days – years.

The station emptied and soon it was quiet except for the clock that clicked from second to second and the constant drip-drip of water from the roof. I thrust my hands deep in my pockets and set off along the platform. In the distance, a light blistered the dark, not moving apparently, until the grumble of the engine made itself heard and the line began to whistle. I positioned myself close to the exit as the train roared in, clacketing past, almost as if it might go straight through without stopping, but then, gradually, it came to a halt on a flush of warm air. The doors opened and the platform filled again with passengers. Doors releasing, hurried footsteps. A man with a briefcase, another man, too old, three girls laughing—

'Leo?'

On my right. I'd been looking the wrong way. I smiled, unsure, but yes, it could be . . . had to be.

'It *is* you,' he said. 'I thought it must be—'

'David.'

A moment's hesitation and he pulled my out-stretched hand into an embrace, his left palm cupping my elbow first, then moving up to my shoulder. I could smell beer on his breath. It made me feel better somehow, knowing he'd downed a few on the train before seeing me. I grazed his cheek, which, like his scalp, was peppered with dark stubble.

'Look at you,' he said. 'You used to wear glasses, didn't you?'

'Contacts now.'

He laughed, the warmth of it both familiar and strange, like waking from a half-remembered dream. He looked older than his – what would it be? Twenty-four years?

'The weather . . .' I said. 'I thought you might be late.'

'No, it was OK.'

'We could get a drink?'

'Don't mind.'

He was flushed, his words slightly slurred. We moved towards the exit, but it was blocked by passengers waiting for taxis and by the time we struggled through I'd forgotten all the things I'd planned to say. There was wine at the flat, a bottle of brandy. No cans, though. A pub would be too noisy to talk about anything that mattered, but desperate as I'd been to find out the reason for his visit, I suddenly felt I wasn't ready for him to tell me.

'Town's not far, just down the bank.'

He nodded. 'Right.'

He had a bag, a big, green army kitbag slung over one shoulder. I hadn't thought to ask where he was staying. It would've been natural to have offered him the sofa, but I wasn't sure I wanted to do that.

'You must've been to Durham before?' I said. 'When you lived in Middlesbrough.'

'No, seen it from the train.'

We began to walk down the hill, slipping and slithering on a patch of black ice. The city spread out below us, the cathedral floodlit, its bright, golden light creating dark spaces on either side of the main tower like the empty eye sockets of a skull. I pointed out the castle beside it, bathed in a colder, grey-blue light. Most people were gobsmacked by this view. Mum had been, couldn't stop talking about how beautiful it was.

David paused to light a cigarette, clicking the lighter impatiently and then shielding the fragile flame in his cupped hands. In the brief flare his face was impossible to read. 'Frigging kills me.'

'What?'

He took a deep, lung-filling draw. 'Trains. Can't bloody well smoke anywhere now.'

'Have you eaten?'

'I had a sarnie off the trolley.'

We continued towards the town in an uncomfortable silence that made cannon crashes of our footsteps.

'You look good,' he said, finally. 'Student life must suit you.'

5

''S all right.'

He started to tell a story about someone who'd got on the train at Darlington. It didn't seem to have a point and apart from asking the occasional question I didn't contribute much. I wanted to absorb how he looked. I was taller by a couple of inches, but what he lacked in height he made up for in bulk, not broad exactly, but muscular. And there was something about the way he carried himself, a contained, angular walk, not looking for trouble perhaps, but more than ready to meet it.

'So you're on leave?' I asked.

'Left after me last stint in Basra.'

'Oh? I thought you'd be army for life.'

'Na – done me time.' A pause. 'Got wounded—'

'Wounded?'

'Friendly fire.' He laughed, breath and smoke streaming from his mouth. 'Thought I might be pushing me luck if I went back.'

'Yes, of course.' I couldn't think what to say. 'Are you better now?'

'Yeah.'

Silence again. It was what I'd feared, that we'd slip into absurd politeness. I wanted to ask him why he was here, suddenly, after all this time, but I feared the answer, and so I pushed on, taking us into the Fighting Cocks. I knew it'd be crowded, but at least there wouldn't be anybody from the university there. In the great divide of town and gown this was very much town.

I edged between sweating bodies at the bar and

managed, eventually, to catch a barman's eye. I ordered two pints of Carling and, after a moment's thought, two chasers.

'Do you mind?' I set the drinks down in front of him. 'I thought with the cold . . .'

He grinned and raised an eyebrow. He'd found a table by the window, but it was hemmed in on both sides by big groups of girls, screeching and chattering like jays. I pulled out one of the stools and sat opposite him.

'Where are you living now?' I asked.

'Moving around. Last few weeks I've been working in Middlesbrough.'

'Right.'

'I've been thinking I might move back.'

'To Middlesbrough?'

'No, I dunno. Just North.'

I'd only ever imagined him living in barracks. Or abroad. Of course I'd watched the news bulletins, soldiers patrolling the streets of Basra or, once, leaping out of a blazing tank into a hostile crowd – and I'd always thought about him. Now I wanted to know how serious he was about moving back, but I was wary of sounding too interested.

He pulled a beermat close to him and tore at one corner. I was drinking quickly, too quickly, but he easily matched the pace. When it was his round he followed my lead and brought chasers back with our pints. We talked then, loudly – we had to, to make ourselves heard over the shrieks of laughter from the adjoining tables – about things that didn't matter, or not to me anyway. Football. The army. Nothing that anybody couldn't overhear.

'Walk back to the flat?' I said. 'It's just up the road. I've got some brandy, I think.'

'All right.'

The cold air felt like a tight band across my forehead. The alcohol had made me feel light-headed, but not − surprisingly, given my usual low tolerance − particularly drunk. Keyed up, perhaps. I tried to remember if I'd eaten. Nothing for a while. When we reached the flat I moved ahead of him, kicking the base of the front door because it was stiff with damp. In the distance, I could hear the yelp of an ambulance negotiating the roundabout at the top of North Road, then several more yelps as it moved on towards the hospital.

'Mine's the first floor.'

We climbed the stairs, David close behind, breathing heavily, crowding me as I put the key in the lock. I had several goes before I managed to turn it. 'Go on in.'

'Do you share?'

'I did in the first year. I thought about getting somebody else in, but it's not really big enough for two.'

I picked up some post − junk I'd looked at once already − and followed him in.

The living room was tiny and crowded. A table with flaps, a two-seater sofa, an armchair and a coffee table filled all the available space. David sat on the sofa while I went into the kitchen to fetch the brandy.

'This is nice,' he said when I came back.

'Not bad. I like the view from the bedroom, it looks down into a wood.'

He'd taken off his coat, no sweater, only a T-shirt underneath, tight across his chest and shoulders. Still did weights, that was obvious.

'What are you studying?' he asked.

'Economics.'

'Yeah?' He pulled a face, half impressed, half jeering. 'Shit. I always imagined you living in a tent on Holy Island, counting puffins.'

I tensed, started to speak, then checked myself. So had I, once.

'Do you like it?'

'Yeah, it's all right.'

In truth I was bored out of my mind, but there didn't seem much point getting into that now. I handed him his glass, filled to the brim, and sat in the armchair. I needed to make eye contact, but I found myself staring at his hands instead. They were flecked with tiny scars, some still pink. He looked along the mantelpiece, focusing on a photograph of me taken during freshers' week.

I stood up and passed it to him.

He barely glanced at it. 'Yeah, it's the one you sent.'

I took it back, feeling a flush of heat to my throat. I'd forgotten I'd sent it to him.

'I nearly looked you up, once,' he said. 'Last October, when I come out.'

'Why didn't you?'

'Because we agreed.' He gulped at the brandy,

his Adam's apple jerking as he swallowed. 'God, is it really eight years—'

'Nine, in July.'

'Doesn't seem that long.' He retrieved a brass tin from his coat. 'Mind if I smoke?'

'No, go ahead.'

He began to prepare a spliff, resting the cigarette paper high up on his thigh. I watched, mesmerised, as if I'd never seen it done before. He sprinkled the tobacco first, tapping it out from one of the rollies, then the hash, melting it into crumbs with his lighter. When he'd finished he didn't light it straight away, but stood up and walked over to the fireplace. He picked up another photograph, Kathryn and me. I waited for him to make some comment, prepared to be offended, and then was more offended by his silence.

My mouth was dry. 'David, what's this about?'

'Where was this taken?'

'Ibiza.'

'That your girlfriend?'

'Kathryn.'

He looked at me – a flicker of surprise? – then took a small square of newspaper from the back pocket of his jeans and handed it to me. The paper had been torn from a larger section and then folded, the edges sharp as though he'd run his thumb and fingernail along the creases. It was only a paragraph, small enough to have been missed altogether. A single quote from the police. I read quickly, swallowed.

'Where was it?' I asked, handing it back.

'In the *Mercury*, last Saturday. Fourth page.'

'Anything else?'

'No.' He shrugged and sat back down. 'I thought you'd want to know.'

'Christ.' I pressed my hands into my eyes and then read the paragraph again. 'Human remains.'

'*Remains*. Not a body.' He stared into his glass. 'You know what I think? They've found a couple of bones, mebbe some little doggy run back to its owner with a ruddy great thigh bone in its mouth.'

I blinked, repelled by the brutality of it, but then I remembered he'd probably seen things nobody should ever have to see. And unlike me, he'd seen them more than once. Of course it had changed him. It would change anybody.

'They'll know a lot more than they're saying,' I said. 'This is what? Five days old? Forensics. How long—'

'You can't think like that.'

'Aren't you worried?'

He lit the spliff, producing a shower of sparks he brushed off the cushion with the back of his hand. 'So they've found a few bones. They aren't saying who it is.'

I stared at him.

'It was bound to happen.' He caught my expression. 'Look, I'm not saying I don't think about it . . .'

Then what? I flattened out a kink in the hearth rug with my foot. Maybe too much time had passed. We'd both had to find our own way of coping, perhaps it was stupid to think there'd be common ground. I shivered. The flat was cold, even with the heating on full blast. I'd stacked the fire ready for tomorrow night when Kathryn was coming over for a meal, but now I bent down and lit it. I watched as flames licked the kindling, seething, making little popping sounds, then I doused the lot with coal.

'How am I supposed to know what you think?' I said. 'You only wrote once.'

'We weren't supposed to write. That was one of the things we agreed on, remember? Besides, did you really think I was going to pour my guts out to you in a letter?'

Silence.

'I thought you should know about the newspaper report, that's all.'

'The police aren't stupid. How long do you think it's going to take them?' I wanted him scared, as scared as I was. 'They can age bones, David, sex them too. Dental records?'

'Does she make you happy, your Kathryn?'

'How long before they find the skull? Teeth?'

'Does she?'

'*Yes.*'

'Good.' He rested his hands on his knees, the fingers on his right hand, stained yellow, lightly tapping. He seemed, if anything, impatient. 'I should go.'

'But we haven't decided anything . . .'

He took his coat from the back of the sofa and swung it over his shoulders.

'We need a course of action. *David.*'

'Action is keep your mouth shut.'

'Just that? Oh, that's enough, is it?'

He tried a smile. 'For now.'

The more concerned I sounded the more ostentatiously unworried he became. It made me wonder why he'd even bothered to come. But then it had always been like that, he'd always been the hard one, only once or twice a crack had opened to reveal the chaos inside.

'Have you got somewhere to stay?' I asked.

'A B&B.'

I said, because I knew I had to, 'There's the sofa.'

'Huh. With you rabbiting on all night? No thanks.'

I walked over to the window. A scattering of snowflakes, clinging to the glass like they wanted to be inside. I could feel his eyes on the back of my head.

'They don't know who it is, Leo.'

'Yet.' I followed him to the door where he hoisted his kitbag onto his shoulder. He was going and I hadn't said anything I wanted to say. 'You better give me your mobile number.'

He took a biro from the pocket of his coat, freeing it from a handful of receipts and cigarette papers, and reached for my hand. I flinched as the ball pressed hard on a vein.

'I'll call you tomorrow,' I said. 'Maybe—'

'Sure.'

At the door we grasped hands, an awkward fumble. A few hours earlier we'd embraced, but we were further apart now than we had been then. He took a breath and for a second I thought I glimpsed something beneath the surface calm. Fear? If it was, it was only one layer among many.

'Well . . .' He nodded and ran downstairs, keen to be away. At the bottom I opened the door for him and he stepped out onto the street, his boots loud on the pavement. Army boots, I saw, polished to a mirror shine.

'Don't worry,' he said. 'Whatever happens, we're in this together.'

There was a peculiar note in his voice. I couldn't be sure if it was a promise, or a threat. I opened my mouth to speak, but he touched my shoulder, once, and then turned, setting off, briskly, into the dark.

2

There was a new crack in the bedroom ceiling, another tributary of the river that snaked into the shadows at the corner of the room. This side of the street had been built over a worked-out pit and was slowly subsiding. The cracks had been there years, getting imperceptibly worse ever since I moved in, but this morning I lay and stared at them as if I were seeing them for the first time, imagining the dark, hollow spaces underneath.

I rolled over onto my side, wincing at the band of sunlight that pierced a gap in the curtains. It had been a restless, dream-fretted sleep. Now I lay in a pool of sweat, heart bulging up into my throat. I told myself it was only the nameless, disconnected fear that follows heavy drinking – I'd gone on with the brandy long after David had left – but I knew it wasn't that.

David. When I'd imagined us meeting again I always thought I'd be reassured by his presence, just for the simple fact I wouldn't be alone with it any more, but I didn't feel that. Not last night and especially not this morning.

If I'd never met him . . .

I got up and wandered into the living room. Last night's glasses still sat on the coffee table. The saucer he'd used as an ashtray was there too, a single butt folded over into a tiny L. The smell made my stomach heave.

I glanced at my watch. Time was somehow important. Kathryn. I'd said I'd meet her in town at midday and it was almost that now. Spurred into action, I dressed quickly, pulling on clothes from a pile on the floor at the side of the bed, and walked out to meet her.

A light covering of snow had settled over the ice making the pavement treacherous. Footprints, fresh, the wide soles of men, the small neat squares of high heels and, running down the middle, the wheels of a pushchair. I'd lost count of the number of times I'd wanted to tell Kathryn everything, in bed, or stretched out facing each other in the bath, but in the end I'd always stopped myself. I knew there was no way I could hope to make her understand, or that I could be sure I'd still love her if she did.

I stopped at the newsagent's on North Road and bought a copy of the *Daily Mail*. No reason to think the story would've been picked up by the nationals, but I felt compelled to make sure. While I waited to pay I scanned the pages, looking for familiar words or pictures. Nothing. As I stepped back onto the pavement I skidded, my right heel scooting out from underneath me. Instinctively, I grabbed the nearest thing to me, the arm of a woman who'd been about to step inside the shop.

'Whoops!' A bullet of tooth-marked gum shot to the front of her mouth. She sucked it back and laughed. 'Nearly landed on your arse there, love!'

'Sorry.'

Her accent. Teesside? Like David's anyway, or perhaps I imagined it.

I continued walking, took the short cut through the Gates shopping centre and came out onto Framwellgate Bridge. The snow had delineated the cathedral, highlighting the individual arches and turrets, turning it into a negative of itself. I pushed on down the steps to the river path. A young man was rowing, strong, leisurely strokes that left a wide, bubble-strewn V behind him. The waves, each one full of reflected snow-laden sky, broke gently against the banks.

Kathryn was sitting on the bench where we usually met, perched on a plastic bag to keep her coat dry, staring out after him.

'I gave your sandwich to the ducks.'

I tried to kiss her on the mouth, but she pulled away and I was left pecking the air. 'My lecture ran over.'

'Didn't think you had one this morning.' She stood up, folded the bag into a square and put it back in her coat pocket. 'You missed them, just now, two cormorants with their wings out.'

'Shags,' I said.

'Oh? I never know the difference.' She pulled back her sleeve to look at her watch. 'I have to be back for one o'clock, shall we just walk a bit?'

She'd twisted her shoulder-length blonde hair, usually loose, high on her head, and secured it with a slide. She was wearing make-up, more than she normally did, but still discreet. Yet there was something, she seemed different, but then everything looked different today.

'Did you look at the leaflets from the estate agent?' she asked.

'Ye-es.'

'Like the look of any of them?'

We'd talked about living together, once, a few weeks ago. She lived with her parents, didn't want to move in with me because the flat was small and dingy and so she suggested we get a place together. In my mind it was somewhere in the distant future, but because I hadn't ruled it out she'd run with it.

She sighed. 'You didn't look at them, did you?'

'I will, this afternoon.'

'You are serious about this, aren't you?'

'Yes.'

'I mean, you do still want to?'

'*Yes*.'

Did I? If I had doubts, they weren't about Kathryn.

That moment each Friday evening when, with a bottle of wine and two glasses ready on the coffee table, I heard her car pull up outside was one of the highlights of my week. One of two. The other was coming back into the flat after she'd left on Sunday evening, the silence and the solitude washing over me, welcoming me back.

She broke from my hand to pull up the strap on her bag.

'I'm sorry,' I said. 'I just didn't get round to it.'

She looked back along the swollen river. Part of a tree trunk had become lodged on the weir, creating great arcs of foaming water on either side. I took her hand and she smiled, tense, but no longer unfriendly.

'So what was it?' she asked. 'Something more important, obviously.'

'A friend showed up.'

'From uni?'

'Home.'

She turned to face me, freeing her mouth from a strand of hair. 'You don't have any friends from home.'

'Not many.'

'None.'

This hurt for some reason, though I knew it was true.

'A boy? I mean, a man?'

'David.'

The moment I said his name, I wanted it back. I'd been good at keeping David at a distance. I didn't even dream about him. It was as though even in my subconscious I'd shut the events of that summer into a room and locked the door. I could be all right, happy almost, as long as I never went inside.

'You've never mentioned him before. What sort of friend is he?'

'I don't know.' I shrugged. 'The sort that isn't really a friend.'

'*Leo.*'

'You know. Just someone from the past.'

'That's weird, isn't it? Him looking you up after all this time.'

I tried a laugh.

'Is he staying long?'

'Not sure.'

A cyclist sped past, splintering puddles of ice, forcing us to step sharply to one side. I swung round to yell at him, but he was already out of earshot.

'What's he like?' Kathryn asked. 'David.'

'Dunno really. We were kids when I last saw him. He's not long been out of the army.'

'A soldier.'

'Yeah, been to Iraq.'

She looked at me, smiling, slightly flirtatious. 'So am I going to meet him?'

'You wouldn't like him. He's . . .' I groped for the words. 'Rather unkind.'

'God!'

'No, that's not what I mean.' I kissed the back of her hand, wanting to change the subject, not knowing how. 'Not sure how much we've got in common now. People move on.'

'At a rate of knots if they're anything like you. You

don't even remember your mother's birthday. I have to go out and buy her a card.'

'She likes your cards.'

'Why don't you invite him round for a meal? I think if he's made the effort to look you up you should nurture it.'

'*Nurture?*'

'Relationships don't look after themselves, Leo.'

Kathryn was the great relationship expert, capable of making the most astonishing assumptions about people she barely knew. She never doubted her own perceptions, though it seemed to me she often got people wrong.

'I think maybe men are better at picking up where they left off.' She opened her mouth and I added quickly, 'All right. A meal. When?'

'It'd better be tonight as you don't know how long he's staying.'

'Yes.'

We reached Prebends Bridge. It was colder, less sheltered. To go across would take us up to the Cathedral and then we'd have to walk through town, too far for the time we had left, so we turned and retraced our steps. We were holding hands lightly by our fingertips, stepping over puddles, when I stopped to probe one with my foot. The ice creaked, fine white lines spreading out in all directions. Black water bubbled up through the cracks.

'So where are we going to take him?' I asked. 'Friday night, everywhere will be booked.'

'I'll cook. Pasta or something.'

I nodded. 'I'll ring him.'

Part of me wanted to show her off. I'd told him I was happy after all. Another, larger, part knew they should never meet.

'Look,' she said, raising her hand, still in mine, to point at the weir. 'One of them's back.'

A shag had landed on a great mass of trapped twigs and branches, its long, serpentine neck gleaming iridescent blue and green.

'They're like owls, aren't they?' she said. 'Birds of ill omen.'

'Rubbish. It's a killing machine with feathers, that's all.'

Though I had thought him beautiful, that crested, regal head, and the wings, the black ominous wings, spread out on either side. We watched him for a while in silence, then turned and walked on.

3

David had eaten hardly anything, saying something about a stomach bug he'd picked up in Iraq and never quite managed to shift. It might've been true of course, but it sounded like an excuse. He pushed his plate to the centre of the table and lit a cigarette.

'That was great, thanks,' he said.

Kathryn smiled and took the plates over to the sink.

It had been an awkward evening. She and David came from such different segments of my life and I'd been anxious to integrate them, but in the end, as soon as he'd arrived, I'd turned into a dim version of myself, edgy and self-conscious, no help to either.

'Leave the plates,' I said. 'I'll do them in the morning.'

'No wonder the flat's a mess,' she said. 'Leo's solution to everything is leave it till later.'

David's gaze shifted to me. I was getting angry, uneasy at his presence, at the amount he was drinking. He was trying very hard to get Kathryn to like him, but his manner reeked of condescension. I was sure he'd got her down as a spoilt little rich girl who knew nothing about anything, and, to be fair, there was this side to her. Her father was rich. He idolised his only daughter and would do anything to protect her. She'd gone on living at home while she was at university, and afterwards, at an age when most people were only too eager to move out. With her long, pale greenish-gold hair and thin wrists she did sometimes remind me of a princess in a tower. But I *liked* that about her. The last thing I wanted was a girl who'd been round the block so many times she'd left skid marks on the track.

She ran hot water into the bowl, calling back to me to open another bottle of wine. I fetched it from the kitchen and sat at the table to open it. My knee bumped against David's under the table, rocking the candle, and we each reached out to steady it.

'You're sulking,' he said.

'And you're being a twat.'

He flicked ash from his cigarette, missed the saucer, made a half-hearted attempt to scoop it up. 'How am I?'

Kathryn came back into the room, drying her hands on a tea towel.

'Why don't we move from the table?' I said.

She chose the armchair, leaving David and me to squash together on the sofa. I crossed my legs, but still felt the heat of his thigh through my jeans.

'You didn't finish telling me your story,' Kathryn said, kicking off her shoes and tucking her legs underneath her.

'What story?'

'About Leo. I asked whether he had a girlfriend.' She smiled at me. 'Well, I didn't, but I was getting round to it.'

David pretended to consider. 'Yes! There was a lass, wasn't there, Leo?'

'I don't remember anyone.'

'No, there was.' He clicked his fingers. 'Sarah? Sheila? Shit, it can't have been Sheila. Anyway, he was in love, I think, for about a week.' He glanced sideways at me. 'She dumped you for me, right?'

He'd made it up, or confused me with someone else. Either way it wasn't true. Perhaps he was trying to be kind, to present me in a more dashing light, but no, it was too mocking for that.

'I expect so,' I said. 'They all did.'

Kathryn laughed. '*All?*'

'Oh, he's a dark horse, our Leo. You'd be surprised.'

The candles on the coffee table flickered in unison, casting gigantic shadows on the wall above the fireplace.

'And you?' David continued, looking directly at Kathryn. 'What do you do?'

'I'm a trainee marketing consultant at Riley and Hambton's. It's not really where I want to be long-term, but it'll do till Leo graduates. Then I think we'll move.' She kept glancing at me, checking my reactions. 'If we're both going to have careers we need to be close to a big city really.'

'Newcastle?'

He'd directed it at me, but it was Kathryn who answered. 'No, London, or Manchester I expect.'

'Had you down as a country boy, Leo.'

'Yes, well, I've changed. And any road . . .' I coughed. Whenever I spoke to David I seemed to slip into his accent. 'Any road' was him, not me. I doubt if Kathryn had noticed, but once or twice I thought I'd caught a flicker of amusement from David.

Kathryn hurried to fill the silence. 'Was Leo really weird? He says he was. Sorry, darling, but it's true. And shy, he says.'

'Not as shy as all that.'

Another smile, midway into his glass as he gulped down the remainder of his wine and reached for the bottle. I got my hand to it first.

'Cheers,' he said, as I refilled. 'Not bad this.'

'You must've found it strange coming back from Iraq?' Kathryn said. 'I mean, I imagine you get locked in, into a certain kind of mode.'

He shifted, glancing at me. 'You get locked into a routine. Takes a bit of getting used to when you don't have to clean kit or do sentry any more, but yeah, it's different.'

'It was the same for Uncle George, wasn't it, Leo?' Kathryn said. 'It took him a while to readjust to civilian life, though he was in the navy twenty-five years, a lifetime really. He makes those pots for gardens these days, you know, strawberry planters. What do you do now, David?'

'Dunno, yet.'

Kathryn nodded.

'I thought about setting up as a personal trainer—'

'Oh yes, you'd be perfect for that.'

'Rich, fat old women drooling all over him?' I said. 'Yes, perfect.'

'Not *all* are rich and fat. I can think of several girls at the office who'd go for it. It's the thing to do now if you're serious about getting fit.'

They chatted on, Kathryn pleased and flattered because David had given her a problem to solve – or she thought he had – and she loved that. I watched her mouth, tongue red from the wine. I thought, one word could blow all this apart.

'Yes, that's right,' Kathryn was saying. 'Your wound, where were you hurt?'

'Basra.'

She laughed. 'Sorry, I meant where—'

'Oh, leg. Left.' He stretched it out in front of him, rubbing a palm up and down his thigh. 'Gives me gyp now and then.'

'Wouldn't that stop you pursuing the personal-trainer idea?'

'Na – it's nowt really.'

I listened as they talked, watching David closely. Kathryn was in full flow, asking him why he'd joined the army. Sorted him out, he said, never regretted it, you had better mates in the army than anywhere else. He mentioned one man in particular, someone he'd gone through basic with who'd been killed last year in Afghanistan. I thought I detected sadness then, but there was something not quite genuine about it.

'I saw this programme, what was it?' Kathryn looked at me. '*Panorama* or *Horizon*, one of those. They followed this group of marines around. Half the time you couldn't tell who was the enemy, terrifying. They even put bombs inside Coke cans.'

'It was roadside bombs mostly when I was there.' He lit another cigarette, sharpening the ember to a point against the side of the saucer. 'We looked in on this orphanage once, a right shithole, not—'

'I'm surprised Saddam bothered with orphans,' I said.

'He didn't. It was a charity thing.' He took a long pull on his cigarette. 'One of the first places I saw bombed.'

Kathryn's hair had fallen loose from the knot on top of her head. She gave him a fleeting glance – interested, urging him on – while at the same time leaning forward to the coffee table to pick up her glass.

'Our bombs,' he finished. 'Not theirs.'

'What happened to the children?' Kathryn said. She looked at me. 'They weren't still inside, surely?'

'For Christ's sake, Kathryn, what do you think happened to them?'

'Oh. God.' She bit down on her bottom lip. 'You don't hear about that sort of thing though, do you? We should, but I mean, here we are and no one has the slightest idea.' She paused. 'Apart from you, David, obviously.'

I stared at the scars on his hands, barely visible in the candlelight, but I knew they were there. I tried to visualise what they must've looked like fresh, dust and grit ground into the skin.

'Well, you're out of it now.' A pause. 'Leo? My God, are you drunk?'

'What?' I'd been rolling the stem of my glass round and round in my fingers and a drop of wine had spilt onto the back of my hand. 'No. Just tired.'

David stubbed out his cigarette and moved to get up. 'I ought to be making tracks anyway. B&B locks up dead on eleven thirty.'

'Stay,' Kathryn said. 'Please. It's freezing out there. I'll make you up a bed on the sofa.'

He raised a hand in protest, but she pushed herself up out of the chair and disappeared into the bedroom to fetch sheets.

He walked over to the window and stood with his hands in his pockets, big toes poking out of holes in both socks.

'Is it OK?' he asked. 'Me staying?'

'Of course.'

I wanted suddenly to ease the tension between us, but didn't know how. Outside thick fog clung to the street lamps, choking the orange light. Minutes ticked past.

'If you get cold just build up the fire,' Kathryn said, returning to make up a bed.

When she'd finished she turned to him and kissed

him on both cheeks, an awkward bump for the second because he wasn't expecting it. Still a northern lad.

'Goodnight,' I said, ushering Kathryn down the hall.

The bedroom was cold, but after the smell and heat of the living room it came as a relief. Kathryn fell onto the mattress, exhaled slowly and spread out her arms and legs to the sides.

'I hate drinking.' She rolled over and rested her head on her hands. 'Are you really tired? You could've stayed up with him, you know, chatted about old times.'

'You're slurring.'

I lowered myself onto the bed and shuffled across until I lay beside her. I kissed her shoulder, softly, moving up to her neck and then her mouth.

'He's lonely,' she said.

'He's got the television.'

She thumped me in the ribs. 'Generally. Don't you think so? I thought so. I wonder if he'd like Julia.'

'Nobody likes Julia, not even you.'

'She's beautiful.'

I reached an arm around her waist and pulled her towards me. Another kiss, brief. I tasted coconut and wine.

'I think he's a bit lost, you know, since the army.'

She fixed her eyes on the ceiling, lifting each arm in turn as I removed her blouse and bra, pushing her hips off the mattress so I could tug off her jeans.

'He's trying to figure out what comes next and who to share it with.'

'You've only known him five minutes.'

I could hear him in the next room, prowling around, picking things up, putting them down again, fingering my life. I kissed her along her collarbone, sliding down to taste the skin around her nipple.

'We should invite them over.'

'Who?'

'David and Julia.'

I took Kathryn's nipple into my mouth. At once her lips parted then closed again, whatever protest she'd been about to make forgotten. With the duvet pulled over my head, I wriggled down on my elbows, leaving a trail of kisses over her stomach. The skin was goose-pimpled, but warm, with deep indentations where the waistband of her jeans had cut in. I paused, breathed, gently nudged her legs apart. She placed a hand on top of my head, gathering handfuls of hair and twisting it around her fingers. I licked and probed until she started to moan. Harder, softer, slower, faster until, *yes*, the cry I'd been working for. I glanced up at her as she swallowed, hot, red cheeks, lips dry. She tried then to lift me up towards her, but I resisted, holding onto her wrists, nuzzling, until I'd drawn out the very last moan.

For no apparent reason I woke early and lay staring into the dark. After a while I got up, felt around for my dressing gown and moved quietly down the hall to the living room. It was surprisingly light, the curtains drawn well back. Moonlight, like spilt salt, glistened on the roofs of the houses opposite.

David was lying on the sofa, one leg stretched in front of him, the other resting on the floor.

'Did I wake you?' I said.

'I was already awake.' Kathryn's candles had burned down to puddles of wax. 'What time is it?'

I peered at my watch. 'Just after five.'

He threw a cigarette packet on the coffee table. The saucer was full of butts. It was difficult to tell whether he'd slept at all, but he'd undressed to his boxer shorts. His chest was pallid in the light, a few flat, dark hairs running vertically down his breast-bone. I caught sight of the wound on his thigh. It looked like a surgical incision, but broader, messier. He drew back his legs to create a space for me to sit, but I chose the armchair.

'She wants to know if you'd like to meet one of her friends.'

'A girl?'

'Julia.'

I watched him stare at nothing, lost suddenly, but took no pleasure from it. 'Well, I don't suppose either of us can really plan anything,' I added. 'Might be in prison by the end of the month.'

He sputtered out smoke.

'What's so fucking funny?'

He didn't answer. Water dripped from a tap in the kitchen onto a plate, a tinny sound that nibbled at our silence.

'Why did you make up that story about me having a girlfriend?' I said.

'When you think of some of the things I might tell her, I'd've thought that was the least of your worries.'

A threat? 'I don't lie to Kathryn.'

'You're not telling me she knows—'

'No, of course not. She doesn't know what I don't tell her, that's all.'

'Oh, I see. Not lies. Silence.'

I looked at him, but his face was lost in a swirl of smoke.

'How long have you been seeing her?' he asked.

'A little over a year.'

'She's got it all worked out, I'll give her that. Careers in the big city.'

'What's wrong with that?'

'Nothing.'

I waited for him to say something. 'I don't need your approval.'

He had the same flicker of a smile I'd seen earlier, but this time our eyes locked. He was seizing control as he always had, but I couldn't afford to let him do it now. He looked away first.

'That shell,' he said, nodding at the mantelpiece. 'Is it from Seaton?'

'Yeah.'

It was a relief to move. I got up and handed it to him. He put it to his ear and I watched the sound of the sea spread over his face.

'You know what I've been thinking lying here?' he said. 'I've been wondering what did it.'

'What?'

'"Scattered remains." What do you think it was?'

'Jesus, what does it *matter*?'

'Foxes?'

'I don't want to think about it.' I looked away. 'I'm surprised you do.'

'You have done though.' He leant forward, met my eyes. 'Haven't you? You've wondered how much is left?'

I wanted to be away, from his bulk, his smell.

'Have you ever been back?'

'Not since Mum moved. She got a job in Hexham.'

He lay back against the arm of the sofa. When he spoke again his voice was barely more than a whisper. 'You know, the only real way to find out anything is to go there.'

'Just turn up, asking questions?'

'Better than sitting around doing nothing.'

I stood up. 'I'm going back to bed. Might just get another hour. Perhaps you should try.'

As I reached the bedroom door I looked over my shoulder, but he'd sunk down out of sight and all I could see was a coil of smoke rising. Shivering, I climbed into bed beside Kathryn who threw an arm across the duvet, but didn't wake. I lay, straight and tense, staring into the half-darkness. I wondered whether he was serious about going back. I'd always known we would, together, but I couldn't have told him that.

I listened, aware of him, the springs of the sofa squeaking as he tossed and turned in the room next door.

David blasting back into my life this way had thrown me completely. It wasn't just his sheer physical strength that made him seem threatening, though that was a factor. More the impression of something violent in him, barely contained, that took me back to the summer in Seaton, and the first time I saw him.

4

It was the first day of the school summer holidays. I'd got up early to meet the tide, but ended up walking all the way from the tank traps at Church Hill to the rocky outcrop at Emmanuel Point. I'd sat on one of the large stones in the front of the dunes and, for maybe an hour, I'd just listened. The chirrup of insects hunting, the seething bubbly sound of fresh kelp on the shoreline. Now, almost midday, it was too hot to do anything. I stretched out on the bed, the fan on the desk tightening the skin on my salt-scummed legs.

Shortly after I'd returned, Olly had come into my room and taken up position on the window seat with his drawing book. He was unusually quiet, concentrating on a sketch. The pencil made a small, scratty noise, the edge of the lead jagged, not smooth like I'd shown him.

'You need to sharpen it again.'

'I'm shading.'

He shuffled the pencil in his fingers, adjusting the angle where the lead met the paper, but it snapped.

'Told you.'

He picked up the sharpener and inserted the pencil, withdrawing it several times to examine the tip, then brushed the shavings off his lap.

'Now you're making a mess.'

Mum had stuck his glasses back together with Elastoplast. It looked weird, like he had a massive zit on his nose. He stuck his tongue out to the side of his mouth and tried once more to achieve the right effect.

'What are you drawing anyway?'

'A crab,' he said. 'Merlin.'

'Wouldn't you do him better if you were looking at him? In your room?'

'No.'

I stared past him. A flock of gulls was flying out to sea, yelps loud, then fainter as they moved out of sight.

He removed the sheet from his pad and scrunched it into a ball. For a while then he was still, the pad on his knees and the rubber end of the pencil hovering close to his right nostril.

'That pencil's mine. If you get snot on it I'll ram it up your—'

He slid me a sideways grin. 'You were going to say arse.'

'I mean it, Olly.'

He held the pencil to his nose, but then – as if it were a lesser crime – stuck it in his gob and bit down on the centre. Now it'd have a ring of teeth marks.

'Go to your own room. Or somewhere.'

'Where?'

'*Any*where.'

He thought, as though considering options, but for Olly, as for me, there weren't many. Seaton was the sort of place that looked bigger on maps, giving tourists the idea we were a proper seaside resort with donkey rides and candyfloss stalls, maybe even a sea-life aquarium. Something to do. There wasn't. Not unless you included the gift shops that all sold the same thing – starfish or conch shells bought whole-sale – and they didn't sell many of those. Or the arcade, which stank of Slush Puppies and pipe smoke. Wendy's House of Hauntings was about the only 'attraction'. You had to pay to get in. People thought it was a joke, like a funny ha ha sort of joke, but it wasn't meant to be.

'That boy's back,' Olly said, looking out of the window.

I shuffled to the side of my bed, leaning forward, but I could only see the wide privet hedge at the far end of the gardens.

'What's he doing?' I asked.

'Do you think it's true?'

'What?'

'About them being bank robbers.'

'Course not.'

'He looks like his dad. Like a mini-me.'

'You can't believe everything Sweet Jesus says.'

Mrs Browning — called Sweet Jesus because she said it at least a hundred times a day on account of her being Irish — did our ironing. Not at our house. She took it away to her house and then brought it back. She always stayed to gossip though, waiting until her tea got cold, drinking it, and then moving the cup around in her hands like what she really wanted, more than anything else in the whole world, was another cup, another hour.

She, like most of the village no doubt, noticed when the cottage next door had become occupied again. It'd been empty all winter and most of last summer when there'd been a rumour it might be sold, but nothing came of it and the owner, an old man called Mr Garrison who lived in Aberdeen, re-advertised it for rent.

So far it was just the boy and the boy's dad and it was him who'd sparked off Sweet Jesus's theories, based entirely on his appearance and, specifically, his tattoos. They weren't, she said, the sort you got in the navy.

I stood behind Olly's shoulder, cautious in case the boy chose that moment to look up. All our windows, most of them anyway, were small, set in blubber-thick walls and the glass was criss-crossed with thin strips of wood that separated it into squares. The boy occupied the whole of one square.

'What's he doing?'

'Dunno,' Olly said. 'Standing.'

'I can see that.'

He was the sort with bristle for hair and trainers with air in the soles, who looked like he'd been in fights and won them, who carried the scars and wasn't bothered, was looking, even, for a run-in that'd give him a new one. He'd be angry because angry was cool.

'How old do you reckon he is?'

Olly shrugged.

Fifteen at least, maybe even sixteen. And much taller than me. He picked up a stone, slung it into a clump of weeds and went over to the patio. A few moments later he returned, dragging a lawnmower behind him. It was ancient, a diesel with a rusted skirt and peeling paint. It should've been obvious it wouldn't cut the grass, but he turned it over onto its side all the same, examining the parts underneath, pausing every so often to drag on a cigarette. I'd seen boys smoke at school, but they didn't hold their cigarettes like that. He had muscles too, big biceps, the kind that look big all the time, not just when you flex them.

'David,' Olly said.

'What?'

'His name. It's David.'

'I thought you didn't know his name.'

'Mum told me. I forgot.'

It changed things, like matching a picture in my sea encyclopedia with something I'd seen a million times in the rock pools. Knowing it, for the first time, its actual name. Sometimes I was disappointed because the name wasn't deserving or even halfway appropriate. Like the sea hare which you'd think would resemble a hare, but it actually looks like a slug. I didn't know what I felt about 'David' – only it wasn't what I'd expected.

'Are you going to make friends then?' Olly said.

'Get lost.' He ducked as I took a swipe at his head. 'Anyway, he's probably only here for the summer.'

'Isn't. His dad's got . . .' He pushed the glasses up his nose. 'Like custard.'

'What?'

'That's what it sounds like. Custard.'

'Custody, you mean?'

He nodded.

I turned back to the window. They probably couldn't afford to buy a house of their own and that was why they were renting the cottage. I already knew their car was an old banger; a Vauxhall Astra which looked like it'd once been red but had faded to a muddy pink. David's dad worked on it most nights, got it started a couple of times, but it always sputtered and died. He came out of the back door now, wiping his hands on an oil-stained rag.

They did look alike, the same stubble head and cork-coloured tan, but David's dad was a different shape, like he was once muscly only there'd been a landslide and the bulk of him had settled around his middle. He said something to David which I couldn't hear and then went back into the cottage.

'I'm going to do my jigsaw,' Olly said. 'Want to do the sky pieces?'

'In a bit.'

David moved to a tall pile of paving slabs, old ones that'd been pulled up and still had concrete stuck to the edges. Nettles thronged the pile, but there was one place where he'd trampled them flat. And there he sat, for ages, smoking, thinking, looking at the sea.

It was only a matter of time before Mum would make me go over and invite him for tea or something equally awful. She was always doing it – making me get to know other kids, but they were 'nice' kids, the sort she thought I should be friends with. Surely even Mum would see David wasn't like that. He was like the boys at the comp, the worst boys, the ones who waited for me by the bus stop every day after school. A predator. And he was next door.

Shit.

Over the next few days David's garden underwent a transformation, the long grass cut and the weeds uprooted to reveal the shape of the borders. All the waste, leaves and branches, and the grass cuttings had been gathered into a huge heap at the centre of the lawn. Now and then David or his dad would throw something on it, cardboard boxes they must've used to move their things, a roll of mud-coloured carpet.

Now, as a slow blue dusk fell across the garden, I lay in my hammock and listened. The occasional snap of a twig, metal scraping, the flint of a lighter

I recognised when, moments later, the smell of woodsmoke drifted over the wall.

I moved to the hole. It wasn't much of a spyhole because the angle was all wrong, but I could still see a fair bit. David's dad was standing next to the fire, a can of lager tilted to take a swig, the back of his neck creased into rolls of fat. When he looked down, poking something with his foot, his neck stretched to reveal white wrinkles.

I searched for David. At first I thought he wasn't there, but then I saw him, hands driven deep into the front pockets of pale blue jeans. He walked across to the fire, standing some distance from his dad, and picked up a stray twig which he began to sharpen with a knife. A proper knife, the hunting kind with a thick blade. When he'd sharpened the twig to a point, he lifted the tip to his mouth and blew on it, rolling it between his fingers to examine his work. Then, like he'd ruined it, he chucked it onto the fire and stood staring into the flames.

He was beat-up-looking. A crooked nose and a scar on his upper lip that shone silver under a sparse covering of hair. He'd have picked at the scab, I thought, peeling back the thin polish of skin again and again until it bled.

A wasp, drunk on pollen, buzzed around my left ear, whirling and spinning like a kamikaze pilot. I batted it away. When I put my eye to the hole again David was looking straight at me. I ducked – stupid, I guess – there was no way he could've seen me. Even so, I held my breath. And held. And held.

Just when I knew I'd have to breathe he returned his gaze to the fire. His dad had gone back in, the garage probably, because I could hear the Astra's engine turning, over and over, and tinny sounds, like he was raking through a toolbox.

I must've coughed, something, because next thing I knew David had raised his arm and there was a loud smack on the wall.

'Get a good look?'

My heart thudded, missed a beat, then ran to catch up. I strolled casually back to the hammock so as to appear I'd been there all the time.

'I said, "Did you get a good look?"'

He scrambled up the wall, swinging a leg over to straddle it. Close to, like this, his size shocked me. Even if he hadn't have been up on the wall he'd have towered over me. His chest, bare, was brown and muscled, the nipples dark like currants and surrounded by fine hair. Scratches striped his arms, the freshest beaded with blood.

'You were spying,' he said.

'I wasn't.'

'You a peeping Tom?'

'No.'

'What's your name?'

'Leo.'

'Leo the lion?'

'Just Leo.'

The fire crackled behind him, occasionally coughing thick grey smoke into the space above our heads.

'That what you do all day, lounge around in your swing and spy on your neighbours?'

'It's a hammock.'

'It isn't level.'

Great. He'd be like all the others. I straightened up, not as a challenge, but it might've seemed that way.

'Don't you know how to fix it?' he said.

'Course.'

He had cheap blue eyes. I made a big show of bending down to claw at a bite on my ankle.

'If you stop scratching it, it'll stop itching.'

I stopped, but the relief lasted only a few seconds.

'You know how to make it stop itching?'

'It's just a midge bite.'

'Stick a knife in it. It releases the poison. I could do it for you if you like.'

I wanted to say I wasn't scared of his knife and that I knew he'd probably only ever sharpened a stick with it, but the words got jumbled and I could only look at him. The hair on his head wasn't really stubble, but greyish-blond down, not spiky at all.

'Scared it'll hurt?'

'No. I just don't want to.'

He was grinning like I'd said something funny. 'You go to that school up the coast. Bradley's.'

'Bradstones.'

He swung the knife at the handle. 'You must be loaded.'

'Why would you think that?'

'You think everybody goes to private school?'

'Mum's good at her job, that's all.'

He shrugged.

I got a whiff of him then, a spicy, sweaty smell that was different from the boys at school. I remembered being huddled together in the bus stop once, eight or nine boys crammed together. Damp wool and chewing gum, groiny smells and salt-and-vinegar crisps.

I stared down at my chest, baby plump breasts and pale skin freckled with blotches. I should've put my T-shirt on, but it was too hot. I clamped my arms to my sides and tried to think of something to say, for he seemed to be waiting, a small, crooked smile on his mouth.

'Mum said you used to live in Middlesbrough,' I said. 'That's where Captain Cook's from, right? Or is it Whitby? I can—'

'What?'

'Captain—'

'How the fuck should I know?'

I rested one foot over the other, skin sticking to skin. I wished I chewed gum. People who chewed gum never looked serious.

'I've seen you before anyway,' he said. 'You were going into the library.'

'Returning some books for Mum.'

'Yeah, right.'

I swung off the hammock and landed squarely on my feet. 'I'm sure you'll like it here. If you're worried about it, I mean.'

'Fuck off.'

'Right.'

46

I decided to back away before I could make it worse and walked back up the lawn. He watched the whole time, or at least I think he did, because when I looked over my shoulder his eyes were still on me, still staring. He'd lit another cigarette and took several long drags, then, before it was even half finished, flicked the butt across our lawn and jumped down into his own garden.

I went back to my room and sat on the bed. The window was open and for a long time it was quiet, only the occasional gull's cry to pierce the afternoon heat.

I felt sticky and bad-tempered. And ashamed of myself, though I didn't know why.

Later, when I was sure he wasn't in the garden, I returned to the spot where we'd spoken. The grass felt cool beneath my feet and the hollow shell of the moon was just visible on a pale, lilac sky. I circled the lawn until I found his cigarette, squashed at the filter where his lips had pressed around it. It was a Superking, the word Super burned away so that only 'king' remained. I took it into my mouth, black ash crumbling from the tip, but was shocked by its bitter smell and taste.

I looked up at their cottage, at the window I imagined was his. The curtains were open. Inside it was dark, just a faint bluish light from a television flickering on the bare walls. I imagined him lying on his bed, arms crossed behind his head, thinking . . . but there I had to stop. I had no idea what boys like David thought.

5

It used to be Dad's job to carry the chairs. Now it was mine.

I walked ahead, Mum and Olly trailing some way behind with the basket. We always went to the same spot on the beach, a bowl of white sand clear of sedge and shielded on three sides by dunes. I set out the chairs beside each other, one for Mum, the other for me, then followed the path towards the shoreline.

On the hottest days, like this one, the sun drummed a rhythm on the top of my head and my arms and shoulders pricked with its heat. I stopped and looked at what the sea had brought in. Driftwood scummed with salt, an old tyre powdered white, an upturned crab shell. I picked up a frond of sea wrack, the bladders pruned like your fingertips after you've been in the bath too long. I raised it to my nose and sniffed.

When I got back, Mum was setting down the picnic basket beside the chairs.

'Can I go for a swim?' I asked.

'I suppose so.' She pushed her sunglasses onto her head, scraping back her fringe. She was wearing kingfisher-green eyeshadow and some of it had speckled on her cheekbones. 'Don't go too far out.'

I'd already changed into my swimming trunks at home so only needed to remove my shorts.

I walked to the pillbox, shuffling through the deep white sand. On my left the dunes ran into the distance. In patches, the sun had bleached the marram almost white, creating shocks of scorched tufts. A couple of ducks muddled through, the male ahead, the female making soft clacking noises as she followed on behind.

The pillbox squatted among the tank traps further up the beach. I clambered over the rocks that half choked the entrance and ducked my head inside. It was dark, the air sour with piss and the floor black where people had lit fires. Broken glass, fag ends, the odd splat of gull shit. I probed half a brick with my foot, astonished when I saw what I thought was a sea slug lying over the top of it, but as I bent down to take a closer look I realised it was a condom. It even had a knot in the end. I'd never seen a used one before.

I moved towards the window. Far away, almost on the horizon, a small white fishing boat jogged across the waves. I raised my arms, levelling them at the boat and fired off several rounds, filling the pillbox with the rattle of machine-gun fire. Then, ducking down to dodge the sand spray from an enemy grenade, I slid, panting, down the wall.

When I looked out again David was there. He was staring at the sea. As I watched, he turned and started to walk up the beach. I drew back sharply and dropped to my knees. If he saw me he'd think I was spying on him again, and he was headed this way. How would I get out without being seen? Rising slowly to my feet, I peered out, but no sign of him anywhere. He'd gone.

I ran for it, not pausing or slowing down until I stumbled into the sea. There I stood, gasping for breath, a wave creaming over my toes and sucking out the sand from between them. Cold. Nice. The next wave, bigger, slapped my knees. The one after that splashed my trunks. I clenched my teeth and inched forward until I was waist height. Behind me I could just make out Mum and Olly, Mum shaking out a towel to lay across her chair, Olly sitting on the picnic basket to unlace his plimsolls. They were looking at one another, talking, but too far away for me to hear the words. Other sounds reached me on the wind, a dog, short-legged and square-shouldered, barking at a stone, voices, yells and laughs from a group further up the beach.

I'd spat into my goggles and was just about to pull them down over my eyes when I saw him again. He was standing on the roof of the pillbox, legs apart, hand raised to his eyes to shield them from the sun's glare. He must've gone up and round through the dunes, and that's why I hadn't passed him. The wind snatched away the occasional plume of smoke that escaped from his mouth. He turned and looked in my direction as if he sensed he was being watched.

So what? I waded to the shore and trudged back across the sand to Mum and Olly. He didn't own the beach. Nobody did.

Mum had finished laying out the food and was midway through changing into her swimsuit, dark lavender blue with wide shoulder straps and a deep V at the front and back. I squeezed water out of my trunks and sat at her feet. I was already nearly dry, calves stippled with sand.

'What's it like?' she asked.

'Nice.'

A gust of wind snapped at the corner of her towel showing a flash of dimpled skin and, higher up, where the suit met her bum, faint papery silver lines. Olly didn't like the sun and had made a tent out of the picnic blanket. He crouched underneath it, only the blunt shape of his head visible.

'Why don't you try to find some dinosaur fillings, Olly?' Mum said.

Immediately he pulled the blanket down and jumped to his feet, spraying the paper plates with sand.

'Drink some water first.'

'I'll find loads more than you,' Olly said.

'They're anthropoids.'

'Don't start that again,' Mum said.

Olly took the bottle she gave him and, using both hands to lift it to his mouth, drank noisily. Water dribbled down his chin and onto the oily slick of sunblock on his chest.

Mum handed me the other bottle. 'I can't believe this heat. Hottest summer since 1911 apparently.'

'They're dinosaur fillings,' Olly said.

'She's not talking about the beads any more, stupid.'

'From billions of years ago.'

'That's just a story Dad told you.'

He pushed up his sunglasses to glare at me. They were prescription and circular with a thick purple frame that Mum said made him look like Elton John.

'Are you coming?' he said.

'No.'

He hurried off. He had a weird walk, all the movement from the knees down. Didn't walk, in fact, he twinkled. Fifty yards ahead of us, where the sand was gravelly with shells, he squatted down and began raking about.

I sat in the chair beside Mum who was examining a large ginger freckle on the underside of her arm revealing, as she twisted the skin round, the black stubble in her armpit.

'Mum?'

'Yes.'

'Do you think Dad meant what he said about me going to France when he's nearly finished the house?'

'I don't know.'

A vertical frown between her eyes; it was an

expression I knew well, the one she had whenever I mentioned Dad, wanting to say something, biting it back.

'Are you very disappointed?' she asked.

'No.'

She sat up, batting away a hovering bluebottle. 'It's all right to say you are, you know.'

'I'm not. I was just wondering, that's all.'

She settled again, digging two grooves in the sand with her heels.

'Don't think I'd like France anyway. They eat snails.'

'I know.'

'Snails move around on mucus. That's like eating snot.'

She laughed, a strand of hair falling into her open mouth. She scraped it back behind her ear with a fingernail.

If she was still angry with Dad for cancelling my trip to France she wasn't letting on, but it had always been like that. They never had fights in front of us, waited till we were in bed, the chimes of Big Ben on the ten o'clock news then voices, his and hers, getting louder.

'I'm sure you and Olly will find plenty to do here,' she said. 'Why don't you ask Mr Cauldwell's son if he wants to do something?'

'Who?'

'The boy next door.'

'His name's David.'

'I bet he doesn't know anyone.'

Pointless trying to make her understand. Some things

Mum just didn't see. She thought *The Silence of the Lambs* was a love story.

'You could invite him to tea?'

'Dunno, I'll think about it.'

Probably didn't even know he did weights. I'd seen him working out, hard not to when every time I'd looked out of my bedroom window he was there. He had dumbbells. Twenty times from stomach to chest, then to the side, twenty, straight up in the air, twenty, sweat jewelling the tip of his nose.

I had started to close my eyes when I glimpsed someone looking down from the top of the dune behind us. For a moment, with the sun behind him, I thought it was David, but he stepped forward and it wasn't. He put a finger to his lips, pointed at Mum, then lunged at her with a roar and grabbed her shoulders with both hands.

'Patrick, you bugger!'

She reached for her sarong, all out of breath, and in one quick movement, stood up and tied it around her waist.

'Pat! You scared me! Not fair!'

So that was him. Patrick. Pat. He'd phoned the house a couple of weeks back wanting to talk to her and when she'd come out of the kitchen to take the call she'd patted her hair in a make-yourself-look-respectable sort of way. I'd wanted to say *phone, not door*, but then she'd picked up the receiver and talked quietly into it, long smooth tones like honey drooling from a spoon.

'My son,' she said, suddenly remembering me. 'Leo.'

'Hello.'

He put out his hand, damp, rope-textured skin. The second our palms locked I wanted to be free. My hands would smell of his sweat. And fish. He was one of the lobstermen who worked out of the harbour, moved to Seaton a few months ago and bought Harold Millban's scabby old boat. None of the other fisherman wanted it. Everyone said it'd cost more to repair than it was worth, but Patrick bought it, did it up himself.

He smiled at me, showing Colgate teeth and a line of silvery-pink gum. When I didn't smile back he put his hands into the pockets of his shorts and tried to think of something to say. I didn't see what was so great about him. Anyone can slap a bit of paint on a boat. Doesn't make you a genius.

'Drink, Patrick?' Mum said. 'I've white wine. Excuse the flask, not very sophisticated, I'm afraid, but it keeps it cold.'

She never brought wine to the beach, not now, not since Dad left. I watched her pour it into plastic cups. Patrick had a wired, overly cheerful look about him, like he wanted something, but was too clever to ask for it straight away. Money, probably. That was it. He was planning to scam her. It happened all the time, maybe not all that often in Seaton, but it happened in other places. You heard about it on *Crimewatch*.

Yabber, yabber. Mum was talking so fast her neck had gone pink and he was staring at her, narrowing his eyes to look her up and down. Smiling. It was a stupid smile really, too big for his face. Weasels had mouths too big for their faces.

'Mum? I'm going for a look about. Mum?'

'What? Yes, all right, love. Where's Olly?'

I pointed, but she'd barely clocked him before she was talking again.

I bent down to put my sandals on, eyes shielded by my fringe so I could continue to watch them. He was staring at her tits, wasn't even trying to be subtle. But he was too young. How young? Twenties, no, thirties, and Mum was . . . ? Older. Forty-five at least.

'Have a sausage roll, Leo.'

'No.'

'You like sausage rolls.'

'I'm not hungry.'

'Why not go and help Olly then?'

She wanted to be alone with him to put knots in condoms like the one I'd found in the pillbox.

'Tusk!' Olly cried, waving a small tusk shell above his head. He ran across to show Mum.

He'd got beads, too, a handful. Patrick picked one off the palm of Olly's hand and held it up, only pretending to be interested, but Olly wouldn't notice. He was lapping it up, in fact, jabbering on about dinosaur fillings and all that rubbish. A few minutes later he came over and tipped the tusk and the beads into one of his socks for safe keeping.

'Told you,' he said.

'Shove off.'

'Want to play Frisbee?'

'No.'

'Go on. It'll be fun.'

'No, it won't. I'll smack you in the head and you'll cry again.'

'But I'm bored,' he said, his voice thinning to a whine.

'So?'

'Bury me in the sand, if you want.'

I looked at Patrick, his head was close to Mum's. He looked like he was going to kiss her, but pulled away when he saw me watching. Olly noticed too and giggled.

'Why don't you bury Patrick?' I said.

Olly ran over to him, interrupting him in mid-sentence and tugging on his wrist.

'I'll go swimming then,' I said.

'What?'

'*Swim.*'

Mum wasn't listening, her attention fixed on Olly who'd already started to dig around Patrick's feet. She joined in, laughing, as she scooped armfuls of sand.

I stood up, irritated by their noise, and set off at a brisk pace. A few minutes later I reached the water, but even as I waded out their whoops and shrieks followed me. I let myself sink under the waves, chin, nose, ears, the whole of my head until all I could hear was the boom and rustle of the sea.

6

I swam out a long way, trod water, spat out salt, expecting to hear Mum calling, but she didn't. I could've bloody drowned for all she cared. I wanted to go back and stretch out on the hot sand, but I clambered out onto the rocks instead and walked in the opposite direction towards Emmanuel Point. I'd explore the caves under the cliffs. Sometimes, after a high tide, things got washed in, like once I'd found a spider crab. Worth a look anyway.

For days the heat had teetered on the brink of a storm, a clammy expectant hush that hung over everything as if the earth had held its breath too long. You felt it strongest on the beach, a tightness in the lungs that made walking tiring.

As I rounded the headland I met a breeze, brief,

but cool. I stood for a moment, tilted my head back and lifted my arms to let the air flow underneath. When I straightened up, there he was. David. Again.

He'd think I'd followed him and so I immediately made as though I was busy staring into a rock pool, every so often glancing up to see what he was doing. He was kneeling close to the water's edge, feeding something onto the hook of a fishing rod. A cigarette dangled from his mouth and several more butts, neatly piled together, lay beside a tackle box.

He turned his head. 'All right?'

He seemed friendly. I moved closer. 'What's your bait?'

'Bread.'

He'd rolled several pieces into small, grey pellets. I watched him do another, squashing it first between his fingers to make it sticky and then using his palms to finish it off.

'Have you caught anything?'

He didn't answer. I figured it was because he hadn't had a bite and he wasn't happy about it. There wouldn't be fish here anyway. Might be able to catch a goby or a rockling, but it wasn't where people usually fished. Dad had bought us nets once but he'd never taken me proper fishing.

'Too many rocks,' I said.

He smoothed out the line between his fingers, but there was a knot, too tight to undo, so he cut out the tangled part and started again. I thought about telling him he should dispose of it properly because seabirds might try to eat it, but I stopped myself in time. I walked around to the other side of him, stepping back when a rogue wave rose up and spat.

'There's a good place further along there, about half a mile.'

'You fish?' he said.

'No. I've seen other people.'

'Right.'

'You can catch mackerel, but not with bread. They use lugworms.'

'Bread's fine.'

'You can dig them up on Cradle Cove. They make casts in the sand. That's how you know where they are. Or you can use limpets. You could get them off with your knife.'

I waited, but he didn't answer. I shouldn't have mentioned the knife. He'd assume I'd been thinking about it. I knelt down. The tops of my thighs were bluish though I wasn't cold. Next to him my pale body and soft flabby legs looked strange, like something that lived underwater. He reached into his satchel, graffitied with odd-looking symbols painted on with Tipp-Ex, and pulled the knife out of a small leather holder.

'Go on then,' he said. 'You do it.'

'A limpet?'

He put the knife into my hand. It fitted perfectly, cool and sleek with grooves where my fingers rested. I moved to the edge of a rock and lay on my stomach, peering into the water. There were lots of barnacles, but hardly any limpets. I leant out and tried to reach one, but I was scared I'd drop the knife.

'Got one yet?'

'No.'

I could've gone for a blue-vein limpet, a cluster of them was within easy reach, but they were too beautiful. Blood rushed to my head. I'd have liked to dip my face in, but I didn't have my goggles. I wrestled with a larger, common limpet until it fell loose into my hand.

'Now I have.' I handed it to him. 'You have to surprise them or they stick.'

'Yeah, all right.'

He took the knife back and used the tip of the blade to scoop the limpet out of its shell. I was pleased to have been given a job, but now stood by uncomfortably with nothing to do. My mouth was dry, saliva congealing on my teeth. I scraped aside a bit of bladderwrack and sat down. It'd crisped at the ends of the longest branches, but the centre was still damp.

I needed to fill the silence. 'You can get razor shells, too. They bury themselves in the sand, but if you pour salt down the hole they shoot up.'

'Shit, it's hot. Do you want a can?'

I didn't know what he meant. He smiled, making me feel stupid. 'Well? *Do you?*'

'All right.'

He crawled on all fours to the edge of the rock and pulled something out of the water, a carrier bag with string looped through the handles. He loosened the knot with his teeth, spitting out salt, and took out two cans of Carlsberg Special. They were the same cans I'd seen his dad drink.

'You do drink, don't you?'

'Course.'

He threw the can at me, but I only got one finger on it and it almost rolled all the way to the sea before I could stop it. When I turned back he was busy again with the rod, feeding the limpet onto the hook. Several times it slipped out of his fingers. Finally, he got it secured and cast out, screwing up his eyes to locate the float and then settling, dropping his shoulders.

'That thing with the salt,' he said. 'Does it really work?'

'Yeah, I think so. I never tried it. Read it in a book.'

'So it might not then.'

I shrugged and opened my can. I had to force down the bubbly sourness, but at least it was cold.

'What's your dad do?' I asked.

'Works at Thornleys.'

Thornleys was a lighting factory in Haresham. Lots of people in the village worked there. It explained why I'd seen his dad leaving the house late at night. They always started new people on night shift. I imagined David alone in the house, watching films in the dark in his bedroom.

'Graham Shipley, this boy at school, his dad's like the UK manager or something. The big boss.'

'Right.'

'He's got a yacht.'

'Kiss his arse, do you? This lad?'

'What? Why would I do that?'

'To get on his yacht.'

I was shocked. 'I don't really know him.'

'Sure.'

I wasn't friends with Graham Shipley, or any of Graham Shipley's mates. They sat in a group two rows behind me. Maybe they knew me, at least they knew the back of my head because they'd used it as target practice enough times. Paper bullets, gob, pencils used as darts. And anyway, it wasn't Graham's yacht, it was his dad's.

'Sweet Jesus, I mean, Mrs Browning, she does . . .' I skidded to a halt. 'Well, she's just this woman my mum knows, she thought maybe your dad was in the navy.'

'Army.'

'Oh, she was nearly right then.'

'Navy's full of wankers.'

A breeze shifted sideways across the water, making sharp curls that sped into the rocks and collapsed softly into bubbles of foam.

'What did he do then?'

'What?'

'In the army, what was his job?'

'Soldier, of course.'

I knew people in the army had actual jobs, like driver, or navigator, or they fixed tanks. I hadn't considered that David's dad might've been an actual soldier.

'He served in the Falklands.'

'Did he kill anyone?'

'It was a war.'

'Mrs Browning's husband was there, I think. She says he never talks about it, which makes me think he might've been Special Forces.'

I paused, hoping for effect, but David looked blank.

'He was away for ages. Her son's in the TA.'

He flicked the limpet shell into the water.

'I don't think they saw Mr Browning for a whole year. How long was your dad there?'

'Fucking hell.' He looked directly at me, mouth open to reveal a chipped tooth.

'What?'

'You always ask so many questions?'

'I just thought . . . I was making conversation.'

He stood up and started to wind in his rod. 'I'm jacking it in. This is crap.'

'Right.'

'Show me this place you're on about.'

'What? For fishing? Oh, yes, all right then. I know where.'

He went ahead, leaping over the gaps between the rocks, occasionally putting an arm out for balance. I was slower, took my own route, dropping into the gaps, climbing up the other side. Once he looked over his shoulder and I thought he might be waiting for me, but then he turned and strode on.

I hurried to catch up, lengthening my strides to match his, but it was a struggle to stay at his side. After a time he was forced to slow down, not knowing which way we were headed.

The best place for fishing was off the rocks right

at the very end of North beach. The only way to get there was to go down a steep cliff path, powdery, ash-coloured dust with loose stones that rolled and plopped into the sea. A few years ago Bobby Myers had slipped and skidded all the way down, breaking his leg in three places. A helicopter had to come and lift him out. The council put up a barbed-wire fence after that and a sign – DANGER, KEEP OUT – but you could easily get under it.

David handed me his rod and tackle box and once he was under the fence I gave them back and followed. He'd turned the hem of his shorts up several times revealing layers of tan at the tops of his thighs, darkest above his knees, a pale creamy yellow higher up.

He walked boldly down the slope, not scared of slipping at all. I tried to do the same, but the toe of one of my sandals snagged on a rock and I ended up scudding down on my bum, hands scrabbling frantically at either side. I snatched a tree root, but it was loose and I let out a gasp as I slid, untethered, to the bottom.

I'd grazed my knee, not enough to make it bleed, but the skin had broken. I picked off the gravel and stood up, swatting away a cloud of sandflies that'd been sucking the rocks.

'I'll cast you out,' David said.

'Me?'

'Just stand here and hold the rod.'

A few clouds, flat and grey like skimming pebbles, had drifted in. I joined him on a ledge that jutted out several feet into the sea. The waves rushed and lulled around, sealing us in.

David cast out, the line whipping the air above my head, and handed me the rod. 'Keep your eye on the float.'

At first the rod was awkward in my hands and I wasn't sure how to hold it, but the waiting and the concentration needed to watch the float felt good.

The wind circled in sharp gusts, creasing the water around the float. Underneath the surface it was almost black.

'Small movements. You have to tease them.'

For half an hour or more we didn't speak, but I knew that was how fishing was supposed to be. David sat behind me. Now and then I got a waft of the smoke from his cigarette or heard him raking through his tackle box.

'Maybe the bait's too big,' I said.

'Bait's fine.'

The sun gleamed off the surface making my eyes water so I kept having to blink and look away. It was obvious I understood nothing about fishing, but I did – and I really wanted to tell him – know a lot about fish. I suspected the fish that swam invisibly beneath us didn't consider a glob of dangling limpet all that appealing.

I gave the line a tug and it snapped tight. 'It's stuck.'

'No, it's not.'

The sun grated on my raw skin. I desperately wanted to sit in the shade or at least dip my legs into the water. I gave the line another pull, but I was frightened of breaking his rod.

'It's—'

'Yeah, all right.'

He stood up and cut the line with his knife then got another limpet and sat beside me, laying the rod over his knees. His fingers were wide, the knuckles big and grained with dirt, but his hand was steady. He used the very tip of his thumbnail to tie a knot in the line where it met the hook. A bead of sweat dropped from the tip of his nose onto the back of his hand.

'There. You cast out this time.' He shifted position so he stood directly behind me and reached around with his arms to take hold of the rod. 'Over your right shoulder, OK? Then sharp forward.'

His hands rested over mine and for a moment I struggled to get my breath. The heat of his chest fused with my hot back, his armpit hair tickling my shoulder.

'Look at where you want it to go. Aim about five feet to the left of that rock.'

He made a small movement and I tried to follow, but I wasn't in time with him and I felt his body tense. Again the muscles on his arms tightened around me and he drew back the rod, throwing the line sharply over my shoulder and then lashing it forward. The float plopped into the water. I took a breath.

'OK,' he said. 'That'll do.'

As soon as he let go my skin goose-pimpled, a thin breeze carrying off our mingled sweat.

'How do you know when you've got a bite?'

'You'll know.'

'But how do I know the line isn't just snagged on a rock?'

He rolled his eyes. 'I can't believe you live by the sea and you don't fish. You tug and the fish tugs back.'

'My dad—'

'*Like now.*'

'Huh?'

'Lift the fucking rod! LIFT it!'

The tip of the rod bent into an arc. 'I've caught something!'

'Now you got to get him in.' He touched the line to get a feel. 'Slow. Don't snatch at it.'

I thrust the rod at him, but he wouldn't take it and instead stood to the side of me, one hand supporting the rod as I wound the line in.

'*Slow.*'

'It's struggling.'

'Easy then, don't pull.'

He jumped down to guide the line so it wouldn't get caught on the rocks. A second later I saw the fish. 'It's a goby!'

'It's dinner.'

As the fish swung nearer he grabbed it and laid it down on the rock between us.

'Dinner?'

Nobody ate them, nobody who fished for fun anyway. You always put them back.

'It's a young one.' I smoothed a finger along the scales. 'They get a lot bigger than this.'

'So?'

'You're really going to eat it?'

'Yep.'

I looked at where he'd been sitting. While I'd been holding the rod, he'd prepared a circle of stones. In the middle was a wigwam of twigs. He unhooked the goby.

'We'll need to find some more dry wood. This stuff'll burn quick.'

I knew fish were caught and put back and it didn't do them any harm. The goby curled, tail, then head, like the plastic fish that come out of Christmas crackers.

'We should put it back,' I said. 'It can't breathe.'

'Smack it over the head then.'

'I caught it, I should decide.'

'What did you think we were going to do?'

'There's a snack van just down there, you could have a burger.'

I wanted to pick it up and sling it back to the sea. I saw myself doing it, quick, before David could stop me, but it was already too late. He picked it up by the tail fin and dragged it towards him. In his other hand he gripped the knife, the handle pointing down-wards. The goby heaved, almost flipped over, but then stopped, suddenly, mouth open in a gasp.

'What are you waiting for?' I said. 'Do it if you're going to.'

'Now?'

He was actually grinning.

'Just do it!'

He brought the handle down on its head. The first

blow did nothing. The second struck it dead. I stared at it; the glassy eye had slipped out of its socket and lay, a bloody disc, over its mouth.

'Fuck!' He laughed. 'You see that? Its eye popped out.'

I wanted to go, right then, to leave him and the goby, but I just sat, quiet, watching him finish building the fire. I'd wasted time, while it flapped on the rock. It was David who'd done the right thing in the end.

When the fire was ready he folded over a handful of marram, scorched dry, and used it as a torch to light the centre, then took the goby and laid it across a flat slab of rock. Carefully he slit down the marble-grey flesh, head to tail fin, exposing the spinal column, gills, bones that ran in neat arcs through the meat. Gulls swooped and circled overhead. He gathered the guts, a fistful of green and purple slime, and threw them into the sea where they disappeared in a frenzy of white wings.

I folded my T-shirt in half lengthways and laid it across my shoulders. Sweat ran over the folds of fat on my stomach and settled in my shorts. Silence again. I had to fill it.

'You know, Bradstones isn't better than any other school,' I said. 'It's just different.'

'Eh?'

'The teachers are pretty strict.'

'They give you a clip?'

'No.'

'Yeah, right, you'd probably sue them.'

'Corporal punishment was abolished in 1986.'

'Fuck, you ever say anything you haven't read in a book?' He sharpened a twig with his knife and drove it through the body of the fish, spreading out the two sides like wings. 'This teacher at my school gave me such a smack—'

'A teacher *hit* you?' I leant forward, elbows up on my knees. 'What for?'

'You think I had it coming?'

I shrugged. 'There must've been a reason.'

He reached for his cigarettes, taking the last one from a packet of twenty. It was squashed and bent so he ran his thumb and forefinger down the length to straighten it.

'We had this maths test,' he said. 'What grade you got decided which level you were put in next term. Only before the exam the test papers went missing.'

'Stolen?'

'By Friday there were copies everywhere, two quid each, even some of the other schools had them. They had to withdraw it, cost a bomb. Real fucking mess. Dodson said I was the last one out of his class so it must've been me.'

'And he hit you?'

'No questions asked, no proof. I got one back on him though, give him a fat lip. I could've got expelled for that, but then if the head had found out he'd hit me he'd have got fired probably. Guess we were even.'

'Did you do it?'

'Huh?'

'*Did* you steal the test?'

'Course I fucking did.'

71

I laughed. Pretty soon I was laughing so hard I couldn't sit up straight. I rolled onto my back, David too, and then his head was level with mine, mouth wide open, laughing, looking at me like he couldn't believe I found it so funny. I didn't even know why I did, it wasn't like it was the most hilarious thing you've ever heard.

It didn't matter. It was enough, that's all, enough to be there on the rock, face scorched by the fire, fingers tacky with fish scales. And laughing. Both of us. Laughing.

7

The air was thick and sticky, the sun shielded for most of the morning behind a thin layer of cloud. Far off, the black hood of a storm hung over Harwood Forest.

We'd been mooching about on the beach since breakfast. Now, bored, David balanced on the dragon's teeth while I drove a stick of driftwood into the sand.

'This is shit,' he said.

'We could go to the arcade?'

'Skint.'

I minded a lot less, this uneventful passing of time, but David was rarely still, always waiting for the next thing to happen. He held his arms out to his sides, the balls of his feet balanced precariously on the points of each concrete pyramid as he jumped from one to the next, to the end of the line and back again.

'Do you know why they're called dragon's teeth?' I said, wriggling my toes into the sand. 'It's from Greek mythology. Cadmus, he was like this Greek god or king or something, anyway, he slayed this dragon and planted its teeth. Then warriors—'

'They're to stop tanks coming up the beach.'

'Yes, that too, but they're called dragon's teeth because—'

'Ah, who gives a fuck?'

He slumped into the sand next to me causing the hole I'd dug to cave in. For a while then he was quiet, one thumbnail scraping out the dirt from under the other, occasionally screwing up his eyes to look up and down the beach. 'I'm going diving.'

'Where?'

He was looking at the Point.

'You can't dive off there. You'll be killed.'

'Not off the top, you nugget. The ledge, halfway.'

Nobody had ever dived off the ledge as far as I knew, nor even thought of doing it probably. It was easy to be fooled by the Point. Tufts of thrift sprouted from the crevices, their pompoms of pink flowers softening the gradient, but behind them the drop was sheer, fifteen feet, perhaps twenty, too high to dive off.

He gave me a look, the dare lighting his eyes, then stood up and set off along the beach. I followed, trying not to trot, and waited beside him as he loosened the laces on his trainers and heeled them off.

It was easy to say from a distance you were going to do it, but underneath, looking up, the dive was massive. I wondered if he'd back out. I hoped he would.

'You don't have to,' I said. 'I mean, it doesn't matter if you don't.'

'I'm not chickening out.'

'I'm just saying, it doesn't matter if you don't. I won't tell.'

It was what I would've been afraid of myself. Taking a dare and then not going through with it was worse than saying you wouldn't. Except I hadn't dared him.

He started to climb, his whole body twisting and flexing like one thick muscle. Across his right shoulder there was a scar, still pink, several more on the backs of his thighs, some of which were oddly circular. I'd only got one, a bracket-shaped ridge on my right knee I did when I fell off a swing at Dad's.

A quiver of excitement bolted across my chest and for a few seconds it seemed the air around us sparked. Then, the first drop of rain, solitary, until seconds later hundreds more smacked off the rocks around us. David carried on, pausing every few seconds to choose where next to plant his feet until finally he pulled himself onto the ledge and stood up.

'You did it!'

'Course I did.'

He held out his arms to the sides, palms up and tipped his head back, sticking out his pink, fat tongue to catch the rain. I looked down at myself, my white body ghostly in the light that had changed from dim grey to silver. His was the same, not as pale, but still oddly illuminated.

Thunder rumbled, a deep throaty sound that seemed to come from underneath us. David replied with a roar of his own, pointing left and right, conducting the sea, and then yelling when a bolt of lightning shot from a cloud and fractured the horizon.

It didn't last long, the storm. We'd only caught the edge of it, the mass of black cloud moving west towards Haresham. The rain, as quickly as it'd come, stopped, and the gulls took to the air again, rawking. The thunder grew fainter. All that was left was steam, clinging to us like a second skin.

David turned on the ledge so that his back was facing the sea. For one heart-wrenching moment I thought he was going to attempt the dive backwards right then, but he was merely assessing the space between himself and the cliff. It wasn't enough to give him any sort of run. For a long time he was still.

'Right,' he said finally. He turned back. 'Ready?'

A razorbill flapped overhead, screeching. I nodded.

It didn't even look planned, for there wasn't a second's hesitation. He lifted off, his body flexing in the air, tilted, glided, smooth as a dart. At first I thought he was too close and that he'd smash onto the rock beside me, but then the sea opened and took him in. A fountain of foam shot up. I scrambled on my hands and knees to where the rocks met the water, but could see only a chain of white bubbles.

Nothing. A minute, two. No sign.

'*David?*'

I looked for blood. There was no way of knowing how deep it was and he couldn't know, not unless he'd checked first and no way he'd done that. If he'd hit the bottom he might've smashed his head. A jut of rock—

'Shit!'

I looked to my right. He was hauling himself out of the water. He came over, his bare feet slapping on the rock.

'You did it!'

He shook his head, tiny droplets of water landing on my legs to roam and tickle among the hairs.

'I thought—'

'Now you.' He was panting, mouth wide in a grin. 'You do it and then I'll go again.'

'What? No.'

'It's a cinch.'

I'd seen him do it, knew it was possible, but I couldn't dive like that. It hadn't even occurred to me I'd have to, that he'd expect it. I looked across the bay. Frustrated, he sat down, reaching for his trainers and pulling out the cigarettes he'd hidden inside. They were sodden from the rain. He closed his fist around the packet and threw it into the sea.

'I'm sorry,' I said. 'I just can't, all right?'

He sighed noisily. 'You saw me.'

'It doesn't matter, does it?'

'It's a rush. Don't you want to know what it feels like?'

I did. I thought I did. I looked over my shoulder.

It'd got higher, or so it seemed, the face leading up to the ledge sharp and toothy. I'd have to do what he'd done, the same route, the same height. I twisted the hem of my T-shirt around my fingers, felt him watching. Doing the dive would make things right again, like when I'd caught the goby. I imagined us, both wet from our dives, high on the thrill, laughing.

'Be a dickhead then,' he said. 'Do it or don't do it. Up to you.'

I stood up, my knees trembling. Excited, he leapt to his feet and led me to the cliff face, one hand on my shoulder, the other raised to point out the route he'd taken. The sun, naked now of cloud, beat fiercely on our backs.

'First your right hand, OK? Then your left foot. And don't look down or you'll throw yourself off balance.'

I gulped warm air, catty with brine, and edged towards the base. David moved ahead of me to show me the first hold, then placed a hand at the bottom of my back and pushed me gently forward. My heart thumped, ears blocked. When both of my hands and feet were on the face he held my ankles.

'I can't,' I said, straining to look at him.

'Don't look at me. Up. Look up.'

I closed my eyes, breath bouncing back into my face off the rock. Carefully, I started to climb. Once I looked down at him through my legs, but I wobbled, dizzy, and dislodged a rock that peppered down the side of the cliff. Grit dug into the pads on my fingers. For a second I couldn't move, legs spreadeagled on the face, a dead starfish. I tried again to see David, but I couldn't risk turning my head. Heard him though, a garble of instructions that made no sense.

Somehow I managed to lift my right leg and get back into a rhythm. I no longer wanted to look down. Easier just to think about getting to the top. I was all right as long as I didn't think about how high I was. When I finally got there I heaved myself onto the ledge, scraping the skin on my stomach on the rock, and lay panting.

'Stand up,' David shouted. 'Stand up so I can see you.'

I got first to my knees, then, leaning back on my heels, I stood up and flattened myself against the back wall of the cliff. I could see the top of David's head and, as he stepped back, his face and shoulders.

'See?' he said. 'Thought you couldn't do it, didn't you?'

A tanker was crossing the horizon, leaving a thick band of dark water in its wake. I tried to bend my knees and put my arms out to a point in front, but the sea swam in circles and I crouched down again to regain my balance.

David was talking, but his voice had become a blur of words again. I just had to do it now or climb back down and that would be harder than getting up. I braced myself and stepped closer to the edge, closer, and then with a moment's involuntary buckling of my knees, I was in the air. I knew I was wrong the second I took off and hit the sea flat.

The water gave me a huge, stinging slap. No breath. Bubbles. Pain.

I opened my eyes, cold and salt rushing into the back of my lids, saw nothing, black all around, then, as I looked up, light. I swam towards it, my lungs bursting.

'HELP!'

A wave slopped into my mouth and I coughed. David was thrashing through the water. I felt him grab me under the arms.

'Stop kicking!'

'My foot—'

I went under again, wanted to, anything to stop the sound of my yelling and the pain that dragged me down. I kicked and surfaced again, choking. I was barely able to keep my chin above the swell. David was screaming.

'*Lie back, keep still!*'

Twice he dropped under the surface and I felt myself drift, out to sea or back to shore I couldn't tell. The tips of my fingers collided with something hard. I snatched for it, clawing for a hold, and with a heave from David, I dragged myself onto the rock. I felt I never wanted to move again, but I'd left no room for him to get out and so I had to crawl forward another few feet.

David clambered up, water running off his legs, dripping from his hair. 'You OK?'

I looked at my foot. Blood was running freely from a big gash above my right toe, so much blood and so fast that in no time there was a red, watery trail back to the sea.

'It's broken it, I think.'

David moved to touch it.

'Don't!'

'It's just a cut.'

'The blood—'

'There isn't much.' He looked at it admiringly. 'Just looks like there is because of the water.'

I bit down, the edges of my teeth pressing into my bottom lip.

'Waggle it.'

'I can't.'

'Waggle it.'

I tried to move my toe, but the pain was too much and I cried out.

'Quit yelling.'

'It's bad, isn't it? Really bad.'

My cheeks burned with the effort of swallowing the pain, but I was excited too. I'd done it. I'd only gone and bloody done it. David ripped the sleeve off my T-shirt, tearing at it with his teeth first, then, when that didn't work, pulling the stitches apart with his hands.

'I must've hit my foot on the ledge.'

He folded the piece into a strip and tied it around my toe.

'I don't remember. Did I? Did you see?'

'Lucky it wasn't your head.'

'You'll have to get someone. I can't walk.'

'You haven't tried.'

I sucked in air through my teeth, saw him stifle a laugh.

'S'not funny.'

'Leo, that was the worst fucking dive I've ever seen.'

'It *hurts*.'

'You should've seen your face. Thought you'd shat yourself! Thought I was gonna get a shit shower!'

I wanted to laugh, but didn't let myself, not wanting, at least not for a while, to admit the pain was numbing to a throb. I was beginning to see the advantages. I'd make the scar bigger of course, you could do that if you picked at it.

'How did you get yours?' I said. 'That scar on your lip?'

The smile wiped clean. 'Kick in the face. Football.'

I don't know how I knew it wasn't true, I just knew.

He looked at the way we'd come. 'We better get you back.'

It was at least fifty yards before you got to the sandy part of the beach. Even if we took our time and planned the best route, there were several wide platforms of rock and some crevices we'd have to jump over.

'You can't carry me.'

'I'm not going to.'

He helped me to my feet and moved ahead, signalling for me to follow in his footsteps. His plan, it turned out, was to haul me up and down the gaps between the rocks, but I felt safer shuffling on my bum. The tide was coming in fast, the last twenty feet between us and the beach already covered by a tongue of sea water. We waded through it, salt stinging the wound, and sat on the sand where I could rest.

'You all right?' he said after a few minutes.

I nodded.

He helped me up and we walked, my arm across his shoulder so I could balance on my heel. When we reached the dune path I put the sandal back on my uninjured foot. The ground had softened, the recent rain releasing a warm, soily smell. We climbed the steps up to the village and passed the golf club-house with its oversized flag smacking in the wind. I'd been looking down, pacing myself, so we were nearly at St Margaret's Church before I saw them. Jaz and Taffy. Shit.

David clocked my change of expression. 'What?'

'Come on. I know another way we can go.'

I turned back the way we'd come, thinking we could cut through the car park and up the narrow lane behind it.

'What are you doing?' David said.

'It's quicker.'

'Quicker? No, it's not.'

Jaz was leaning over the wall that edged the cemetery, plucking the heads off daises. He hadn't seen us, but would do if we didn't get a shift on.

'Who are they?'

'Nobody. Dickheads.'

I didn't want to say bullies. Anyway, to call Jaz Donnelly a bully didn't do him justice. He was actually insane – psychotic – as well as good-looking and tall and the sort of stupid where it doesn't matter because being hard makes up for it. He lived oppos-ite my bus stop and for some reason, though I didn't think reason had a lot to do with it, he took my school uniform as a personal insult. Like I was saying I was better than him because Bradstones was a private school. But I never *said* anything.

I measured the distance between us and them. Considering how scrawny he was, Taffy was fast, but nothing like as fast as Jaz. He held Cadwell's Sports Day record for every race, and not just because no one dared beat him.

'David? This way.'

'What's the big deal?'

Jaz looked over, confused. He was used to finding me alone. Without hesitation he got up off the wall and strode towards us, leaving Taffy mid-sentence. I limped a few steps, hoping David would follow, but he just stood, staring at Jaz as he approached. Jaz was bigger, but then he was bigger than most kids. Six foot probably.

'Hurt yourself, Leo?'

It was the first time he'd used my name and it surprised me so much I couldn't think of anything to say. He looked at my foot, the makeshift bandage David had made now pink and flecked with grit.

'What you do, uh?'

I froze. Jaz's eyes roved over me, up and down, then switched to David.

'Who's your mate?' He exchanged a glance with Taffy. 'Boyfriend?'

David tensed, but he didn't say anything.

'Must be. Yeah, got to be, hanging around with bum magnet.'

Too late to run. I'd never get away anyway, I could barely walk. I couldn't see David's face, but he must've been smiling because Jaz's face tightened.

'What? I say something funny?'

'Yeah, you're a real fucking comedian.'

Surprise flickered over Jaz's face. I took a deep breath. We were as good as dead.

I tugged on David's arm. 'They're not worth it.'

'Yeah, we're nothing, right, Taff?'

David's chest rose and fell, one breath, the only one he seemed to have taken. They'd never leave him alone. Not now. I wanted to tell them. David was nothing like me. I wanted to say it. Then, David, who'd been so still, so controlled, lunged forward. He grabbed Jaz by the throat, shoving him backwards with so much force that he tripped over his feet. David fell on top of him. The two of them wrestled, but David had him good, fingers clamped on his throat. I looked at Taffy. He was staring down at them, mouth open. Stunned. We both were. Jaz's face was tight in pain. I'd never seen him scared, didn't even know he could be, but he was proper shitting himself.

'Come here, Leo,' David said.

'What?'

'*Here.*'

I went and stood over them.

'Hit him.'

'He can't breathe.'

'*Hit* him.'

'No, look, let him go.'

A squeak of trainers on tarmac. Taffy had legged it,

sprinting off down the road as fast as his legs could carry him.

'I don't want to.'

'Hit him, for fuck's sake.' He pushed Jaz's head into the ground, tightening his hold on him, crying out in frustration. 'You think it's all right for him to talk to you like that?'

'No—'

'Tell him to say sorry then. DO IT.'

Jaz looked at me, one eye bulging, cheeks purple.

'Just say it, Jaz,' I said.

He croaked, but David just squeezed harder.

'He can't say anything! You're holding him too tight!'

David let go. Jaz spluttered, spit bubbling out of the corner of his mouth. He got to his feet and rubbed his throat, red, except for the white circles where David had dug in with his fingers. He backed off, stopped as if he didn't know what to do, then David took a step forward and Jaz decided, turned, and ran off.

I let out a long breath.

'What you let them talk to you like that for?'

'It doesn't matter.'

'You could've had him. All you had to do was punch him.'

'I didn't *want* to, OK?'

He walked in front of me, trying to get me to look at him.

'They're nothing, it's not—'

'Leo, you don't sort them out they'll be on your back forever.'

I knelt to adjust the bandage on my foot.

'You fucking *want* that?'

'I don't mind. I can rise above it.'

'Rise above it?' He grabbed my wrist. 'That's what your mam tells you, is it? Jesus H. You're a fucking joke!'

'I didn't ask you to help me.'

'Coward.'

'I could sort them out if I wanted to. I'd—'

'Yeah, right, you'd shit your fucking pants.'

We stood for a moment, eyes locked, but it was David who looked away first. He shrugged elaborately and walked off.

After a few minutes I limped slowly back the way we'd come, down the steps and back to the beach. The sea was huge, a wall of slate blue. I made for the pillbox, knowing that in there it would be dark, empty.

I hated Jaz, more than I'd ever hated him, and I wished now I'd hit him. But I hadn't. Hadn't. I slid down the wall to the floor and pressed my fingertips into my eyes. Sooner or later I knew I'd have to go home, but I didn't want to. David would be there and I wasn't ready to face him. Shit. I'd ruined everything. In just a second I'd ruined everything, but it wasn't my fault. It wasn't. It wouldn't have been fair for me to hit Jaz like that with David pinning him down. But now David would think I was soft, what they said I was. A poof. He wouldn't bother with me any more. Probably go off and make friends with Jaz. They belonged together. And I didn't belong anywhere.

I unzipped my shorts and tried to take a piss. At first it wouldn't come, then a spurt hit the wall. While I peed I gazed around the pillbox. I was familiar with the graffiti, though some had faded or blackened with smoke. Today, though, there was something new. A word scratched into the concrete. A name. DAV. Started, but not finished. I zipped up my shorts and picked up a stone to scratch the last two letters onto the wall and DAV became DAVID.

8

Durham Market Place, late Saturday afternoon. I'd shopped at the stalls then headed home along the muddy path that ran alongside the allotments. The brassy winter sun was fading, probing the bare hawthorn hedge. I stopped and looked through the knotted branches. A furl of blue smoke rose from a wood fire in front of a row of cabbages, thick, veined, beaded with dew. Further back, a line of dead sunflowers, their spectral heads drooping.

At home I showered and changed, hoping to wake myself up, but felt no better. The evening stretched out before me. I was going out with some mates from my course, but now felt I mightn't bother. The meal with David and Kathryn had been exhausting, not least because I had replayed it over and over in my head all day. I switched on the television and flicked through the channels.

A roll of laughter outside, then the buzzer, loud, insistent. I ran downstairs and opened the door. A black wind blew spikes of sleet into my face.

'David.'

He'd been looking at the upstairs window, but seeing the door had opened he walked towards me. He had his bag and was dressed in the same clothes he'd worn to dinner last night.

'Freezing my bollocks off out here.'

I moved to let him past and then followed him up the stairs. Once inside the flat I stood, rubbing my arms. So much of him, a smell of cold, of wet wool, damp hair and cigarette smoke. Something underneath, almost feral, which made me aware of how close we were standing.

He sat on the sofa and pulled a cushion onto his lap. 'Can I take you up on your offer?'

'Offer?'

'Staying here.'

'Oh, right. Of course.' The thought of him staying at the flat made me uneasy, as though I were revealing more of myself than I was prepared for. I wasn't ready to have my life exposed. 'I'll be going out though.'

'With Kathryn?'

'No, with some mates. She's at a hen party.'

He hadn't shaved, but there was still the shine to his boots and his shirt had crisp army folds. He lifted his legs so that just his feet hung over the side of the sofa and lit a cigarette. The movement was familiar, the way he held it in his mouth, the concentration as he bent over the flame. At the station I'd wondered if I would recognise him, but the real shock was realising how little he'd changed.

'Well . . .' I said. 'I'll give you my spare key.'

'Mind if I have a shower?'

'Now? There might not be much hot water. I've just had one.' A pause. 'You're welcome to try.'

He nipped his cigarette, rested it on the saucer and pushed himself from the sofa. I thought of leaving him to it, but sat down, listening to the patter of water on the floor and the sudden gulp of silence when he switched the shower off. When he appeared again he was naked and in the few seconds before he wrapped a towel around his waist I caught a glimpse of his cock, swinging.

He ran a hand over his head. Tiny droplets of water funnelled down his neck and chest. 'You sure it's OK, me staying?'

'Of course. It's probably better you're here. That you're—'

'Close?'

'Available.'

He slid past me, reaching for his cigarettes. He looked depressed, or perhaps just tired.

'Look, come if you like,' I said. 'It's just some mates from uni. A group of us are meeting for a drink in town.'

'All right.'

He grabbed his bag off the floor beside the sofa and disappeared, returning a few minutes later dressed in dark jeans and a black polo neck. It suited him, like a skin.

We set off together towards the town centre, David with the tips of his fingers tucked into his front pockets. A fine rain had begun to wash away the curds of dark slush that had gathered at the sides of the road, but he hadn't bothered with a coat. Soon his jumper was jewelled with silver drops. He lowered his head, shielding his face from the wind, taking great strides I did well to match. As we crossed Elvet Bridge a freezing gust from the river snatched our breath, but once we pushed open the door of the pub we were met by a fug of warm bodies and beer.

Most of the crowd were already there, perched on stools by the bandit. Michael. Nick. Graeme. I introduced David and the group spread out to welcome us in.

I went to the bar, but David was quick to follow and walked up and down looking at the pumps. Once I'd got a round in he helped to carry the drinks back to the table. I tried to appear normal, laughing loudly at their jokes, drinking too quickly. I'd been nervous about how David would fit in, but it wasn't long before I realised I'd been worrying about the wrong thing. A couple of times he gave me a look, signalling what I took to be disapproval of the others, or of me, or of the life I'd created. His manner was, if anything, arrogant, and as time passed I could sense his antagonism growing. They were an OK bunch, a little pretentious perhaps, though I hadn't thought that until I saw them through his eyes.

When he went to the Gents he was gone so long I thought he might've left. Part of me was relieved if it was true, I resented the way he made me feel like an outsider in the group, but then he reappeared at my shoulder, carrying a round of pints and chasers on a tray.

He handed Nick his drink first.

'Thanks,' Nick said, looking startled, 'but I don't do shots.'

'What?'

'Someone'll have it. Graeme?'

Graeme shook his head. He was still holding the last pint which he'd barely touched. David opened his mouth, but I interrupted him before he could speak. 'I'll have it.'

Michael, who'd started talking to a group at one of the nearby tables, waved Nick and Graeme across. David turned to me, lowering his voice. 'I thought all students were pissheads.'

'The way you're necking them nobody could keep up.'

'These your mates?'

'Ye-es?'

'Nowt.' He tossed the whisky back. 'Wouldn't have thought they were your sort, that's all.'

'What does that mean?'

He didn't answer, glancing over his shoulder to a couple who were sitting directly behind him. I felt him tense and thought perhaps it was because the man was talking loudly.

'It's a fucking embarrassment,' he was saying, pint

an inch from his lips. 'Squaddies are all the same. Thick as shit. I mean, pissing on the Iraqis, taking bloody pictures of themselves doing it?'

David took a step backwards, knocking their table.

'Leave it,' I said. 'What's wrong with you?'

'Doesn't know what he's fucking talking about.' He picked up his cigarettes. 'Stay if you want. I'm going to try that Lloyds place.'

'*David?*'

'What?'

'Just . . .'

'Come then.' He knocked back his beer and pushed my chaser towards me.

I could feel his anger growing, knew I had to get him away and soon, but I felt bad about leaving. As we got to the door I turned back to wave at the lads, but they were deep in conversation.

Darts of sleety rain found every patch of bare skin. Once I peered over the edge of Elvet Bridge, the lights from the pubs and restaurants reflected in the dark water, but David kept moving, head down, and I had to run to catch up. In the Market Place we passed three girls huddled together outside the Tavern, eating chips from a carton. They'd kicked off their heels, must have been bloody freezing, but they didn't seem to care. David crept up behind one of them and snatched a chip.

'Oi!' She spun round ready for a fight, but softened when she saw him. 'Got garlic sauce on, mind.'

'S'all right.'

'Not if you're gunna snog your lass later.'

'Who says I've got a lass?'

'Aw, diddums. Want to come home with me for a cuddle?'

'Aye,' her friend laughed. 'Your Mick'd love that.' She looked us up and down. 'You two bouncers?'

'Bouncers?' David glanced at me. The girls turned in my direction, a line of cleavages and three-barrelled bellies. 'Yeah, right.'

'Bloody hell,' the big blonde said. 'It's him off *Ant and Dec*. Dec, or Ant. Shit meself if I woke up with you. Think I was in the fucking jungle. "I'm a celebrity get me out of 'ere!"'

A cackle of laughter. 'Just kidding, love. You don't really like look 'em. Wanna chip?'

'No,' I said. 'Thanks though.'

We walked on and had reached the barriers that closed off the Market Place when one of the girls shouted after us. As we turned she lifted her skirt to show us her arse, a fat white peach halved by the red slash of her thong.

David laughed and waved.

'I take it you don't have anyone?' I said.

'Have anyone what? Oh, a Kathryn, you mean? No.' For a moment I thought he'd stopped, but he went on. 'You love her, Kathryn?'

'Yes.'

'Fucking hell, Leo. Lurve, shit, you're — what are you? Twenty?'

'Twenty-two.'

'You even know why you're with her?'

'Yes. I can't imagine being with anyone else.'

'Bullshit, Leo. Fuck! You know it is.'

'How do you know what's right for me? I'm not fourteen any more.'

'You are what you are.'

'And you're drunk.'

So was I, or at least so thick-headed that once we'd got inside Lloyds I lost track of time entirely. Might've been one hour, or several. We talked little, the music was too loud anyway. He might easily have pulled, a couple of girls had looked over, but he seemed content just to sit and drink.

Before the lights came up we left and started to walk home.

'I got some JD in my bag,' he said, leaning into my shoulder.

I'd had enough, but I knew he'd want to go on drinking. He stumbled into the path of a taxi which swerved, beeping its horn. I hauled him back.

'Oh Leo, Leo, Leo, Leo. You're lost.'

'No, I'm not.'

'Phi-lo-soph-fuckly.'

A thick fog was replacing the sleet, freezing fog, or it would be in a couple of hours. I shivered and drew my coat tighter around me. A few yards further on he broke loose and staggered into the doorway of Clinton Cards, unzipping his flies for a piss. I watched him hunched in the corner, a puddle forming around his feet, steaming as it trickled onto the pavement. When he turned round he was trying to light a cigarette, his face swaying over the flame.

'Come on,' I said. 'I'm cold.'

A man and his girlfriend had stopped ahead of us, the man with his hand edging up the hem of the girl's blouse. It was the guy who'd been sounding off about squaddies earlier. I hoped David wouldn't recognise them, but he tripped, swore, and looked up at the girl.

'Sorry. Mouth. Soap.'

They broke from their kiss and laughed.

'Hey, you're that gobshite from before. *British Army*. You should fucking say that.'

The man frowned and, instinctively, or perhaps responding to pressure from her boyfriend's hand, the girl took a small step back.

'David,' I said. 'Leave them be.'

'No, he was expressing an opinion about "squaddies". I'm interested.'

'Yeah. So what?' He looked amused, but had turned his body round to face us, braced. 'We shouldn't even be fucking there, mate.'

'You British?'

'Why?'

'Only you talk like a Paki.' David stepped forward again, grinning. 'You know what happens in war, *mate*? People get fucked. And they get fucked all kinds of different ways—'

'Come on,' I said. 'Leave it.'

I took hold of his arm at the elbow, but he shrugged me off.

'So what if they piss on a few Iraqis? You know what they'd do to us, what they have done?'

'What's your problem, huh?'

'They're fighting for your freedom, you and your fucking ugly girlfriend.'

'What did you say? You believe he just said that?' The girl had been wary until now. She edged out of the doorway. 'You can't say that!'

'He's just drunk,' I said. 'He doesn't mean—'

'He said I was ugly.'

'You are,' David slurred. 'Park a fucking truck in that mouth, but big enough for your cock though, hey? Big man with a big cock. You, you couldn't fight a fucking war, you, you wanker—'

The man swung at him, missing with his right arm, but a second later he landed a blow to David's ear that knocked him off his feet. As I ran forward to separate them the girl yanked on my arm. I glanced at her, back to the fight. David was up again, spinning and stumbling down the street with the man in pursuit. He grabbed David's arm and they fell, a knot of struggling dark backs on the greasy cobbles.

Most of the punches landed nowhere, but the man got a knee on David's chest and for a moment he was pinned, taking punch after punch. I pulled the guy's leg at the ankle and reached for David's arm, but missed. The girl ran towards her boyfriend.

'It's all right, Mo! Leave him!'

David managed to swing his fist, a smack as it made contact and then blood from the guy's mouth spattered on the street. As he wiped his chin, dazed, one hand groping for something to hold onto, David kicked him twice in the stomach. I watched, able to move, but didn't. I could've stopped him, perhaps, but

I didn't. Seconds later, though it felt longer, I grabbed his arm. He spun round, fist raised.

'It's *me*.'

His eyes were wide, saliva and blood dribbling down his chin.

'For fuck's sake. Stop!'

He yanked his arm free and spat a gob of blood onto the street. 'I'm done.'

A crowd had gathered. Somebody shouted, 'Ring the police,' and immediately David was off, sprinting ahead of me, spitting as he went. I ran after him, but as I turned onto North Road I slowed to a walk. No police vans, but I cut through the bus station just in case, hoping David would be back at the flat. He'd have to be, had nowhere else to go.

I found him in the living room hunched over his bag. He pulled out the bottle of Jack and unscrewed the cap. He was pretty fucked up, his left eye closed, weeping at the corner, and there was a deep cut over his left brow. I handed him a mug from the draining board and watched as he poured some in. He drank half, then offered it to me.

'Jesus.'

'Suit yourself.'

I made a square out of some kitchen roll and put it next to him, but he ignored it. 'You're going to need stitches.'

'It's fine.'

What the hell had just happened? I was numb, burning. I couldn't believe he'd risked getting arrested. Like we needed that. I sat opposite him. He was trying to make his lighter work, but it sputtered and died.

'Sit down,' I said, taking his cigarette and lighting it for him on one of the gas rings.

The smoke caught the back of my throat and I coughed. He gave me a Quasimodo smile, his one working eye wincing.

'Want to tell me what the fuck that was all about?'

'Yeah, I got jumped.' He pressed the kitchen towel to his cut. 'Fuck knows what you were doing.'

'The police, David? I mean, Christ, why not just save us some time and invite them bloody round?'

He gaped at me.

'Lie on the sofa. It might help slow the bleeding.'

'I'm all right.'

Silence.

'You could've killed him.'

'The guy was a wanker.'

'Right.'

'What? *What?*'

'David, you were the wanker.'

'Fuck off. Where were you? Not that I needed you, I had him—'

'Yeah, big man, sure, we all got a look at your big hairy balls.'

He swung round in his chair. 'What are *you* gunna do about it?'

'You're out of control.'

He turned his back to me. In the distance I could hear sirens, ordinary enough for a Saturday night, but the sound cut through me. I had to get away from him. At first I thought I'd go to bed, couldn't risk going back out, but I ended up in the bathroom searching the cabinet for plasters. There weren't any. I settled on some cotton wool and a wound pad.

'I thought you'd crashed,' he said, when I returned.

He'd abandoned the mug. Easier to get his mouth around the head of a bottle, he said, with a wink that didn't quite work. 'Had a punch on him. Give him that.'

'Hold still.'

I cleaned the cut and fixed the pad over it, securing the edges with tape. He held his head up, occasionally swigging from the Jack. When I'd finished I chucked the bloodied cotton wool into the sink.

'What was it all about, David? Do you know?'

He started to speak then spread his hands. 'Na – forget it.'

'Go on.'

'Waste of time.' Silence, then it seemed to burst out of him. 'You know, out there I saw this guy have his arm blown off. You want to know what he did? He picked it up in his other hand and carried it. And you know something else? I wasn't "traumatised" or owt like that, but I just think that guy – never mind me – *that* guy deserves a bit of fucking respect. Instead of that you get some greasy prick shooting his mouth off about sodding, stupid squaddies.' He laughed. 'Aw, what's the use?'

It was the first time he'd talked properly about Iraq. And now I understood that the body in Harwood Forest had been, for him, the first in a long line. He could never look back on that summer and feel what I felt because violent death had filled all the years between. I was alone with it. He was alone.

He stood up and staggered into the living room, knocking a lamp over, laughing again.

I followed him. 'Sit down, for God's sake.'

He collapsed onto the sofa with the bottle of Jack resting on his chest and then, suddenly, seemed to choke. I thought at first he was being sick, but he was crying, hard, dry sobs that shook his chest. I reached out to touch his shoulder, but he pulled back from me.

'I'm all right,' he said, wiping a tear from his cheek with the heel of his right hand.

Silence.

He wouldn't look at me and I didn't try to touch him again. 'I'm tired. I think I'll turn in.'

'You know something, Leo?' He was peering up at me with his one drooling eye. 'If we could start again, you and me, Seaton, you know what I'm saying? I wouldn't change a single fucking thing.'

I shook my head. 'You don't mean that.'

'I do, you know.'

'Get some sleep.'

I wanted to sleep. God, I needed to, but once I'd undressed and lay down on the bed I knew I wouldn't. His words played over and over again in my head. How much would *I* change of that summer? All of it? Everything, or nothing? Not nothing, that was mad. I thought I heard David come and stand outside the bedroom door, but a second later the sofa groaned under his weight. I rolled over, wrapping the duvet around my head to block out the images that now flooded into my mind. David standing on the dragon's teeth in Seaton, me wriggling my toes in the sand, and in the distance, Harwood Forest, a dark smudge on the horizon, coming closer.

9

It was late afternoon when I left the pillbox. As I headed home, hot and sweaty, midges fizzed about my head.

When I reached the back gate of David's cottage I stopped and peered around the privet hedge. He was bouncing a football on his knee, now and then letting it drop to his foot before lifting it up again and heading it at the space above the kitchen window. I liked the sound it made, soft against his knee, then harder, echoing off the wall. He hadn't noticed me and, though I had been dreading it, I was relieved to see him. It felt like coming home, as though a new space inside me had been created for him to fill.

I walked up the path into his garden.

'There you are,' he said. 'Where've you been? I rang your bell.'

'Oh.'

'I've got something to show you.'

He seemed different, hyped up, though he didn't say anything about the fight with Jaz. I wondered whether I needed to say something, but then he nodded for me to follow him, bouncing the football in front of him and then hoofing it over my head where it landed in the knotted branches of the hedge.

'Dad's asleep so you'll have to be quiet.'

A mouse's tiny skeleton lay on one of the slabs on the patio. I stopped to look at it.

'Shit, Leo, you coming, or not?'

'Yeah.'

We walked through to his kitchen. Five or six lager cans on the table, bent double, and an ashtray overflowing with cigarette ends.

'Nights. He has to get wasted or he can't sleep. This way.'

A pile of clothes spilt out the open door of the washing machine. I got a whiff of their oily smell. All of them were either dark green or black and some of the T-shirts had Thornleys logo on the chest.

He led me through into the garage. After the brightness of the sunshine outside it was black and I stood in the doorway, breathing darkness, until David found the switch. A damp, mould smell, but something else too, sharp. He pulled a chord and we blinked. Once my eyes adjusted to the light I could see the sharp smell was sawdust, a dusting of it spread over a long workbench. David moved to a big filing cabinet at the back and tipped out some keys from an empty jar of pickled onions to unlock the top drawer.

'You can't tell anyone you were in here, OK?'

'OK.'

'Swear.'

Jokingly I said, 'Cross my heart and hope to die,' but then I realised he had meant it. 'All right. I swear.'

He reached inside the drawer and pulled out something wrapped in a towel. Bulky. First, he held it tight to his chest, as though whatever was inside might struggle and break free, then he placed it gently on the workbench. It looked like nothing, a cloth with a few black marks on it, boot polish maybe, no way to tell what it was from the shape, but as he began to unfold the towel I caught a glimpse of the handle. Black, sleek.

'It's a gun,' I said.

'Pistol.'

He finished unwrapping it, unfolding each corner of the towel carefully until it was done. I stared at it, silent, my breath held.

'It's a Glock 17 … 9 mm.'

I knew I wanted to touch it.

'Dad doesn't know I know about it, but I saw him cleaning it once.' He pulled out a box from the drawer where he'd got the gun. 'Keeps the bullets here.'

'Is it loaded?'

'He never loads it.'

'What's it for?'

'It's a gun, stupid, what do you think it's for?'

'Has he used it?'

'I don't think so. Just takes it out every so often and cleans it.'

I reached out a finger to touch it.

'Watch it! If you mark it he'll know.'

I brushed my hands down my T-shirt to take off the sweat. I could still smell the sea on us both, mixing with our own smells and those of the garage. Even the gun seemed to have an odour, a cold-night-air smell. I picked it up.

'It's light.'

'Yeah.'

I brought it up to shoulder height and took aim with my finger hovering over the trigger. 'Shit! It's like—'

A footstep. We spun round, colliding with each other. I nearly dropped the gun.

'*Olly.*'

He stood in the doorway. 'Mum said I had to come and get you.' His words were gobbled, a lolly making one cheek bulge. 'What are you doing?'

I slipped the gun to David who hastily wrapped it back in the cloth and returned it to the drawer. He was out of breath, a rash of sweat beads glistening over his cheeks.

'Go away, Olly.'

'I know what you've got. I've been standing here ages and ages.'

I lunged at him meaning to give him a dead arm, but David pulled me back.

'What did you see?' David asked.

Olly stared at his feet, unsure now. He looked at me, to David.

'He didn't see anything,' I said. 'He's just a big liar.'

'I did. You had a gun.'

I tried to dive at him again, but he ran back into the kitchen. I cornered him by the sink. 'We didn't have anything and you didn't see anything. Right, Olly?'

He shrugged.

'Shhh!' David said. 'You won't tell anyone, will you?'

Olly shook his head, mouth clamped shut, nostrils flaring.

'You can't believe him,' I said. 'He'll say anything.'

David took a step towards him, but when Olly backed away he stopped. 'Look, Olly, if you don't say anything, if you keep it a secret, I'll show you something better.'

'What?'

'I've got a gun, too. I'll let you hold it if you like?'

'*You've* got a gun?' I said.

He was still looking at Olly, who stood with one foot resting on the top of the other. He looked from David to me. It was the best offer going.

'It's in my bedroom,' David said. 'You've got to be quiet though, not a sound.'

We kicked off our sandals and followed him upstairs, me in front, Olly behind. David's dad was snoring, one big snore followed by a long silence then another hiccuping snore that made us all stop dead in our tracks. David beckoned us along the landing. His was a tiny bedroom, only enough room for a single bed and a chest of drawers, a portable telly on top with a coat hanger instead of an aerial. Navy-blue sheets on the bed. Olly and I sat on the edge, lifting our legs when David rummaged underneath. He pulled out a canvas bag, unzipped it and spread back the two sides.

'It's an air rifle,' I said. 'A boy, I mean, this lad at school has one.'

'This is different,' David said. 'It's the dog's bollocks, this is. Dad got it me when he split with me mam.'

I lifted it up.

'Careful.' He pushed the tip of the barrel away from him. 'It's loaded. You've got to point it to the ground all the time except when you're taking aim.'

'Air rifles can't kill you though, right?'

'You got one in the head you'd know about it.'

I brought it up to my shoulders and peered through the sights, scanning the things on top of his dresser for a target, a comb, box of matches, a photograph. It was of a woman, blonde, pretty, smiling.

'What do you use it for?'

'Rabbits.'

'You kill them?'

'No, I read them bedtime stories. You want to hold it, Olly?'

He shook his head.

'He's chicken,' I said. 'Just ignore him.'

'I *do* want to. I want to hold it.'

'No.'

'*Please.*'

'NO. What are you doing following me around anyway? Get your own friends.'

His bottom lip wobbled. For a second I wanted to say sorry. It wasn't his fault he didn't have anyone. He was weird. He smelt of Frosties.

'What do you with them?' I said, turning back to David. 'The rabbits?'

'Eat them, of course.'

I pulled a face. 'Gross.'

'You eat what you kill, that's the rule. Everyone knows that.'

'Yes. Right.'

'I'll take you with me next time I go out with it.'

'OK.'

I tried to sound casual, but my heart thumped and skipped a beat. I didn't believe we'd kill anything. We'd aim at cans probably, pretend to be snipers. All the same, I knew I wanted to do it. I was nothing like David, which made no sense of me liking the feel of the rifle in my hands, or of the fact that I knew, right then, I'd be good at firing it.

10

The gun changed everything. Not the air rifle, the other gun hidden in its nest of soft cloth. The night before our first hunting trip I dreamt about it, woke remembering how it had felt in my hands.

I'd wanted to be up and out of the house before anybody else was awake, but then I heard a thud as Olly jumped down off his bunk. I put on my dressing gown and followed him downstairs. He was sitting on one of the breakfast chairs in the kitchen, index finger stabbing the remote control of the portable.

'It's broke,' he said.

'Because you broke it.'

I put on a cartoon for him, but he'd lost interest and poured salt onto the counter to play with. I got on with making sandwiches – thick slabs of bread and ham bought specially from Prices.

Olly watched me closely. 'You're making a picnic.'

'Provisions.'

'Why?'

Four slices, two each. Proper ham too, the meaty kind cut from the bone. Olly picked a grape from the fruit bowl and began peeling off the skin with his teeth. 'That Dairy Lea's mine.'

'I'm only taking a bit.'

'Where are you going?'

Not saying would only make him more curious. He'd go on and on about it till I told him. 'You'll blab to Mum.'

'I won't. Promise, I won't.'

'I'm going hunting. Rabbits.'

'You can't kill them.'

'That's what hunting is, melonhead.'

He was quiet for a moment, choosing the word. 'Murderer.'

'It's not murder if you eat them.'

'If you're going to eat them why are you making sandwiches?' He lifted his dressing gown from where it had slipped off his shoulders. 'I'm coming with you.'

'You'd freak. We're going to kill Bugs Bunny, you'd have a fit.'

'You're going with David, aren't you?'

I wrapped the sandwiches in foil.

'You've got to let me come because Mum's going out with Patrick.'

'Since when?'

'Forever.'

'You'd better be joking.'

'Mum said.'

As if on cue Mum appeared in the doorway, humming. For a second she paused, clearly having forgotten what she'd come in for. She was holding a pair of jeans with the tags still on. She never wore jeans, but they were too long for me so they had to be hers.

'Mum, tell Leo he has to mind me.'

'Would you?' She rooted around in one of the drawers in the dresser and pulled out a pair of scissors.

'I'm going out.'

'Sorry, I meant to tell you last night.' She tutted, busy with the tag which had knotted itself on the zip. 'It's just the morning then you can go off.'

'I can't change my plans now, it's too late.'

'He's going—'

'Fishing,' I said, throwing Olly a glare.

'Since when do you like fishing? Are you going with that boy?'

'David,' Olly said.

'You're spending a lot of time with him.' She smiled. 'We'll have to have them round, him and his dad, what's his name again? He told me—'

'Can't you take Olly with you?'

'*Leo.*'

'Why are you going out with Patrick?'

'Because he asked me. What, Olly?' He was pulling

at her nightie, stretching the material tight around her waist.

I could see the outline of her breasts silhouetted against the thin cotton, the ripe plum circle of a nipple. I turned away to look out of the window.

Far out the sea was a heaving steely-blue mass, but for the occasional snap of white when a wave rose and fell. I remembered Mum, wading out for a swim, her lips pressed to a seam. She swam with her head erect to keep her hair dry. Dad, on the beach, newspaper laid over his furred chest, watching.

'We're only going to Haresham,' Mum said. 'Pat knows somewhere I can get a clock to replace the one in the hall.'

Dad had bought it in Guernsey. It might've even been a wedding anniversary gift, I couldn't remember. It was special anyway, or it had been once. 'I like the clock.'

'Well, it doesn't work and it'd cost more to get it fixed than to buy a new one. Oh, come on, Leo. Olly can go with you. Bring him back at lunchtime. I'll be here then.'

'No, he can't.'

'For heaven's *sake*.'

'He CAN'T.'

'Give me one reason.'

'He thinks fishing is murder.'

She laughed. 'It's not murder if you put the fish back in the water, Olly. And you will, won't you, Leo?'

'*Mum*.'

I wasn't being selfish. Guns and Olly wouldn't mix. He was the most accident-prone kid I'd ever met.

Mum glanced at her watch. 'Oh God. Just this once. Just do it.'

She gave me a pleading look, slung the jeans over her shoulder and went upstairs. I scraped the coils of fat from the ham into the palm of my hand and emptied them into the bin. Near the top lay one of her bras, kidney beans from last night's chilli inside the cups. I stared at the straps, grimy grey with old skin and sweat.

'Told you,' Olly said.

'Shut up! You're coming, aren't you? You tell Mum we're shooting rabbits though and I'll kill you. Got it?'

He blinked.

'Get dressed then, while I finish this.'

Hoppers Wood was really part of Harwood Forest, but it had its own name because it stood alone on three sides. It was only at the very top, where it narrowed to an hourglass waist, that it joined Harwood. I took us via one of the farmer's fields, the earth ploughed and baked into ridges that crumbled under our feet. We followed the hedgerow, its thorny branches jutting out at sharp angles, at war with themselves.

Olly stopped to pick a wide strand of grass to blow.

'Put it down. There isn't time for that.'

'It's hot.'

'It'll be cooler in Hoppers.'

It was farther than I remembered. We picked our way through a dense thicket of bracken, the undersides of the leaves heavy with seeds. As we batted back the fronds, a cloud of insects swam into our faces. I felt the skin on my arms and legs crawling with them. Once we got to the other side I brushed myself down. They were beetles mostly, black, tiny, one or two with a flash of red on their abdomen.

'I got one in my ear!' Olly said.

'No, you didn't.'

He shook his head, tried to turn himself upside down and nearly lost his balance. Right way up again, he looked at me and grinned.

'Come on, you idiot.'

The path ahead was brambled, a knotted mass of tripwire. It wasn't clear which way to go, for the undergrowth all looked the same, clearings dotted with the sinewy trunks of saplings and moss-covered rocks. Other areas were thick with trees, their roots jutting from the earth like bones.

'Wait.' Olly was panting, red-faced. He sat on a rock to pick the sticky pellets of sweetheart off his tracksuit top.

'Why did you put that on? Take it off if you're hot.'

It got stuck on his wrists as he pulled the sleeves over his arms. I yanked it off and tied it around my waist. For a while then he stopped moaning and we moved at a quicker pace.

All the while the light changed, grey to yellow to

green. In places, the air seemed cooler, but then heat would blast onto our backs from an opening in the canopy. I looked around, tried to work out what was west. I wasn't sure we'd come far enough in, but then I saw it, a flash of green through the trees. I'd found it, the Bankside, a steep grassy hill on the far side of the wood.

'You have to keep quiet, Olly. All right?'

I was worried David would have seen us coming and be so annoyed Olly was with me that he'd have gone on alone. Then, a rustle and snap of fern. Several yards to our right, David's head appeared. He stepped forward. He was dressed in heavy boots and army camouflage trousers like they wore in the TA. He had a rucksack, too, and a bucket hat pulled well down over his face.

Olly and me were dressed all wrong. I was wearing a bright yellow T-shirt still covered with the black specks of insects and Olly was wearing a white vest.

'There wasn't anybody to watch him,' I said. 'He'll be quiet.'

He looked furious. 'Did you bring the things I asked for?'

'Yes.'

I handed him the small round tin of boot polish from the side pocket of my rucksack. I didn't understand why we needed to camouflage our faces, but I quite liked the idea. He did his own, daubing two thick lines on either side of his nose and passed the tin back to me.

'I want some,' Olly said.

I ignored him and put several stripes on my own face.

'You were supposed to be here an hour ago,' David said.

'I got up early, but Mum said I had to look after him.'

He sighed. 'OK, I guess. There are still a few moving about.'

'On the Bankside?' I said, but he didn't answer.

We walked, David leading, until we reached a barbed-wire fence that ran all the way along the boundary between the woods and the hill. It had fallen here and there, the wire mingled with brambles.

I handed Olly his tracksuit top. 'Put it back on.'

'It's too hot.'

'It'll stop you getting bit.'

A bee worked at a foxglove, visiting each bell in turn from the large heavy ones at the bottom to the smaller, tighter buds at the top. Olly eyed it nervously, flapping his hands about his ears when the bee buzzed near his face.

David had already climbed over and moved into the long grass on the other side. It reached his bare waist, soughing gently against his sides as he walked. He'd slung the rifle over his head so that it rested diagonally across his shoulders.

I lifted the wire of the fence so Olly could climb under, but one of the barbs snagged his top and he cried out.

'Duck, stupid!'

He dropped to his knees and crawled on all fours until he was clear then stood up and brushed his palms down his chest.

David turned, impatient, waving us to follow. When we reached him I looked from right to left, scanning gorse bushes and clumps of wild garlic. The spot he'd chosen was a natural dip in the land with a wide view of the Bankside. 'I don't see any.'

He put a finger to his lips and laid the rifle carefully on the ground beside him before shuffling down to lie flat on his stomach. I tugged at Olly's wrist, but he stepped across David and settled next to him.

'You see the holes up on that little rise?' David whispered.

I couldn't see anything. He took my hand and I followed his line until I saw a pockmarked area of ground. The grass had been nibbled flat and the bare earth was dotted with black pellets around the entrances to the burrows.

'I'll take first shot,' he said. 'Then you.'

He unzipped the rifle from its carrier and then raked around in an old tobacco tin for a bullet.

'I still can't see any.'

'You've spooked them,' he said. 'They'll come back as long as we're quiet.'

'They don't look like bullets,' Olly said.

'Pellet.' He put one in Olly's hand. 'You can keep that one.'

I'd have to let him have it even though I knew he'd probably show it to Mum. If I tried to take it away he'd scream himself into a fit. Besides, I didn't want to spook the rabbits again.

We crouched down. Minutes passed. A centipede with rust-coloured armour marched over my hand. Nothing. I could see areas where the dew was still silver and the darker tracks of paw prints through it, but no rabbits. A rustling overhead as a blackbird lifted off a branch. Olly shuffled.

'Keep still,' I mouthed.

'The grass is making me itch.'

David wet his lips, concentration narrowing his eyes. His ears were red, the lobes bulging with hot blood and feathered with tiny blond hairs. I felt his muscles tense. He lowered his head, level with the sights of the rifle. A rabbit was bumping down the hill, sniffing the air. It stopped to wash itself.

Now that I saw one, so alive, so unaware, I wanted to spook it, but I couldn't move. I expected David to fire, but he was still, holding his breath, index finger poised. Finally, he squeezed the trigger and the silence cracked with a judder and a whistling thud.

A flash of white scut and the rabbit was gone.

'Shit. Missed it.'

I breathed out. Sweat had trickled from my scalp and gathered at the corner of my eye. 'Do we need to get closer?'

'Range is good.' He handed me the rifle. 'Your shot.'

We'd have to wait for the rabbits to settle again, he said, but I could take the next one. A pulse throbbed in my neck.

'Then you,' he said, ruffling Olly's hair.

'He's only here to watch.'

'I want to be a hunter!'

'No way.' He was pale, but for two spots of pink on his cheeks. I glanced at David. 'He can't shoot.'

'I want to!'

'If you don't shut it I'll take you back.'

'Shhhh!' David pressed my shoulders down against the grass. I was glad he didn't challenge me about Olly. There were some things I had to decide.

'Shuffle down more.'

My hands sweated on the metal. It felt awkward, either because I was holding it wrong, or because holding it at all was peculiar. David straightened my arm, picked a tuft of grass that was too close to the sights, then, on a shared breath, we settled.

It was nearly an hour before another rabbit appeared, smaller than the last, perhaps a juvenile. I was amazed by how quiet Olly was being, but then I realised he'd fallen asleep with his head against David's side.

I trembled, the anticipation I'd held in my muscles for so long making them weak.

'Aim behind the eye,' David whispered.

I narrowed my focus to the gun's sights. Two, then three rabbits, all from the same burrow.

'Focus on one.'

But how was I supposed to choose? My eyes darted from one, to the others, and back again. They nibbled grass, scuffed at patches of dry earth with their hind legs, rose up and sniffed the air for danger. For me.

David's breath was hot on my shoulder. 'Now.'

I closed my eyes.

'*Now!*'

I squeezed the trigger, then, seconds, minutes, I don't know how long. I saw the trees, an ash key spiralling down. At first I thought I'd missed, but then David was over me, pummelling my stomach.

'Get you, you jammy fucker! First bloody shot!'

'Did I kill it?'

He got up and walked towards it. 'Shit. Clipped it.'

'What?'

'Doesn't matter, happens—'

'It isn't dead?'

He fetched his knife from his rucksack and handed it to me. 'You can either slit its throat or put another one in its head. No, wait, gun's better, but in the head or we'll have to dig out another bullet.'

The sound of the shot had woken Olly up. It took a minute for him to figure out was happening then he started to snivel, his cheeks puffing in and out. 'Don't, Leo, don't.'

'I can't do it,' I said.

'Just go over there and bang, finish it.'

'I can't.'

'Then take the knife.'

'You do it.'

'It's your kill.'

'Not like that. I can't—'

'For fuck's sake!' He glanced at Olly. 'He's going to bust a fucking gut in a minute. Just do it.'

Our eyes locked. I looked at the Bankside and the body of the rabbit lying on the ground beside one of the holes, its back leg kicking spasmodically. I knew from the way David was looking at me that he wasn't going to do it. I stood and walked slowly towards it. Its grey flanks puffed out shallow, quick breaths. I wanted it to get up, it must've been stupid just to lie there as my shadow fell over it. Blood oozed from a hole directly behind its shoulder. *Die. Just die.* I knelt down to touch it, my hand lightly resting on its damp fur. When I took my hand away the fur was flattened in the shape of my fingers.

'Keep still.'

It was looking at me. I saw myself in its eye.

'In the head!' David shouted.

I took aim, swallowed and then pulled the trigger, turning my head sharply away at the last moment. When I looked back it was in time to see the final twitch.

Olly and David came up, David with his arm around Olly's shoulders.

'I want to go home,' Olly whimpered.

I wanted to go home too, but I couldn't say so.

David picked the rabbit up by its hind legs. He was so high on the kill you'd have thought he had done it and, for a second, I actually believed it had been him, but I felt the rifle in my hands, heavy now.

'I better take Olly back,' I said.

'No.' The rabbit dangled limp against David's leg. 'Now we've got to cook it.'

'Is it really dead?' Olly asked.

'Yes.' I put a hand on his shoulder. 'Come on, I'll take you home.'

'No one's going.'

'He's scared.'

'Are you?' He knelt in front of Olly. 'I don't think you are. I think you're brave.' He held the rabbit up. 'Do you want to touch it?'

Olly shook his head.

'All right.' David took the tin of boot polish from his pocket and smeared a straight line across Olly's forehead, two more in diagonal streaks over his cheeks. 'There.'

Olly hiccuped. 'Do I look like a hunter?'

'Yeah, you do. You look like me. Want to help me build a fire? Over there, beside the fence where we came over. Collect some wood, little sticks, but make sure you only pick the dry ones.'

Olly was unsure at first, but determined, pleased to have been given a job. He stood up and wandered off, lifting his bare legs up high through the long grass. Now and then his chest heaved.

'He hasn't seen anything like that before,' I said.

'Yeah, like you have?' David lit a cigarette. 'You did it though. Shit, you looked amazing, you should've seen yourself, the way you stood there and then bang.'

'Yeah?'

'Fuck, yeah. Scared the shit out of me.'

I felt the thrill then. Up to that point I'd worn what I'd done like a dead skin, but now, David looking on, I was pumped up. 'I should've killed it out right.'

'You'll get better. Wasn't bad for your first time. Come on.'

We walked back towards the fence, choosing a spot and then brushing away the leaves to reveal bare earth. David took the knife from his belt and laid the rabbit out, smoothing his fingers along the limbs, gentle now.

'You want to do it?' he said.

So much blood for one dead thing, but yes, dead. The pulse in my ears quickened. I blinked, two red spots behind my lids, and then knelt beside him. He put his hand over mine and, together, we made the first cut.

11

The days struggled to let go of the sun, holding, with each night, a store of heat that rose in the morning from the ground in a misty haze of damp, warm air.

I was stuck inside with Olly who'd got a bad bout of hay fever. Mum had bought him two new jigsaws to keep him occupied because he had to stay indoors, but she'd only been able to get one day off work which meant I had to watch him until the afternoon when Sweet Jesus was taking over. I sat at the kitchen table peeling the pith from an orange I didn't want.

'We could go rock pooling?' Olly said.

'You can't go out, stupid. Anyway, tide's in.'

He was doing it all wrong. Everyone knew you did the outer edges first, but he'd got bits everywhere.

He tried to fit two pieces together, pressing down on them with his fist, but they didn't go.

'Don't do that. You'll bend them out of shape.'

'It goes.'

'Oh, whatever.'

He swivelled around in his chair and went over to the fridge to get himself a drink of orange, the white pudge of his ankles juddering with each step. He always looked fat when he had hay fever, not just his lips and eyes which swelled up like a pufferfish, all of him. He got eczema too. Sometimes he clawed at himself so much Mum had to bandage his hands.

'I want to go out,' he said.

'Well, you can't and that's that.'

He pursed his lips and leant over the jigsaw, the sleeves of his pyjamas knocking several pieces onto the floor.

'I'm just going next door.'

'You can't. You have to stay with me until Mum comes home. I'm sick.'

'There's nothing wrong with you.'

Olly would blab if I went out. Even if I made him promise not to, he would. Nearly three o'clock and still no sign of Sweet Jesus. I sat down again, shoving the top of Olly's jigsaw box onto the floor.

'Hey!'

'Pick it up then, blob.'

'Don't call me that.'

'Sniffling, itching, bloater blob.'

Sweet Jesus's voice in the hall. I jumped up, almost colliding with her on my way out.

'Where are you going?'

'Next door. Mum said I could.'

'She didn't tell me.' She eyed me. 'Back for dinner then.'

I chucked the orange at her, which she caught, laughing, then turned her attention to Olly who was already in mid-flow telling her about his hay fever. Mrs Browning's mutterings of Sweet Jesuses. Before I'd got out of the door I heard him change tune, whining, wanting to come with me, but I was gone.

I hurried round to the utility room at the back of David's cottage and knocked on the door. It was ajar. He had to be in. A fly strip hung from the ceiling, the meaty carcasses of several bluebottles suspended, wings glossed green. One, still alive, writhed but with each movement only got itself more stuck.

As I walked into the kitchen I called, heard David answer, a muffled word, but I couldn't tell where it was coming from. I called again.

'Out *here.*'

Outside. A butterfly kissed my wrist and bobbed over the wall. Still no sign of him, then he poked his head round the door of the shed and beckoned me over.

'I found the key,' he said. 'Dad doesn't know I've got it.'

'Is he at work?'

'Double shift.' He pushed open the door and stood to one side to let me in. 'You coming in or not?'

It was packed inside with junk, but for a clear patch on the floor where it looked like David had sat. Paint sheets in a pile, speckled blue, and next to them, a stack of seed trays with shrunken soil inside and the odd brown stalk. My foot knocked against something, a box, filled with rusted metal, bits of broken machinery knitted together with cobwebs. Bags too – different kinds of compost and several plain black sacks. I shuffled a few steps further in, but there was hardly any space so I shoved some plant pots out of the way. A black beetle scuttled into the space I created, then changed direction, heading for a gap between the bags.

David knelt down, his face illuminated in the great slab of light that shone through the small window. A feather lifted in the swoosh of air I'd created and brushed against my leg.

'That's how she gets in and out.'

He was pointing at one corner of the shed where one of the slats had broken in half, rotten. I didn't see her at all at first, but then she lifted her head and I saw her eyes. A cat, sleek and dark. Kittens too, three of them, though I'd thought at first the shapes were her paws.

David fetched a tin of tuna from a plastic bag and pulled back the lid. She yowled, several miaows bunched together, and nudged David's hand, lifting her front paws and marking him with the side of her face. The kittens dropped blindly from her teats.

'OK, wait. It's coming.'

He put the tuna onto a saucer and mashed it up with a fork. Once she was tucking he moved over to the kittens.

'The ginger one is Red, the tabby is Tio and the black-and-white one, that's Boris.'

'What about her?'

'Blackie. It's a bit naff, but I couldn't think of anything else.'

'No, I mean where did she come from?'

'Stray, mebbe. She might've lived here and the owners left her when they moved.'

'I don't remember anyone having a cat.'

He picked up Red by the scruff and handed him to me then lay Boris across his palm. Blackie was tucking into the tuna with greedy licking sounds, not bothered at all about us touching her kittens until Boris let out a high-pitched cry. Even then she only looked and once he was quiet again she settled at the saucer.

'They're great, aren't they?' he said.

'Yeah.'

He cradled Boris in his right hand and stroked his head with one finger. He was tiny in comparison to David's hand, could probably close his fist right around him, but David was gentle, lifting the kitten up to his face and planting a kiss on each of his two front paws. I shuffled back, legs straight and pushed together so I could lay Red in the furrow between my thighs.

'Rest your head back,' David said.

'What for?'

'Just do it.'

Our voices had a strange quality, not exactly an echo, but made more important by the tiny space.

The plastic bag which had carried the tuna tin advanced across the floor on a faint breeze from the gap in the slats. I lay back and David put Boris on my chest. I added Red. The two of them went limp, their tiny mouths opening and closing in silent mews.

'When do you reckon she had them then?' he asked.

I shrugged. 'They're pretty small.'

Their claws were the same pearly white as the underside of a razor shell and they pricked my skin, leaving tiny pink spots. David lay beside me. He wore pale, tea-coloured shorts and had the biscuit smell of suntanned skin.

'I reckon they're all boys,' he said. 'You think?'

I turned Boris around and lifted his tail, but I wasn't sure what I was looking for. They were probably too young to have anything. I thought of Olly and felt a twinge of guilt. He'd have liked the kittens. When I rolled Red over onto his back it made him yowl so I turned him back. 'Do you think we should find them homes?'

'This is their home.'

'Your dad'll let you keep them?'

He didn't answer, smoothing Boris's whiskers from his face until he started to purr. It was a strange sound, too big for his body.

'We could bring her fish,' I said. 'The ones we catch.'

'Yeah. You got to keep this place secret though, that we come here, I mean. You can't tell my dad, or your mam. It has to be just ours, for the kittens and for us.'

'All right.'

'Dad thinks the key's lost.'

He lifted Boris off my chest and put him back onto the blanket. His tan had darkened, but for the tops of his thighs, an occasional white flash just visible above the line of his shorts. It didn't look real somehow, painted on.

'We can make it nice,' he said. 'Clean it up. Bring stuff from the house as long as it's nothing anyone will miss.'

'I've got some pillows in my wardrobe.'

He lit a cigarette. As he lowered his head to return the lighter to his pocket I noticed he had the beginnings of a bruise, a dark whirl at his left temple.

'What did you do to your head?'

He blew the end of his cigarette until the ember burned bright. I could see the start of a black eye, too, hardly visible from frontways on, but from the side the ridge of his cheekbone was tipped yellow.

I put Red on the blanket with the others and faced him. 'You been in a fight?'

'It's nowt.'

'Does it hurt?'

'Not any more.' He looked at me, scowled. 'Don't wet your knickers. It's nowt.'

'It doesn't look like nothing.'

He didn't say anything. I ran a finger across the swelling on his cheek.

'Doesn't look real.'

'It's real.'

'Like special effects.'

He looked up, a flicker of a smile.

'Did you get jumped then? Who'd you fight with?'

'My dad, all right? I got a hiding.'

I shrank from him. I'd never had a hiding like that. He must've done something pretty bad. I wanted to ask him what it was, but I was frightened of it coming out wrong so we sat in silence listening to Blackie's engine purr. She was washing the kittens, licking their fur into flat, dark streaks.

I glanced at David. He had that look again, the one I'd come to know, but not understood. There'd always been the feeling in the quiet moments between us, lying on the beach to look at the sea through the gaps in our toes, fishing off the rocks, that he owned the silences and I had to wait for his attention to turn back to me. Now, lifting his head to stare at the space in front of him, I saw the time in between hadn't been filled with silence at all.

'Why?'

'Why what?'

'Why did he hit you?'

'He was just looking for a fight.'

He ground out his cigarette on the floor, using the butt to move the ash into a line. I moved closer to examine the bruise, but he flung a hand at me and blew the last stream of smoke into my face.

'You think I need a fucking cuddle? You don't know a fucking thing. You don't know what it's like. Bet you've never even had a fist in the face, have you?'

'It's not my fault.'

'Huh. Leo the lion.'

I sat, silent, chewing my thumbnail. The whites of his eyes held tiny red veins and his lids at each corner were crusted with sleep.

'You could punch me,' I said. 'If you want.'

'What?'

'I'd know then, wouldn't I?'

'Don't be stupid.'

My voice shook, but I rolled forward onto my knees and straightened up. 'Go on.'

I stuck out my chin, but he just stayed looking at me, sucking in a breath softly through his teeth. I waited, then he clenched his fist and lunged at me, pushing me to the floor and pummelling me in the stomach. We rolled over, laughing, a clatter as a plant pot toppled over. We fought to pin the other down, using knees or elbows so our hands were free to pinch and slap. He won easily and sat astride my ribs, panting.

'I could've taken a punch.'

The skin on his thighs stuck to my waist, peeling off each time I struggled and then sticking again. I wriggled some more, but it was useless to even try. He bent over me, his face an inch from mine. I could smell his breath, fanning my cheek, musky, mixed with the fishy stink of tuna and the kittens' warm fur.

He placed his hands either side of my head. 'Why would I want to hit you?'

His right hand touched my neck. My pulse throbbed against his palm and blood burned my cheeks. Rolling off me, he landed a slap on my ear and gave a yell of triumph so loud Blackie was startled and, claws skittering across the floor, she shot out though the broken slat.

12

The fair occupied the site of the old community hall and all the football field behind it. For two days in August the entire village congregated there and the sounds echoed across the headland. Gone were cries of gannets and kittiwakes, the rustle of sand shifting, the pop of animals blowing mud bubbles on the beach. Instead, laughter, whoops and whistles, the bass dum-dum of music, metal against metal, and the grumbling chug of the generators. Even the smells were different, diesel fumes, foot-trodden grass, doughnuts slick with melting sugar, hot dogs in steaming pots, and the buttery waft of fried onions.

The men who came with the fair were unshaven and rough-looking. It was always the women, their wives and girlfriends, who were the most interesting. They wore belts around their stomachs, fanny packs David called them, where they kept the money they took for the rides. I liked them because they laughed a lot, great gravelly belly laughs with a rasp they got from smoking too much. They cajoled and flirted with you to play the stalls: darts, brooms with hooks, coconuts, tennis balls, even popguns.

I looked for David. We'd arranged to hook up beside the dodgems, but he wasn't there. I sat on the steps leading up to the pay station and waited. Behind me the cars bumped and a girl screamed. Opposite, a miniature railway slowed to a halt and the kids that'd been waiting climbed into the carriages. A boy who was too fat for his seat held on to the bars in front of him, cheeks blowing out breaths as the train pulled forward.

Mum, Olly and Patrick were on the other side of the ground near to the burger van. Patrick handed Olly a large stick of candyfloss. At least I didn't have to hang around with them all night. And if I wanted candyfloss I'd get my own.

The evening sun faded. Gradually, bulbs and spot-lights lit up, some clear, others casting red and blue shadows on the faces of passers-by. Jaz and Taffy were among them, but they didn't see me. They had burgers wrapped clam-like in green napkins. I watched them until they disappeared into the crowd and when I looked back David was there.

He was standing outside the beer tent next to a group of four women who sat beside a low bamboo table smoking. He said something to them and they laughed. I caught his eye and he waved me over.

'All right?' I said.

'Yeah. You been on anything yet?'

I shook my head and he lit a menthol cigarette. I noticed the women were smoking the same. They smiled at me, but smoke got in my eye and I had to blink through the sting. I'd only ever seen David in shorts or jeans, but he'd dressed up, a white shirt and navy trousers with loafers, same as his dad.

'Dad says he'll get us a drink later from the tent.'

'Oh, right.'

I glanced over my shoulder. Patrick was lifting Olly into one of the miniature railway carriages, Mum standing several feet back with a camera raised to her face.

'I've got plenty of money anyway.'

'How much?'

I pulled out the note to show him. 'Twenty.'

'Not last long that. Every ride's two quid each.'

He didn't seem to have brought any money with him, or if he had, he didn't offer it. It didn't matter.

I suggested a plan which included the best rides, namely the waltzer, the Calvados which was basically a ship that swung from side to side, and the dodgems. If there was anything left we could do a couple of the stalls.

We stood in line for the waltzer, waiting longer than everyone else so we could get a car to ourselves. The siren wailed as we moved off, slow first, wheels grinding on the rails, then faster and faster until I felt the knobbles on my spine jar against the back of the seat. My breaths spun out of me in short hiccuping laughs.

I looked at David. His head was thrown to one side, mouth open wide to reveal a nicotine-stained tongue. The bruise had darkened and I suddenly felt I wanted to touch it, but then the carriage swung and he was thrown against me, his nose jarring off my chin. A rush of blood swam up my chest to my head.

When the waltzer finally came to a stop and the bars were raised I stood up, giddy from the swirling in my stomach. I was relieved when David suggested we buy hamburgers at the van. I put loads of ketchup on mine to take away the taste of the grease, but it'd already soaked into the bread.

'What shall we do next?' David asked.

I took a gulp of the can of Fanta we'd got to share, but the bubbles made me queasy so I handed it to him. 'Rifles are a quid a go. Two goes each?'

I handed the money to the man at the stall. I knew the sights would be skewed and that's why it was impossible to hit the cans. There were three, but the bottom two would be nailed down. You couldn't reach them to prove it, but everyone knew they were. In theory, if you knocked them all down, you got one of the prizes hanging from the highest rail. Top prize, another reason why the cans were nailed, was a Nintendo game.

'Go for the one in the middle,' I told him. 'That way you might hit something on a ricochet.'

'Cheers, Prof, but I do know how to shoot.'

The man put his hands in the pockets of his jeans which were worn and speckled with pink and white spots like he'd just finished painting something. I looked at him and he smiled, showing a line of small grey teeth.

'The middle one,' I said again.

David handed me the can of Fanta to hold.

Even though I was a better shot, and even though I'd paid, the gun was still his. He wanted to let me know it too, which is why I didn't argue when he took first pop.

He fired the first shot quickly, a tinny sound, but none of the cans moved. The second shot took out the top can, but the last missed altogether. Tight-lipped, he handed the rifle to me, but I waved it off and moved down to the next one in the line.

My chest tightened, a sudden drop in the breeze bringing a still, heavy beat to my head.

I fired twice and missed.

'Give the gun back to Dave.'

David's dad had appeared behind us. Immediately I handed the gun back.

'What've I told you, Dave? You didn't have it down on your shoulder. How do you expect to hit anything like that?'

He took the rifle out of David's hands and looked up the sights. He smelt of aftershave and beer, over-powering. Behind his left ear there was a rolled-up cigarette, tobacco sprouting from the end. A woman tottered across and linked his arm. She wore a short skirt with high, white boots. I imagined her legs sweating in them, pools between her toes.

'Jack,' she cooed, 'I need a drink.'

'In a minute.'

He fished in his trouser pockets, pulling out notes, lots of them. He held them in his teeth while he looked for change. In the end he handed over a five-pound note to the man.

'If he still hasn't hit anything after that you come and find me.'

The man grinned, stuffing the note into his jeans pocket.

'What's so funny?'

'Didn't say nothing, mate.'

'Don't you think he can shoot? He's been on a proper firing range and shot a long sniper rifle. I don't suppose you know what that is, do you? They used them in the Gulf.' He turned to David. 'Show him. Show him you can do it.'

'Come on, Jack, you said you'd buy me a drink.'

'I said in a minute, didn't I?'

He shrugged her off. For a second she looked like she'd have a go at him, but her face softened and she draped an arm over his shoulder.

'Not like that.' He snatched the rifle back from David and took aim himself. 'Here. Like this. Then bang, bang, quick. Don't be wriggling about. Your arms are jelly.'

I wanted to say that the cans were nailed down, but I didn't. I just stood, two or three feet back from David, willing him to hit something. He fired again. Missed.

'Fucking useless.' David's dad shoved him in the chest to move him out of the way.

'Steady on,' the man said. 'It's just a game.'

'You got your money, didn't you?'

He nodded and stepped back, not wanting to get involved.

David's dad fired off two rounds and all three cans fell. The woman cheered and clapped her hands, shiny nails crossing at the tips. The prize was a football and pads from the top rail, but as the man reached up to take it down, David's dad said: 'Not that. Give him the teddy.'

David took it and stared at the ground. A flush had swept up his chest to the roots of his hair. When it faded he was white under his tan. He hadn't said anything.

'Howay, love. I'll get you that drink.'

And with his hand clamped to the left cheek of the woman's arse, his dad walked back over to the beer tent.

'Come on,' I said. 'Let's go, huh?'

I just wanted to get away. David followed me out of the fairground, silent. Even when we were in the village, which was quiet and deserted, he didn't say anything. I moved slightly ahead and headed towards the beach.

The sky had hardened to a blackish blue, pressing down on the sea like a giant plunger. We sat in a furrow between two dunes, the stalks of the marram shining silver and bending over to carve arcs into the sand. Far out, the lights from two ships blurred together and then separated as they crossed paths.

I looked at David. His colour was starting to return. 'He got lucky, that's all,' I said.

When he didn't answer I put an arm across his shoulder, but it was a mistake and he stood up, backing away from me like he'd been stung.

'You think I fucking care? You think I give a shit?'

'No, of course not.'

'He's a wanker. The big I AM. You see him with that slut? He doesn't care about her, she's just a trophy, somebody he can push around and yell at. Not like that, you useless fucker, like this, I told you, are you thick or what? No brain?' He smacked his head with his fist. 'Nothing there, nothing there, is there?'

'David.'

'Nothing, you're stupid and worthless and a fucking embarrassment. Just like your mam, crazy fucking slag.'

'David!'

He kept punching himself, harder and harder. I wrestled with his arms, but he wrenched them free.

'STOP!' I pushed him back into the sand and sat astride him. He struggled then lay still. 'Just stop it, OK?'

He turned his head away from me. A tear, fat and glistening, rolled over the bridge of his nose.

I wanted to say something that'd make it right. I wasn't what my dad wanted either and I wanted to say it, that I knew how he felt, but I hadn't got the words.

Breaking free from my grip, he wiped his nose with the back of his hand. I thought he'd calmed down so I started to move off him, but he pulled me back and then just looked at me, eyes wet, mouth open.

'You're all right.' He sniffed. 'You know that?'

'Yeah. You're all right too.'

He laughed and wriggled out from under me to sit on the sand, hands resting on his ankles, now and then heaving a breath. I lay back and stared at the sky, huge, freckled with stars.

'Look,' I said. 'There must be billions.'

He tilted his head to look up, smiled, but said nothing. He didn't need to. It was amazing, that stretch of black ice so crisp and clear you could imagine sliding on it. That, and the sea underneath, the incessant murmur of waves in the darkness ahead of us, a low rumble as a bigger wave spoiled up the beach. And us, the spaces between the wind and the sea when it was quiet, just our bodies shifting, stomach gargles, and breaths. David's words playing in my head. *You're all right.*

After a minute or two he lay back on the sand beside me and lit a cigarette. With each long puff the tip crackled and spat until it had burned all the way down to the filter. He nipped it between thumb and forefinger, sucking out the last drag, then flicked the butt high into the air, an arc of orange against the black, then gone.

I turned to face him, a laugh threatening to burst out of me. Despite what had happened with the rifles, with his dad, I'd done things right. His dad was a big man with no brains and what did it matter what David could do or couldn't do with the rifle because the sights were skewed anyway and if you didn't know that then you weren't worth the bother and that was all.

He saw my expression. 'What?'

'Nothing.'

'You're grinning like you just found out you got a third knacker.'

I shrugged with my elbows, fingers locked behind my head, and turned back to the sky.

'Go on.'

'Nothing.'

He rested his head on his hand to look at me. 'Close your eyes.'

'What for?'

With a big sigh I closed them tight. At first nothing happened, then I felt his hand on my stomach. I flinched thinking he'd deal me a slap, or pinch the band of skin showing at the hem of my T-shirt. But he didn't, just slowly spread out his fingers.

I opened my eyes. 'What you doing?'

'Closed.'

'Why? What for?'

'Cos I said.'

When I closed my eyes again I felt his hand move down, resting for a brief second on the buckle of my belt and then settling on my cock. My hands immediately grabbed his wrist to push him off, but his arm was rigid. I felt myself harden against his fingers, tried to sit up and wriggle free, but he shoved me back onto the sand.

'It's all right,' he said.

Part of me wanted him to feel, maybe he'd think I was big, but then if I wasn't . . . He pulled my hand towards him and pressed it on his hard-on. I could feel the length of it even with his zipper in the way. He was bigger, but not by much. The skin on my palm tingled.

Slowly he began to rub me, back and forth through my jeans, once or twice side to side so that he almost gripped me. I turned my head away, cold sand against my cheek, felt him rock against my hand. His breathing was different, or the waves were different, I couldn't tell them apart. My face was hot, but I couldn't stop, not touching him, or him touching me, not even when I kicked at the sand and tried again to slap him off.

A second later I came into my pants, my backside jerking up and down as I rolled to face him. My knees knocked against his, but he wouldn't let me have my hand back and kept it on his cock, his hand covering mine until he'd come too, eyes pressed tight, mouth open in a silent scream.

One breath held, released, and he was still. When he finally looked at me it was only for a second, then he laughed, stood up and raced towards the sea, stripping off his clothes as he went. I followed at a sprint, trying to catch up, lungs bursting with night air. As I got to the water's edge, David was taking off his jeans, pulling them over his socks and shoes, then his pants, slinging them back out of the reach of waves.

He pummelled his chest with his fists and then leapt into the water, great bounding strides that took him beyond the breaking waves.

'Come on!' he roared.

I laughed and looked back to the beach, to the lights of the fair and the Calvados that still tossed people high above the ground. Then, with an answering roar of my own, I followed him into the dark.

13

I knew something was wrong the moment Kathryn walked into the restaurant. She hesitated in the doorway, looking tense. When she couldn't immediately see where I was sitting, I stood up to wave her over, but she merely nodded and as I bent across the table to kiss her she pulled back. I was left taking an awkward bow.

'You OK?' I asked.

'Fine.'

It was unusual for her to be late, but she offered no explanation and picked up the menu, glancing up and down it impatiently. It was happy hour, half-price pizza, and there was a queue of students at the door waiting for tables. Once the waiter had taken our order, I looked at her more closely. Her face was flushed, shadows from the candle on the table flickering across her cheeks and collarbones. Her long fingers delicately folded a napkin.

I reached for her hand. 'Are you sure you're all right?'

'Hectic day.'

She appeared to relax a little then, meeting my eyes, but flitted from one subject to the next with hardly a pause. I convinced myself it was stuff I needed to hear. Normal things, plans for her father's retirement, work. Once or twice she stumbled on the words and looked out of the window at the river. Framwellgate Bridge was floodlit in golden light, the arches sitting on their own reflections to make perfect circles in the dark water.

'It's pretty, isn't it?' she said.

I turned back to her, but the conversation stuttered along, never really getting going. Even so, watching her, I felt my cock stir. My eyes shifted from one detail to the next, the underside of her wrist, the way her bottom lip glistened from the wine. I was safe as long as I stayed in detail.

'Have you seen David?' she asked.

'He's staying with me.'

Her eyes widened.

'For a few days.' I took a breath, losing her hand to reach for my glass. 'Makes sense. No point him paying for a B&B.'

'No, I suppose not. I didn't know he was planning to be in Durham so long.'

I shrugged. I needed to elaborate, but the truth

was I'd no idea how long he'd stay and every time I tried to think ahead I was stalled by endless what ifs.

'Have you given him a key?'

'Of course.'

At once I realised my mistake. Kathryn still didn't have a key to the flat, partly because I hadn't got round to having one cut, but partly, also, because I wasn't ready for her to have one. I could see it hurt. I was about to say something about getting her one, but she spoke first.

'Well, if he doesn't mind the sofa.'

'What's wrong, Kat?'

'Nothing.'

'Yes, there is. Something.'

She gave a small laugh. 'I've got this awful feeling I don't know who you are any more.'

I took a gulp of wine. 'What a peculiar thing to say.'

'Is it?'

'I'll get another key cut—'

'It's not about the sodding key . . . Shit.' Laughter from one of the nearby tables drowned out what she said next. I leant forward. 'Since when do you brawl in the street, Leo?'

'What?'

'Jamie saw you.'

Jamie was Kathryn's younger brother. Could he have seen the fight? I tried to remember his face in the group of people who'd gathered to watch, but they'd just been pink blurs.

'It was just a scuffle.'

'But you were fighting?'

'No.'

'You're saying Jamie imagined it?'

'No, I'm not saying that. David and this guy had been arguing. It got out of hand—'

'To put it mildly. The guy's arm is broken. Did you know that? Jamie was the one who called the ambulance.'

God. 'No. I didn't know.'

The pizzas arrived. We sat for a moment, staring at them in front of us.

'I was trying to break it up.'

'That's not what Jamie says.'

'Then he's *wrong*!'

Her eyes flickered, a moment of shock at my raised voice. A young couple with a child turned to look. I leant towards her again, but she sat back, refusing contact.

'So it was just David?' She raised an eyebrow. 'Is that what you're saying? You weren't involved?'

'I'm not saying it was just David. I was there, so yes, I was involved, but—'

'Why are you letting him stay with you?'

'I'm just . . . helping him out. Look, I know it's not great for us, but you can still come back to the flat. There's no reason for you not to stay over.'

'With him next door? No thanks.'

I brushed her hand with mine and held onto it when she went to move it away. 'He just needs a place. Hard for me not to offer.'

She let her hand rest for a moment and then

withdrew it to lift her knife and fork. 'I imagine he's changed quite a bit since school.'

Her change of tack was smooth. No longer confrontational, but still pressing hard for the information she wanted.

'We didn't go to school together.'

'Oh? I thought that's how you knew him.'

'No. He lived in the cottage next door for a bit . . .'

'How long?'

'A couple of months, then he moved.'

'Wow.' She shook her head, smiling in disbelief. 'Must've been quite a couple of months.'

I could see how odd it must seem to her, though in my mind that summer had gone on for years.

'You must've got really close. For him to look you up after all this time.'

'Quite close.'

She curled a strand of hair behind one ear. 'He's not what I expected.'

'I thought you liked him?'

'I don't know him. There's just something about him, a feeling you get.'

'Arrogance?'

'Unhappiness, I think, I don't know. He seems to be looking for a fight.'

'You only say that because of what Jamie told you.'

'It's more than that.'

'That's fair, I suppose. He was aggressive as a kid, not one to back down.'

'You're different when you're with him. The meal, the three of us, you were quite unlike yourself.'

'I don't see how.'

'Almost wary of him and yet, at the same time, there was something else. I was watching you, it was as though you, I don't know, you admired him.'

Her words struck me with such force that for a minute I couldn't say anything. 'I don't think I do, particularly.' I shifted in my chair. 'Do we have to talk about him?'

She looked at me, a note of surprise, but then obliged and the conversation limped along a different path. I thought, it doesn't feel right any more, this, not a relationship really, more of a situation. And yet I did want her, didn't I? Perhaps we just needed more time together.

I settled the bill, our silence coagulating around the things that hadn't been said, then I helped her into her coat and we walked outside.

'Funny you should use that word,' I said. 'Admire. I don't think it's true. I never wanted to be a soldier or—'

'Not for what he does.' She paused, struggling to find the right words. 'You were looking at him while he was talking and I just thought "I haven't seen that expression before." And now he's staying with you.'

I attempted a laugh, but it dissipated quickly. 'I hardly know him.'

'He means a lot to you.'

'Why on earth would you say that?'

She pulled back from me sharply. 'You say you don't want to talk about him and then you start doing it.'

I reached for her hand, but she snatched it away.

'Perhaps I should invite him out, just me and him, see what all the bloody fuss is about.'

'Christ, Kat, it's like you're jealous! Why would you want to go out with him? It's ridiculous.'

'Frightened he'll tell me something I don't know about you?'

'There's nothing you don't know.'

'I don't know anything.'

'That's just fucking dramatic.'

'He knows you better than I do. How do you think that makes me feel? Fourteen months we've been together. He knew you for a couple of months, eight years ago, and now you're living together.'

'I'm putting him up for a while. Jesus!'

'Listen to yourself.' Snowflakes had clung to her eyelashes; she blinked, wetting her cheeks. 'It's more than that, Leo, you know it is.'

'What? What is it?'

'It doesn't matter.'

We were halfway up the steps to the bridge. I pushed her back against the wall and put my arms either side of her, blocking her attempts to walk away. She looked down, lips pleated together. 'Does he have some kind of hold over you, Leo?'

'I don't know what you mean.'

'Are you afraid of him?'

My hands slipped on the wall, wet, slimy with algae.

'I don't understand this. I thought I would if I spoke to him, but it's you I can't fathom.' She met my eyes. 'Do you even want us to be together? Really, do you?'

'Kat . . .'

'Answer me!'

'Yes. You're attaching far too much importance to this thing with David. You and I are all that matter. He's really not important. Look, I'll tell him to go if it means that much to you.'

She raised her head, smiling. 'Of course I don't want you to tell him to go. That's ridiculous.'

'Your parents are away, aren't they? The two of us . . .'

The snow was falling into her hair, suspended for a moment perfectly intact before slowly melting. She freed herself from me and wrapped her coat tightly around her, walking up the last few steps onto the bridge.

'Kat?'

'I don't know, Leo. Perhaps you're right and I'm making more of it than—'

'I love you.' I'd no idea if I meant it, but I knew how much I wanted it to be true.

She faced me, a flicker of doubt, then, 'I love you, too.'

We shared a smile and walked together to the taxi rank where there was one already waiting. We climbed into the back seat, hands held. After a few minutes I turned to look at her. Her face was illuminated by the street lamps one second, in darkness the next. I sometimes felt alone with Kathryn, particularly in the last few days, but that didn't matter now. I moved closer and put my hand on her left thigh, feeling my cock strain against the buttons of my jeans. She turned to me and smiled, a moment to get lost in.

When we arrived at her parents' house she led the way up the path, searching in her handbag for her key. I slid my hands gently up her skirt, encouraged when she laughed and wriggled away. There, we were far enough from town to feel as though we were somewhere else entirely and it's what I needed. I needed her. Kathryn. She was the reality of my life.

When we were inside she'd barely set her keys down on the hall table before I kissed her.

She gasped, laughing again. 'Upstairs.'

Halfway up I kissed her neck, got the delicate smell of her covering my nose and mouth. She pushed me away, fingers lightly hooking over mine, leading the way. I focused on her ankles, the pale skin on the backs of her knees. God, it hadn't been this good in a while.

When we reached her bedroom I waited while she moved cushions and cuddly toys from the pillows. It still had the look of a child's room, fairy lights, rosettes pinned on a noticeboard, but alongside there were other things, more grown up, artists' postcards, pink Velcro rollers, a bowl of lavender on the dresser.

She was turning back the sheets. Impatient, I pulled her onto the bed on top of me. Her hair fell against my face as I kissed her again. Gently I pushed her legs apart, inserting one finger, then two. Her breaths were ragged, fast, and as I rolled on top of her she scrabbled for the belt on my jeans, her green eyes full of determination. She grasped my cock and guided it inside her, but it was an awkward fumble. Seconds. I closed my eyes, saw David's face, heard him, smelt him. I cried out in frustration. Always there. Always.

'What's wrong?' she said.

'Nothing.'

She stopped, looked at me, panting breaths onto my cheek. I felt myself go soft. Jesus. I took my cock in my right hand, tried to wank it hard again, grunts stuttering against the pillow.

'It's all right,' she said.

No, it bloody wasn't. I couldn't even make love to her. I buried my face in her neck then, frustrated, turned her over and spread her buttocks apart. Immediately I was hard again. I wet my fingers in the juice of her cunt, fast now, frantic, smearing her arsehole before attempting to get inside. I wanted to take it slowly, but I jerked forward and came.

Minutes later, I don't know how long, I opened my eyes. Kathryn was breathing heavily, her back tense, fists clenched around the duvet. I reached out to touch her hair, pulled back. Shit. She rolled over onto her side and without saying anything, switched off the bedside lamp.

We lay, half holding hands. I'd never felt further away from her. Still she said nothing. Gradually, her breathing slowed, deepened. When I was sure she was asleep, I pushed back the sheets and dressed. I'd never felt such an overwhelming sense of failure and knew, looking at her, knees curled up, I couldn't be there to see the expression on her face when she woke. I ordered a taxi and sat in darkness in the living room to wait.

14

The streets were wet, one or two of the drains over-flowing from where the snow had melted. Only ash-coloured slush remained, banked up on the kerbs. I paid the taxi driver and looked up at the flat. No lights. David must have gone to bed, or out, but still I hesitated. He had to go. I had the sense of moving to the margins of my life, with my friends, my course, now with Kathryn. I needed to confront him and yet had no idea where to begin. For all I was thrown by his physical presence, I was also comforted by it. A contradiction that weighed heavily on me.

Upstairs, I put the key in the lock, but when I pushed against the door it was on the chain. I banged on the door and waited, no noise from inside. Again, louder. Finally, a light came on, and a few moments later David's face appeared through the gap.

'Leo?'

'Take off the chain.'

'I thought you weren't back tonight.'

He looked bleary, like he'd just woken up. 'Come on. Let me in.'

A voice from upstairs. Female.

'Can you . . . ?' David said. 'Just a few more minutes, half an hour.'

'Who's that?'

'Howay, Leo.'

'Someone's there?' I pushed against the door, but he shoved his shoulder hard against it. 'For God's sake, David, it's my flat.'

'I said just give me some bloody time, no need—'

'Let me inside.'

'No.'

I took two steps back and kicked the door, more to make a point, but I broke the chain. He stumbled backwards, then, seeing where I was headed, scrambled to his feet. 'Just *wait*!'

I charged through into the living room, getting angrier, turned, walked back on myself. No one. He wouldn't . . . the bedroom. I flung open the door.

For a brief second I saw Kathryn, her long blonde hair covering her face, but of course it wasn't. She straightened up, looked at me. Then. No. Not even the right bloody sex.

'You get a canny look?' he said.

He had to be fifteen, sixteen perhaps, at the most.

Only really his face that gave away his age, for his body was well defined, a few hairs on his chest. I opened my mouth to speak, but made no sound. He stared at me for a moment and then casually picked up a sweater off the bed. As he drew it over his face, I moved to leave the room, but I was still standing there when he caught my eye again. He looked amused.

I closed the door and went to find David. He was in the kitchen, cigarette in one hand, a pint glass of water in the other.

'You might've let him get dressed.'

The flat reeked of sex and cheap aftershave. My heart was thumping, cheeks hot. I sat on the sofa, spilling an ashtray full of butts on the floor. No, it hadn't been Kathryn, but I'd thought it. Christ, what the fuck was happening to me?

David went back inside the bedroom, spoke, his voice, low, apologetic, and then the boy's, coarse, pissed off. I listened to them come out the bedroom behind me, whisper in the hall for a minute and then the door closed. David had put on a pair of jeans and rested the cigarette in his mouth while he did up the buttons.

'His name's—'

'I don't give a fuck what his name is.'

'Danny. He works in Wilson's betting.'

'I can't believe you picked up some rent boy and fucked him in my bed.'

'The sofa would've been a challenge.'

'You think it's a fucking joke?' I stood up, circled him. 'You bring some fucking kid here, lock me—'

'He's not a kid.'

'What would you call him?'

He thought, choosing the word. 'Knowledgeable.'

'You make me sick.'

'Cos I fucked him? Last I heard that was still—'

'Yes, that's it.' I laughed. 'This is about Kathryn. You're getting your own back for that night when she was here.'

'What? What you on about? I fucked some lad, OK? And I did it in your bed, so what?'

'Mine and Kathryn's.'

'Haven't seen her in it lately.'

I turned my back on him, felt the muscles in my stomach tense. I was filled with rage, but still I couldn't *do* anything.

'Frightened I've got spunk on your sheets?' He looked at me. 'Or maybe you're just jealous.'

'That you shagged the arse off some lad? He's not my type.'

'Isn't he?'

I held his gaze, looked away. 'I want you out of here, David.'

He laughed.

'I want you OUT! You hear me? This isn't a fucking brothel.'

'Ah, quit, will you? You sound pathetic.'

I launched myself at him, but he dived to my right, stumbled and then fell, jammed between the sofa and the coffee table. He put his hands up in front of his face, laughing.

'Ah, you're not worth it,' I said.

'Oh come on, Leo.' He stood up and straightened. 'I think you're making something out of nowt.'

'Have you spoken to Kathryn?'

'No.'

'What did you tell her?'

'When would I have spoken to her?' He shook his head. 'What's the matter with you? Things not as rosy as they were, that it? You had a tiff?'

'You must've said something to her.'

His eyes widened. 'Shit, you thought it was her, didn't you? You thought it was Kathryn in there?'

'Don't be stupid.' For a few seconds I had thought that, even though I'd left her asleep in bed. 'You're a fucking joke.'

I walked to the window remembering how that morning I'd found his stubble in the sink. How long had I stood staring at it before I washed it away? Christ. Kathryn's words replayed in my head. *Does he have some kind of hold of you? Are you afraid of him? I don't understand.* I didn't either, but I knew I had to try. From the moment he'd come back into my life I'd felt suspended in a sort of dreaming, confused state where images were too vague to make any sense and sounds were sharp and repetitive. Voices, my own or David's, a combination of the two.

'This has to end,' I said.

The distinctive sound of a ring pull being tugged back. I turned back to find him sitting in the armchair, a can of lager resting on his knee. The living room stank of beer and stale cigarette smoke. His clothes everywhere, several sweaters and shirts which had fallen in a heap on the floor. I pushed the coffee table back to sit on the sofa and a plate with crusts of toast, edges curled up, fell to the floor.

'You're a fucking slob.'

'Tell me what happened with Kathryn.'

I laughed.

'You know, you're pretty uptight for a student. It'll clean up.'

'Not by itself.'

'Then I'll do it, in the morning.'

'It *is* morning.' I sighed, irritated by my nagging, unable to stop.

He brought the can to his mouth and his face was lost to me for a moment. When I caught his eye again his expression was hard to read.

'Have a drink.' He pulled a can from a four-pack by the side of the chair and threw it to me. For a while then we sat in silence, only the occasional rattle of the boiler and the wind pressing hard against the window.

'It must be difficult for you, not telling her anything.'

'I haven't, if that's what you're getting at.'

'And what about me?'

'What have I told her about you?' I thought of telling him about Jamie seeing the fight, but it felt like old ground. 'Not much. She can't see any good reason why you and I would be friends.'

The corners of his mouth turned up into a smile. 'We're more than that though. Aren't we?'

I stared at him.

'The connection,' he added. 'All those years. I never stopped thinking about you.'

He had been staring at the dead fire, but now turned to look at me, his right eye still swollen and so bloodshot there was no white at all. Suddenly he produced a rolled-up newspaper from his side and handed it to me. It was a weekly, not one I bothered to check.

'Nothing new really. I was going to tell you earlier, but I thought it'd ruin your night.'

I snatched it from him, filled with panic, and flicked through the pages, irritated when I couldn't immediately find the story. He settled, resting his head on the back of the chair. It was only a few paragraphs, but from the facts which were so familiar to me now, having read and reread the first report, new words leapt off the page.

'Forensic testing.'

'You knew they'd do that,' David said.

They'd know who it was. Days now. Everyone would know. I opened my mouth to speak, but my chest had tightened and I had no breath. I coughed. 'We should go the police.'

He laughed. 'Are you mad? Fucking hell, Leo.'

'Tell them, before they get to us.'

'Now there's a plan!'

'It's our last chance to put things right.'

'Right? Listen to yourself. You and your fucking conscience.'

I stood up and threw the newspaper at him. It hit him squarely on the face.

'Careful,' he said. 'I'm not in the mood for your shit.'

'They think it's *murder*.'

He shook the newspaper at me. 'Where does it say that?'

'It's implied.'

'Just newspaper crap. They're bound to juice it up.'

I spread my hands out on the mantelpiece and stared into the mirror above. 'It might suit you to think we're together in this, David, but think about it—'

'I don't need to think about it. You and me, Leo, the whole way. Either of us mess up over this and it's both of us in the shit.'

'Tied.'

'If you like.'

'Then what's your plan?'

'I don't know.'

I smacked my palms off the mirror. It shook, but it didn't break. 'I can't take this.'

'No, you'd rather go and blab. Why doesn't that surprise me?'

I turned to face him.

'For God's sake, Leo. Isn't it time you grew a spine?'

'You arrogant . . .'

I swung my foot at him, striking him on the knee, but a second later he had me by the throat, his right hand pressing on my Adam's apple. I didn't pull back and so we stood, eyes locked, breathing hard.

'Go on,' I said, hissing out the words. 'Hit me.'

He backed down, spinning away from me with a groan of frustration.

'Things have changed, David.'

'Have they?'

We stood staring at each other then I turned, grabbing my coat. I needed to get out of the flat. Anywhere, towards town, or wherever my feet took me. When I reached the traffic lights that led over onto Crossgate I paused. I didn't want the lights of town and so turned and ducked into St Margaret's churchyard. Ahead of me were the lopsided stones of the graveyard, tottering down the hill, cracked tombs where the ground had given way underneath them. Hollow spaces, I thought, flooded tunnels filled with broken shale and smashed props.

I walked along the path between them until I reached the trees at the far side. Their naked, entwined branches criss-crossed the blue-black sky.

I couldn't stay with Kathryn, didn't want to go back to the flat and face David. And so I stood there, rain dripping from the trees onto my face. I was alone. Nothing to do. And nowhere to go.

15

I woke at dawn to a fist of wind slamming against my bedroom window. Last night when we'd walked back from the beach it had been a soft skin-on-skin sound, but through the night it had grown stronger and now it was a battering ram that shook the windows in their frames.

I lay on my side, arms wrapped around me, duvet tucked in under my chin. David hadn't said anything on the way home, not as we'd dressed silently on the beach, pulling on dry clothes over wet bodies, not as we'd walked up into the village and through the empty streets. Even when we'd gone our separate ways at the back gates, when I thought he'd be bound to say something, he'd walked up the path and gone inside without looking back.

I threw back the duvet and kicked it off the bed with my feet. Bum magnet. ~~Shirtlifter~~. Pots brown, our Leo. Jaz and Taffy had been right all along. I was a poof and David had seen it in me. I'd ruined things for good this time. What had happened on the beach had been his idea, but it was me who had made it happen. He wouldn't have done it with anyone else.

I dressed and went downstairs. Another gust, fiercer than the last, rasped down the chimney and spat black ash onto the hearth. I called Mum, got no answer, but then saw her out of the window. She was standing on next door's drive talking to Mr Cauldwell. It was several seconds before I worked out why he looked different, but it was because he had a suit on. Mum's hair was flying up around her face and she was trying to pin it down with one hand. I heard her laugh. Mr Cauldwell smiled. I'd never seen him smile either, it looked all wrong. I watched his tie flap around his face until, with one swipe, he caught it and held it against his chest. He was trying to impress her. He'd even sucked his stomach in.

I looked for David, but he didn't seem to be around, then he came out of the cottage with a suitcase and loaded it into the boot of the car. He had a suit on, too. I'd only ever seen him in jeans and shorts. He looked surprising, older, though it was more than that. I went to the back door, but met Mum coming in. Behind her I could just see the car pulling off the drive.

'Where are they going?' I said.

'It's started raining, felt a drop just then.'

'*Mum.*'

'Oh, a funeral. Leeds, I think.'

I stood, jostled by the wind, staring out after them. 'When are they coming back?'

'I don't know.'

'Didn't you ask?'

'No, Leo—'

I grabbed my sandals and pulled the straps over my heels.

'You can't possibly want to go out in this?'

I slammed out the back door, Mum calling after me, but I was caught by a gust of wind and propelled forward. I was unsure where to go at first, the day now yawned in front of me. I turned along the main street and half ran, half staggered to the village green. The two huge oaks in St Matthew's churchyard cast out their long branches, feeling for the ground as though to stop themselves falling. Where? As I rounded the corner of Jenkins Avenue I skidded to a halt.

Ahead of me, the beach. The once-distinct line of sea and sky had been scrubbed and scoured to a uniform grey. Waves rose, walls of chewed-up sand as high as ten feet, scrabbling up the beach in huge arcs of bubbling foam. I thought of all the stuff that the sea would spit out, suck and rake over and then of David when he'd stood high up the ledge at the Point. I blinked, but still saw him, a white shape against the cliff face.

He must've known he was going away last night, but he hadn't said anything. It was a stupid thing to keep a secret and funerals were arranged, they didn't just happen overnight. Maybe he was going for good and that's why it had happened.

Thunder cracked, barely discernible over the crash of waves. I made my way to the greeny-grey line of jetsam and mooched about, raking over a clump of bladderwrack with my foot. It was probably only for one night, he'd be back tomorrow, at least I hoped he would be.

When I looked up again I saw a dark shape in front of the dunes. For a moment I was convinced it wasn't a person at all, but some marine creature washed up. Her body had that look, a smooth shape, but with hair that flared wildly around her shoulders in thick clumps.

I walked closer. Her pale legs were pulled tightly up to her chest and her head rested between her knees. She was looking at a collection of shells and other things she'd gathered in a pile between her feet.

'Hello,' I said.

She raised her chin to me, startled at first, for she clearly hadn't expected to see anyone either, then she smiled.

'The flag's up, you know,' I added.

'I wasn't going to swim. I lay in the water over there though, there's a pool.'

'OK.'

I liked the fact she didn't seem to be afraid of the wind. She was skinny and it might be strong enough to pick her up. I sat beside her, catching a whiff of the sea's rot in her hair as she twisted it round her index finger. Fine strands lifted up and danced around her head.

'Look.' She held out her forearm, goose-pimpled, the tiny blonde stalks erect and shivering. 'It's the electricity. Your hair's doing it too.'

I ran a hand over my head, hairs clinging to my palm. We looked at each other and grinned.

'Do you want to see something?'

'What?'

She fished around in the pile at her feet and held up an egg sac.

'It's a mermaid's purse. What do you think they need money for?'

'Who?'

'Mermaids, silly.'

'Nothing to do with mermaids. That's just what they call it. A dogfish lived in it.'

She looked inside the narrow opening and then smoothed a finger over the leathery casing. 'Not any more.'

'They're sharks really, only little ones, but—'

'Was it a boy or a girl shark?'

'Dunno. They live inside for nine months, like a human baby, and then when they first come out, they're blind.'

She stuck her little finger through the hole at the top. She wore a bracelet, a sliver of gold that went around her wrist twice.

'Where's your mum and dad?' I asked.

She pointed at the small coffee shop on the front. As she rolled her head back I saw she had breasts, small mounds of fat with erect nipples. 'They're having breakfast.'

The Parlour. Fry-ups and burgers during the day, a restaurant at night. Mum took us there sometimes for pancakes. It had a row of floor-to-ceiling windows that overlooked the beach, blinking in the sun. I squinted and could just make out two figures sitting opposite each other at one of the tables.

'I only eat Cheerios,' the girl said. 'They have Weetabix.'

I tried to think of something to say. She was beautiful. Her swimsuit was tight over her body, her ribs visible all the way down, and on her stomach it folded over in wet ridges and ballooned into a pocket of air over her crotch. A trickle of seawater leaked from it making a damp patch on the sand between her legs. She traced a pattern in the sand with her finger, a figure of eight, but before she'd finished drawing it the wind brushed it away and she had to start again.

'I found some treasure,' she said. 'I'll show you, if you want?'

'OK.'

She got up, spraying me with sand, and ran up the side of the steep dune behind us. Once she fell onto her hands to balance herself, arse up, and I saw where the sand had stuck to the bony points of her bottom, two pale circles like a second skin. I swallowed over my tongue, suddenly swollen.

I followed and found her standing over a pile of clothes, a skimpy peach-coloured T-shirt and lime-green shorts with a scalloped hem. She lifted them up to reveal a collection of dolls. Not baby dolls, these were long-legged and skinny like Barbie.

'The sea gave them to me. They're from the storm.'

She knelt in the sand and arranged them in a circle around her. They were all the same, blonde plastic hair, big tits and a pink dress. The odd thing about them was the poses she'd put them in, one with its head between its legs, another balanced on all fours. I watched as she picked each doll up in turn, making small adjustments to an arm or leg.

'There were loads of them, like millions in this giant box that just floated right out the sea. I've only got twelve. A roof came off one of the caravans too, not ours, someone else's.'

'Oh.'

'My name's Snowy Stokoe.'

'That's a funny name.'

'It's my porn name. You take the name of your first pet and your mum's name before she got married and put them together. Snowy was my goldfish. I wanted a white rabbit, but Dad said no. What's yours?'

'We haven't got a pet.'

'Oh. Well, what was your mum's name before she married?

'Pemberton.'

'Right. And you haven't got a pet. I'll invent one for you.'

She pushed her dolls aside and thought. She had a tooth missing. I tried to remember how long ago it was I lost mine.

'How old are you?' I asked.

'Shhh! I'm thinking.'

She placed her index finger on her chin as though

to demonstrate the fact and then, suddenly, raised it and pointed it at me.

'You shall be Peanuts Pemberton! My friend's dog was called Peanuts. He poisoned himself licking creosote off their fence.'

'My real name's Leo.'

'I'm Alice, but as soon as I'm old enough I'm going to change it to Ruby.'

She offered no explanation for this, but instead pushed her tongue through the gap her missing tooth had made and rolled forward onto her knees to whisper in my ear. 'I'll let you poke me if you want.'

'What?'

'White cats are deaf too.' She rolled her eyes. 'I *said*, I'll let you poke me.'

I felt a flush rise to my cheeks at the thought of what she meant, though I couldn't believe it.

'You're not very clever, are you?' she said.

'Oh, I see. No, thanks, you're all right.'

She shrugged. 'Suit yourself.'

'Thanks though.'

'You're welcome.'

She smiled, delighted with the polite exchange.

I'd not taken long to decide about poking her and none of the reasons I tried out on myself really worked. Nothing to do with the act itself anyway, which I was sure would feel exactly like inserting my finger into a small clam.

'What's the matter with your foot?' she asked.

'I smashed it off a rock when I was diving.'

'Does it hurt?'

'Not any more. I just have the bandage on to keep the dirt out.'

Her feet were very wide at the toes and on the big toe of her right foot there was a silver ring with a tiny dolphin.

'You on holiday with your mam and dad?' she asked. 'It's just I haven't seen you at the caravan park.'

'I live here.'

'We're going home today. I live in York.'

She crossed her legs, pulling one ankle over the other like a Buddha. I noticed she had a large plaster on one of her knees.

'I was spinning,' she said. 'Fell over. It happens when you go really fast.'

'Spinning?'

'Don't you know what spinning is? I could show you if you like?'

She got up, put her arms out to the sides, tilted her head back and then began to swivel tightly in a circle. Her hair flew about her shoulders, dark blonde, straggly, long enough to touch the curve of her bum. She slowed, staggered, and flopped onto the sand beside me, green eyes shining.

'It makes you feel drunk.' She steadied herself on my arm with both hands. 'Like you.'

'I'm not drunk.'

'You make me feel drunk, silly. That's what I meant.'

'You're a bit young to be my girlfriend.'

'But you fancy me, don't you?' She wet her lips with the tip of her slim tongue. 'Your eyes went funny when you were watching me.'

I ran a finger over her plaster. She tore it back and showed me the cut, tiny, but deep.

'If I blow on it, it feels nice. Go on, you blow.'

I took a deep breath and blew which made her laugh, a nice laugh, like she was being tickled. I did it again.

The dunes were like a cave, cool, spiky sand, and still, but for the marram higher up that tossed in all directions. The heat beat down, thick, almost waxy. Alice laid out her towel carefully, flattening herself on it as though she were sunbathing. Above us a solitary cloud looked down, forming a clean ring at the centre like a bruise healing.

I looked at her lying there, the ridges of her ribcage rising and falling. She was very white, but her armpits and the hollows of her collarbones and neck were almost yellow. I thought, we can stay here forever. I liked being with her. She opened one eye to look at me, closed it again.

'You're funny,' I said.

'I'm an enigma.'

'What's that?'

She turned onto her side, posing her head on one hand.

'It means I'm like an abandoned ship in the middle of the ocean, or a horse that gives birth to twins. You know, if the twins are girls they can't have babies? I mean when they grow up. Because they're a freak of nature.'

'I didn't know that.'

'I'm a twin. I had a brother who had a heart too small for his body. He died.'

I tried to imagine it, a boy who looked like her. The same bony hands, feet with long, curled toes. She shifted her legs apart, a scissor shape, and then put my hand on the chilled bony mound at the top of her legs. Her hand rested on top of mine, pressing it down and then she closed her eyes, the lids fluttering.

I felt a jolt in my shoulder and a prickling of the skin around my groin. I'd have been happy to stay there, but then she opened her mouth and pushed out her lips for a kiss. I didn't know that's what she wanted, not for sure anyway, so I didn't do anything, the corner of her towel flapping around my ankles. She pulled herself up and, with a wriggle, fixed her mouth onto mine. Her lips were cold; I felt her eyelashes on my cheek. She let out a breath and a soft groan, deep, like it came from the base of her throat, then she pulled back sharply and laughed.

'There!' she said, ducking away from me to stand up. 'I've got to go now. My dad'll be looking for me.'

She gathered up her things into the crook of her arm and held out her towel as a carrier to receive the dolls I collected up for her.

'Do you have to go?' I said.

She smiled and, shooting a quick glance behind her, kissed me again. This time it was a colliding of lips and teeth. I could still feel her though, a warm sugary fizz that lasted far after she'd gone, running, fast as hare through the dunes, out of sight.

16

We followed the path through the dunes, once cordoned off, but the fence was now half buried in sand, the posts fallen in places and brittled with salt.

Mum had put on a floaty skirt and jewellery, a fat wooden bangle on her wrist. Make-up too, a pink slick across her lips like sugar melting. She'd made a big deal out of a trip on Patrick's boat, even arranged it with him so that I could steer, but I hadn't asked her to. I'd have to stand at the wheel with him, his sweaty hands on my wrists.

'Oh, come on, Leo, you've no one to play with.'

He'd been gone six days. 'We don't *play*, we hang out.'

'You might surprise yourself and actually have some fun. Possible?'

I was about to reply, but she skipped ahead with Olly.

When we reached the end of North Beach we walked down to the harbour, but despite the breeze that had been steadily picking up all morning, the wooden slats of the jetty blasted heat up into my face.

Patrick was on his boat. He looked up, showing off his gummy grin. 'My crew.'

'She's beautiful,' Mum said. 'Isn't she, boys? *The Fantasia*. What a lovely name.'

Olly looked like he'd bust a gut he was so excited. 'Can boats be boys?'

'No.' Patrick laughed, lifting him under his arms and swinging him onto the boat beside him. Mum next. As her feet left the jetty she shrieked, falling against him when he set her down. A second when they looked at each other, smiling. Whatever. She'd think she was in a movie probably, yeah, right, *The Silence of the Lambs*. Before he could get me I climbed aboard and sat next to Olly at the back.

'Right,' Patrick said, quickly undoing the moorings. 'Are we ready for off?'

The water inside the harbour was murky and shallow, but once we were past the other fishing boats it was deeper. Waves smacked off the bow. We bumped along following the shoreline in the direction of Cradle Cove.

Mum and Olly were loving it, shrieking every time one of the terns that were following us swooped close to their heads. I looked up, watching one ride the air and then dive down, beak open to reveal the slash of angry red.

'Want to steer a bit?' Patrick said.

I wasn't bothered, but Mum gave me a look and so I got up and stood beside him at the wheel.

'You can take us in, if you like. Put your hands either side on the wheel and aim for the middle of the beach.'

He stood behind me, crowding me, now and then putting one finger on the wheel to make a correction. It took forever for us to reach the cove. By the time I felt the bottom of the boat scuff the shingle I was more than ready to get off.

'He's good, Jeanie. A natural.'

I sucked in my bottom lip. Her name was Jean, not Jeanie.

I was first off, swinging over the side and paddling towards the beach, but Mum called me back to carry the brolly. I wouldn't have to stick around. I'd do my own thing. Mum straddled the side of the boat and slid down, splashing into the water just as Patrick reached forward to help her. He got Olly instead who was jumping about with excitement and holding up his arms ready to be lifted. I turned away and waded to the shore.

'Hang on a second, Leo,' Mum called after me. 'Somewhere by the trees. Then we've got shade if we want it.'

She and Patrick walked ahead, him telling some joke, her laughing, the picnic basket balanced between them. Her skirt trailed in the fine shingle, darkening at the hem where it had picked up a fringe of tiny shells. She looked happy, swinging her sandals in her other hand as she walked. Hard heels, tough, yellow skin. I remembered the woman I'd seen having sex in a cave last summer, her heels rolling dents in the sand and him, some bloke, on top, his backside pale as a crab's belly. Then, as though it was part of the same memory, I thought of David and me, stripping off our clothes and running into the sea.

When we'd picked out a spot everyone got on with helping to unload the basket, even Olly, who lifted out the blanket and then sat in the middle, diving at the corners. Mum just laughed. I felt sick. The smell of diesel fumes clung to my T-shirt. I watched a blue-bottle suck on the skin of a chicken leg.

'Can I explore?'

'What?'

'*Explore*.'

'Aren't you hungry?'

'No.'

She threw me a nervous, don't-screw-this-up-for-me smile which I blanked with a bored look.

'Just for a bit then. Take Olly.'

I rolled my eyes, but she wouldn't want to tell me off, not with Patrick there. I got up and strode down the beach, not bothering to wait for Olly who had to run to catch up.

'Go the other way,' I said.

'We have to stay together.'

'Look for shells or something. I'm going for a look about.'

'I'll come with you.'

'*Alone.*'

He stopped then, twisting the material of his shorts around his fingers and exhaling a deep nasally breath. I left him and continued along the shoreline. The water was warm and shallow. Further out, Patrick's boat rocked, a faint trammelling of waves against its sides, the occasional bump and slosh of water.

I trudged on with the sun on my back until I was as far away from the others as I could get and then turned and walked up through the dunes. As I ran down a steep hill and crossed the lane on the other side, the sand gradually changed to soil. I slowed to a walk. Across a field of spiky stalks a farmhouse shimmered in the heat.

Funerals were one day. Not six. He should've told me he was going.

'Found you!'

Olly stood behind me, grinning.

'Get lost. I told you I was going by myself.'

He hummed a tune, ignoring me.

'Whatever. Just stay back.'

I picked up a rock and placed it on top of another, much larger, then scraped the ground with my feet, looking for shells or pebbles to hurl at it. Some that were too big, others I didn't like the feel of.

Several misses, then a hit. My pebble had bounced off the rock and landed at the mouth of the hole. I walked over to take a closer look, heaps of bleached tussock grass outside, not rooted. Bedding. A den, no, not a den, a set. I knelt down and peered inside. It was perhaps two feet across at the widest point with a deeply shelving entrance and camouflaged well, tussock grass capping the roof, only visible if you approached it directly from the front. I tried to work out the depth, at least three feet, more probably. Tunnels. I ran a finger across claw marks in the soil, a few roots with bright white tips that looked like they'd been chewed back.

'What do you suppose made it?' Olly said.

'Badgers.'

'They might be in there watching us.'

'Don't be stupid.'

'They might.'

'They've got more than one entrance, stupid. They would've heard us the second we got here and run off.'

Olly knelt to look inside, his chubby white hands placed squarely on either knee.

'Go in,' I said. 'Have a look.'

'No.'

'There's nothing in there.'

He shook his head. 'You do it.'

'I can't, can I? I'm too big.'

'I don't want to.'

'You're such a crybaby, Olly. You never want to do anything.'

'It's dark.'

'Of course it is, it's a set.' I picked up a pebble and threw it at him, narrowly missing his arm. 'You're scared. You're always scared.'

'I'm not.'

'You blubbed when I shot the rabbit. Do you know how embarrassing that was? I told you you'd freak and you did.'

'Shut up, Leo.'

'Fair enough, we'll just sit here and do nothing. Makes a nice change, huh? Nothing. Nothing. Nothing.'

'We'll go back and find Mum and Patrick, then.'

'Mum and Patrick don't want us there. Haven't you figured it out yet? They're probably having sex.'

He looked at me.

'Oh, just shove off.' I'd been cruel to Olly ever since David had left, knew I was doing it, but couldn't stop. I snapped a loose thread off my sleeve and wound it around my thumb pumping blood up until the nail was red as a bite. 'You make me sick, you're all over him and you don't even know who he is.'

'I'm not.'

'Mum's in love with him. And she wants you to love him too, so you won't mind when she marries him.'

'She won't. You're just mad because—'

'Quit whining, you're giving me a headache.'

He looked at the set. 'All right, I'll do it. I'll go in.'

'You won't.'

'I said I will.'

'You won't do it.'

He dived for the set, scrambling forward quickly on his hands and knees. I stood up, excited. He got in as far as his shoulders, but then got stuck.

'Wriggle,' I said. 'What can you see?'

His voice was muffled, underground.

'What can you see?'

'Nothing.'

'Wriggle yourself further in.'

'It's dark.'

'Of course it is. I'll give you a push, OK?'

'No, don't push.'

'Ready?'

'*Don't.*'

I grabbed his feet, palms flat against his soles of his sandals. Surprisingly he shot forward with very little effort. I heard him scream, shock, but then he laughed.

'Well?' I said. 'What do you see?'

'Nottttttthing.'

As I let go of his feet the tussock on top of the entrance shifted. At first I thought it was just the breeze making the grass shiver, but then it started to cave in and the soil on the top was sucked down.

'Olly, get out!'

'What? Leo, there's—'

The roof collapsed, sudden and silent.

'Come out!'

He yelled, something, a word I couldn't hear, then nothing. Silence.

'Hang on! I'll pull you.'

I grabbed his ankles and yanked him backwards, but he was trapped. I tried again, put all my weight into it, digging my heels into the soil at the entrance and leaning back as far as I could, but he didn't move. I dropped to my knees and started to scrabble around his waist, scooping out soil with both arms, but each time I moved more soil slithered into the space I'd made.

'*Olly?*'

The sun beat a tattoo on my head. Shit.

Mum and Patrick were at the other side of the cove. It'd take too long to reach them, then get back. I looked inland. The farm was at least a mile away. No people. No cars on the road.

'I'll get help!'

I told myself there'd be an air pocket. Like in earthquakes. He'd have air. That's all he needed. That's why he wouldn't answer me, because he was conserving air. He'd know that. I ran, stumbling, falling down the soft sides of the dunes to the beach.

'Help!'

They were a hundred yards away, but I could see them, two figures in a shimmering haze and the brolly, snapping against the wind. I waved my arms, shouted, but a gust snatched the words away.

It was Patrick who saw me first. He got to his feet and put a hand at his brow to shield his eyes from the sun.

'Help!'

Mum's face, flushed with wine. She was looking at Patrick, laughing, then she stopped, puzzled, and looked in my direction. When she saw me running she stood up, her wine glass dropping onto the sand.

'Olly,' I said, when Patrick reached me. I tried for a breath, my mouth was dry. 'He's . . . stuck.'

I ran ahead though he was quicker. Several times

he had to slow until I pointed and he ran on again. I wasn't sure how far behind Mum was, but I could hear her, panting. I darted into the dunes. Right. Left. Stopped. Where? Sand. Grass. The damp, dark soil where I'd dug.

'There!'

His legs were still sticking out, not moving. Patrick lunged forward, skidding onto his knees and grabbed Olly's ankles. Mum was in the way, trying to help, clawing at the soil with her nails like some frantic dog, whimpering.

'Oh God, oh God. Olly!'

She was terrifying, her face like I'd never seen it before. Patrick yelled at her to get back.

Several more heaves, a minute, maybe more, and then Olly shot out like a cork. There was soil in his ears. Patrick rolled him over, more soil in his mouth and nostrils.

'DO something!'

Patrick put his head on Olly's chest. 'Not sure he's breathing.'

Mum shook Olly violently by the shoulders. Patrick shoved her off. I put a hand on her back, her dress was soaked with sweat.

Don't let him be dead.

No one heard me, perhaps I hadn't said it out loud. I was afraid, mumbling, pleading and yet aware, at the same time, of another part of me that stood back, enjoying the thrill.

Olly's face was purple. Patrick struck him hard between the shoulder blades and then roughly stuck his index finger into his mouth to free it of soil. I thought, it's no use, he's gone and Mum knows it too and that's why she sounds so bad. I put my hands over my ears, but heard Olly, an odd choking sound, then he coughed.

'All right,' Patrick said. 'He's breathing. We better get him straight to hospital.'

I hadn't meant for him to get hurt. I hadn't.

Once we were back on the boat I sat with my hands gripping the side. We heaved over the waves, the engine whining so loud it drowned out the shrieks of gulls. Mum put Olly across her knees, wrapping him tight in the picnic blanket so that only his head showed. She cradled him to her chest, every so often looking at me, then past me, lips tight.

His cheeks were streaked with tears, hair dusted white. I wanted to say sorry. Sorry. I'd have crawled in myself, but it had been nothing to do with me. I'd wanted Olly to do it.

Patrick had radioed for an ambulance as soon as we'd got on the boat and so it was waiting on the quay when we arrived, blue lights flashing. Olly looked better, not so purple.

Mum picked him up and handed him to Patrick while I moored the boat. I didn't know how, couldn't think of the right knot, spent too long on it, making Mum shout.

'Mum!'

'Stay with Patrick!'

'I want to come!'

She went in the ambulance with Olly and I couldn't

see, then just a glimpse of him sat up on the bed inside with an oxygen mask covering his face. When the paramedic closed one of the doors I ran forward.

The other door slammed shut. The siren yelped, once, then drove off.

'Come on.' Patrick put a hand on my shoulder. 'I'll take you home.'

It wasn't very far so we walked, him ahead, me trailing a few feet behind. I felt cold though it was still hot. When we got back to the cottage, I told him it was OK and he could go, he didn't have to wait with me, but he made me a drink of orange. Cordial, too strong. I didn't want it anyway. We sat opposite each other at the kitchen table, not talking. Eventually, he got up and walked over to the window, hands in the pockets of his jeans. I could see him trying to think of something to say and once or twice he opened his mouth to speak, but then closed it again. He looked fed up.

When Mum came back she had Olly with her. He was lying against her chest. Patrick and I both rushed into the hall to help, but she said she could manage and carried him straight upstairs. She was gone ages. When she finally came into the kitchen she didn't even look at me, just washed her hands at the sink.

'He's asleep.'

'Best thing,' Patrick said.

'Thank you, Pat. I can't tell you how—'

'It's fine. Look . . .' He glanced at me. 'You need to be together. Call me later?'

They exchanged a few more words in the hall,

quiet so I couldn't hear them, and then she came back and stood in front of me, pressing her hands into her eyes.

'What were you doing, Leo?'

'Nothing.'

'Olly's not got half the bloody beach in his mouth for nothing.'

'I didn't know it would collapse.'

She turned away. 'Oh God, just go to your room.'

'He *wanted* to. I didn't make him, Mum.'

'*Now!*'

I went upstairs, hands clamped over my ears as a plate clattered and smashed. At Olly's bedroom door I stopped and looked inside. He had bunk beds left over from when we shared a room. Even now he always slept in the top bunk, but Mum had put him on the bottom. He was lying on his back, asleep, eyes swollen and puckered like a baby rat. I wanted to cry, but couldn't.

I went into the bathroom, locked the door, and splashed my face with water. When I raised my head to look in the mirror I tried to make the tears come, but still they wouldn't. I stared at my reflection for a long time, water dripping off my eyelashes and the tip of my nose. I was changing, a different expression, a different face. And I didn't know who it was.

17

Patrick chose to sit on my bed, right on the edge like he was expecting to have to get up again quickly. He cleared his throat and clasped his hands together, rolling one thumb over the other. I might've said something to make it easier, but then it hadn't been my idea at all.

I thought of Mum downstairs, waiting, trying to stop herself from standing in the hall where she might be able to overhear us talking. There hadn't been much talking so far.

He took a breath. 'So. What sort of stuff do you like?'

'Huh?'

'Football?'

'No.'

He looked around, settling on my bookcase. 'Astrology?'

'Astronomy. I had to do a project on the planets for school.'

He nodded.

'Just cos I've got books about something doesn't mean I'm interested in it.'

'Right.'

I walked across to the window. Several times since David had left I'd thought I'd heard their car pulling up outside, but when I'd gone to look it hadn't been them. Now, I was sure I heard the distinctive sound of the engine clicking over and when I pressed my face against the glass I could just see the bonnet. A car door slammed and then the car was reversing off again, revving, then nothing. A minute later I saw David walking down to the shed. He was carrying a tray. I watched him balance it against his hip while he unlocked the door and went inside.

'Jeanie – your mum – thought we might talk . . .'

I wanted to run out and join him, but I was afraid suddenly. How were we going to talk about what had happened on the beach before he left? I felt it was like a long time ago and sometimes, these last few days especially, I'd wondered whether it'd had even happened. Perhaps I'd dreamt it.

'Olly and the foxhole. Among—'

'It was a badger set.'

'And leaving the fair. Just going off. Your mum was worried.'

'I didn't go off.'

'We couldn't find you.'

'I went to the beach.'

'In the dark?'

My face burned.

'Look. I know you probably don't want to talk to me, but your mum thought what with your dad not being around.'

'He is.'

'Not here.'

'He's in France. I can go there whenever I like or he can come here and—'

'I'm not a threat, Leo.'

I examined the cuticle on my index finger. I could ring Dad, ring him right now if I wanted. I thought of the last time when I'd got the Frenchwoman. She couldn't understand me at first, said something in French and the line went quiet like she'd put her hand over the receiver. A laugh, hers, and Dad's voice in the background, too faint to hear, then the line went dead.

'Whether you like me or not doesn't really matter.'

'No, it doesn't.' I stared at him. 'You're just shagging my mum.'

His mouth tightened. I thought he wanted to hit me, but he looked at his hands instead and sighed a deep breath.

'Your mum thinks, lately . . . you've been a bit mean to Olly. On top of that, you're going out a lot and this not saying where you're going—'

'I'm not a kid.'

'She thinks David—'

'What about David?'

'Some kids are just trouble.'

'You don't know him. You don't know me. You're just shagging my mum. Maybe you want her money, or you just want to see what you can get from her, but I'm not stupid.'

'No.' He stood up and thrust his hands into the pockets of his jeans. 'You think you've got me all worked out, don't you?'

'I didn't know I was supposed to be working you out.'

'Maybe you've picked the wrong guy to wind up. If you were mine—'

'I'm *nothing* to do with you.'

'Your mum's worried about you. She's upset. I don't like it when she's upset.'

'I don't care what you like.'

'You've been acting different.'

'I'm like this all the time.'

'Show some consideration for her. No one expects you to be thrilled about me, but you might be a little less selfish.' He went to the door, stopped, turned back. 'If you loved her you'd want her to be happy.'

'You don't make her happy. You—'

He left, cutting me short. I stayed at the window for a few minutes, gazing down at the shed. There was light now, poking out under the door, a candle perhaps. I listened, muffled voices downstairs. Patrick would be telling Mum what a great job he'd done. Sorted me out. I pulled my trainers out from under the bed and sneaked downstairs to the back door.

It hadn't looked it from inside, but a wind had got

up and as I walked to the end of our garden all that had been still came alive. The apple tree gestured wildly and I could hear the waves clawing up the beach. I walked round to the shed and knocked.

'It's Leo.'

He opened the door, just wide enough for me to see his face. He looked startled, then grinned and let the door swing open.

'Red's opened his other eye.'

'Great.'

They were asleep, lying so close together it was impossible to tell one from the other, but when David leant over them, Red lifted his head and peered out through half-opened lids.

'You were gone ages,' I said.

'Yeah.'

'Where'd you go?'

'Funeral then this caravan place in Wales.'

I waited for him to say some more, but he merely shifted to get more comfortable, lying on the floor next to the kittens, one hand propping up his head, the other smoothing the fur on Red's chest. He stroked him under the chin and instantly got a purr.

'You didn't say you were going on holiday.'

'What?'

'Holiday.'

'I didn't know, did I? You think he tells me every-thing?'

I wondered if now was the time to talk to him about what we'd done on the beach, but it didn't seem right. I'd thought he might be angry about it, but he didn't seem to be thinking about it all. I was relieved at first, but I'd thought of little else since he'd been gone and so, as we sat there, silent, aware of his body close to mine, I grew restless. He really wasn't going to say anything.

'Do you want to do something then?' I said, finally.

'Like what?'

He lifted Tio's tail and blew softly on the tip. I was amazed by how gentle he was with the kittens. He loved them.

'We could go to the beach,' I said, adding quickly, 'There was a storm while you were gone, a big one. We could look for washed-up stuff.'

'Right.'

'A bit of the church roof come off.'

'Oh. All right.' He sat up, waiting for me to get outside first, before blowing out the candle and locking the door.

On the walk down through the village a warm wind blew in gusts around us, but on North beach, with nothing in its path, it turned into dancing dervishes that whipped our calves. We raced to the waves, got as close as we dared to their deafening, brutal clash, chasing them as they were sucked away, laughing, sprinting back up the beach before the next ones could get us. Once, he looked at me, his T-shirt clinging to his sides, outlining the muscles on his chest and shoulders. It didn't matter what had happened before, things were good.

'Come on,' I said, sprinting away from him up the beach.

I led us through the marram, pushing on along the path through the dunes though I didn't know where I was going. When we reached a patch of sand clear of sedge I dived onto all fours and rolled onto my back. David made as if he was going to stamp on my chest with his foot, but then dodged at the last second and collapsed onto the sand beside me. A small high-pitched whining alarm from an insect, then silence. Sandwort and mouse-ear shivered on the banks around us, their smell strong and sickly.

I imagined Patrick, Mum and Olly on the settee watching *EastEnders*, Olly in the middle. I didn't know what I hated more, that Patrick'd had the nerve to tell me to sort myself out, or that Mum had asked him to do it.

'What's the matter with you?' David said.

'Nothing.' I stopped, started again. 'Him. Mum's boyfriend.'

I hadn't called him that before, not out loud anyway. It made me angrier. 'He came to my room for a chat.'

'Oh. What about?'

'Dunno. Stuff. I just hate him, that's all.'

'Cos he's doing your mam?'

'Yeah. No. Ah, I dunno, forget it.' I plucked at some grass. I wanted to tell David everything that had happened while he'd been away, Alice and Olly, but I couldn't find the words. I looked away, blurted out, 'He thinks he's my dad.'

'Oh. So?'

'He isn't.'

'Yeah? Doesn't matter though, he's all right, isn't he?'

'He's *not* my dad!'

'OK. Bloody hell, I was just saying. You could—'

'He's nothing to do with me!'

I ran, leaving David sat there. I didn't stop, ran as fast as I could until I reached the harbour where I skidded to a stop. A minute later David was beside me, hands resting on his knees, gasping for breath.

'You off your naffing trolley? What did you run off for?'

I scanned the cottages on either side of Pier Road. Even if someone was looking out, it was too dark, they wouldn't see. I led the way, confident.

'Where we going, Leo?'

'You'll see.'

When I reached the quay I stopped. Far out, the moon, small and high, drew a faint silver line on the water. A few stars pricked the sky, but it wasn't dark yet. I kept going until we were on the main jetty, our footsteps hollow on the slats. All the boats were moored, some out in the harbour itself, others tied side by side on the jetty rings. Rigging clicked against masts and now and then there was a creaking sound and a knock when one boat nudged another.

I squeezed past a stack of lobster pots, taking in a mouthful of their fishy stink. A lobster's pincer poked out through the netting. I looked for the rest of the body, but it was just an arm, ripped at the shoulder.

Patrick's boat was the last one in the line. *The Fantasia*. It was a different colour in this light, blue grey, instead of white. It bobbed up and down gently.

'His,' I said.

'Who?'

'Patrick's.' I looked out over the bay. Further out, where the lights of the village didn't reach, it was black. 'He'll need a tow. He won't like that.'

I knelt down to undo the moorings, wrestling with the knots. I wasn't sure I'd go through with it, but soon the boat was free. I held on to the rope in my hand.

David laughed. 'You're fucking nuts, you.'

I could've tied it back on the ring, thought I might, but then a gust of wind tugged the boat and I felt the rope tighten and then go slack in my hand. I let go. At first the boat didn't move, but then it drifted a few feet from its neighbour. Before I could change my mind I lifted my foot to the bow and gave it a shove. It swung away, water slapping against its sides.

'Shit!' David said, half laughing, half amazed.

I laughed too, watching it floating free. I couldn't believe what I'd done. David's mouth was open, the whites of his eyes shining. We should've legged it then, but I wasn't afraid we'd be caught. I grinned, watching the boat slip further and further away, turn, drift.

'Fuck me. I thought when you wouldn't hit Jaz, I thought maybe you were soft, but *shit.*' He tugged my wrist. 'We'll be dead if anyone sees us.'

We ran back up the jetty, laughing, full of it. I was barely able to keep up with him, but happy, drunk on his words. David had made me dive from the ledge, he'd made me shoot the rabbit and skin it. But this, it'd been me. All me.

★　　★　　★

By the following morning I was convinced someone would've seen us. Hours passed as though they were days. Mum'd gone to Haresham with Patrick, leaving me to watch Olly. It was late afternoon when she got back and I half expected Patrick to burst through the door behind her in a rage, but he wasn't with her. She called us through to the kitchen and put out some cakes she'd bought from the baker's.

She seemed all right, not mad. 'Tuck in.'

I chose an eclair which slid in my fingers as I took the first bite. Olly took the one with rice crispies on the top, but then made a face out of them on the table. I watched as it took shape. Eyes, nose, mouth in a grin.

Mum sat beside me. 'OK, Leo?'

'Yeah.'

She leant over the cakes, but didn't have one, just picked off a strawberry decoration and popped it into her mouth. 'How did it go with Patrick?'

'Huh?'

'Your talk with him.'

'Can we go out with the nets tomorrow, Mum?'

'In a minute, Olly. I'm talking now.'

'Fine,' I said. 'It went fine.'

She waited for me to say more, but I shoved in another mouthful of eclair, fingering the loose cream into my mouth where it squirted onto my cheeks. I hoped Olly would start rabbiting on again, he did usually, but he was adding eyebrows to his face.

'Someone set Patrick's boat loose last night. Had a hell of a job getting it back.'

I didn't dare look at her so I stared through the window. A wren bobbed about on the lawn, picked at the grass.

'A couple of the fishermen are jealous of him. He does a lot better than most.'

I looked at her.

'I know. Grown men. Can't prove a thing, of course. There's no damage done, thankfully, but it's pretty pathetic all the same.'

'Yeah.' I grinned at Olly who looked puzzled at why I'd suddenly pay him any attention. He smiled back, a rice crispie stuck to his chin.

'Maybe you could both go out with the nets?' Mum said.

'What? Oh yeah, sure.' I couldn't have said no, not after everything that had happened. I pulled back from the table. 'Tomorrow though. I was going round—'

'David's. All right then.'

She looked disappointed. Maybe I'd stay, have another cake, but I was desperate to go to the shed. We had plans to make it our own, add things, take away the junk and dump it in a skip in the next street though I wasn't up for doing it today. The air was cool now, but it had been hot and I was tired. I knocked on the door three times and went inside.

David was lying beside Blackie and the kittens. I slumped onto the beanbag and gazed at them, asleep on their teats. It wasn't long before I closed my eyes and drifted off to sleep.

When I woke David was still in the same position.
'You were talking.'

'What did I say?'

'Dunno. Blah, blah, blah.'

I tried to collect the images together. David buried in the sand, sinking, only his head visible. Gradually this too began to sink and I'd scooped away the sand, around his chin and mouth first, then moving down his body to find an arm or a leg I could pull. I'd had to work quickly, seeking out edges, scrabbling for something, some part of him I could get my weight under, but all the time the sand kept changing, hard, easy to shift, then soft, caving in on itself, replacing all that I'd moved with more.

'What was it about?'

'What?'

'Your dream.'

I shrugged and sat up, wiping the corner of my mouth with my sleeve. The kittens were awake now, suckling again. Blackie looked at me through half-closed eyes. I wondered what it felt like, those tiny teeth on her pink skin.

Tio was the strongest. Often he'd shove Red and Boris aside to get the teat he wanted. They'd started playing too, Boris liked to bite Red's paws and once or twice Red would squeal and roll over.

Sometimes, at night, I worried about them, imagined a fox might get through the hole and take them, or Blackie would get run over and they'd be waiting for her to come back.

'When do you think they start eating proper—'

'Shhh!' David sat up. 'Did you hear that?'

'Just the wind.'

'No. It's Dad.'

I looked at my watch. It was only half past four and he didn't finish work till six. I lay back. Sometimes you heard a car door slam on the street outside, or voices, a dog barking, and it felt really close. David was looking at the door of the shed.

'Relax,' I said. 'Do you want to go back to the house?'

'No.'

I stood up and looked out through the roof window, but saw only the dusty green leaves of the privet. Then, a footstep on the path outside. David's dad put his head round the door.

'What the hell are you doing here?'

He looked at me, then David. 'Start talking.'

'Just messing about,' David said.

My heart was beating fast though I didn't know why. He came in and stood in front of us. At once the shed felt tiny. His bulk, suddenly there, sharpened everything, the smell of old compost, the moon's glow through the window that illuminated David's fingerprints on a glass. He couldn't be mad. It's not like we'd wrecked the place.

'We weren't doing anything.' I said. 'Just feeding the kittens.'

'Kittens?'

I must've looked at them for he took a step towards the blanket, his heavy black boots a millimetre from Blackie's head.

'She gets in through the slat.'

He dipped his head and peered at the gap. David was looking at the floor. I nudged him, but he didn't speak.

'Do you know how many kittens a single female cat can have in one year, Dave?'

He didn't answer.

'Thirty. Sometimes more. Not only that, but the kittens grow up, have kittens themselves in no time.'

I looked at David, then his dad, confused. I felt a laugh rise up inside me. It seemed like such a funny thing to say, like a joke with no punchline. He knelt beside the kittens and then picked up Tio, pulling him off the teat and holding him up by the scruff of his neck. He was purring, a drool of milk on his whiskers.

'Strays, huh?' He held Tio at eye level, and blew on his face, which made him cry.

'He's friendly,' I said.

'Feral.'

'No. Blackie probably belonged to the girl who lived here last.'

'Hand me that bag, Dave.'

It was the plastic bag I'd bought sandwiches and magazines in, last week sometime; we'd used it for rubbish ever since. For a while David just sat there, still.

'Come on! Hand it to me!'

Silence, made all the more empty because it'd been so unexpected. So loud.

'Please, Dad. Don't.'

His dad grabbed the bag himself, emptied the contents onto the floor, orange peel, cigarette butts, a Coke can.

Suddenly David came to life, scrambling on his hands and knees to where his dad was standing with the bag. He grabbed the handle, a tug of war he lost when the handle snapped. His dad clipped him across the head and David fell backwards into a slump on the beanbag beside me.

'What are you going to do?' I said.

'They're not pets, not these ones. They're wild.'

'We're going to find them homes. Put a notice in the post office.'

David let out a strange, strangled sound. Blackie hissed, ears flat, and then backed away and shot out through the slat. I watched, unable to move, as David's dad picked up Boris and Red and put them inside the plastic bag. Tio rolled onto his back as Mr Cauldwell's hand bore down. I stared at the bottom of bag, bulging.

I was waiting for David to do something, say something, but nothing.

'I'll take them home,' I said.

'Get out of the way.'

Then, suddenly, there was no time. None of his movements were fast or hard. He had an unstoppable momentum, the quiet force of someone who knew what he was doing was right and he couldn't be stopped. He put the handle of the bag over his wrist and rolled up his sleeves, taking his time to smooth out each fold and curl it cleanly over the next. Looking at him, I thought, he's enjoying it, a joke. Any minute he'll let them go.

I looked again at the bag. They wouldn't be able to breathe. If I took them outside, hid them in the hedge, Blackie would come back and find them and maybe take them off somewhere else. Somewhere safe.

David was rocking back and forward, locked into himself, biting and chewing his bottom lip. His dad grabbed him, forcing him up to his feet. Outside, up the path to the house, the bag swinging from his dad's hand, the other clamped around David's wrist.

The breath in my lungs vanished. A minute, two, then I ran after them.

Downstairs was in darkness, but upstairs a light was on and I could hear running water, echoing, and voices, his dad's deep, insistent, David's in reply, quiet, trembling. I began to climb the stairs, but with each step my legs grew heavier. If I was slow enough I might miss it, but I wanted to keep going, had to. I made myself walk forward until I stood in front of the bathroom door. David was sitting with his back against the tub, sobbing, shoulders rounded.

'Stop snivelling,' his dad said, then, to me, 'Go home, lad.'

The bath was ringed in a scummy brown and the water, perhaps a foot in depth, was a pale yellow.

'Give me the bag, Dave.'

I saw now that it rested in David's lap and for a second I was filled with relief. The kittens would be safe, but then David passed the bag up to his dad's waiting hand.

'Don't! David!'

The kittens squirmed behind the thin plastic, tiny eels. They were frightened now. I heard one of them cry, thought I recognised the mew as Red's.

'What are you *doing*?'

I reached for the bag, but met David's outstretched arm. He shoved me back. 'Just go home, Leo.'

'What?'

'Go.' He looked at me, pleading, shaking his head. 'You can't do anything.'

I covered my ears, unable to bear the sound of plastic, the rustle and the silence as it sunk under the water. I lunged forward, met David's hand on my throat, firm, yet gentle, pushing me back against the wall.

It didn't take long. No cries, no thrashing, no bubbles. When it was over his dad lifted the bag up, water streaming out of the holes in the bottom. He put it on the floor next to David and wiped his hands down the back of his trousers.

'Get this place cleaned up,' he said. 'You can put them in the bin.'

He tapped the side of David's head as he pushed past us out of the bathroom. I wanted to hit David for doing nothing, for not stopping it. But I hadn't stopped it either. I could've done. I could've taken them and run.

The front door slammed and a few seconds later we heard the car start on the drive, rev, pull away, and then grow faint in the distance.

'Are they dead?' David asked.

I couldn't speak.

The bag was tied at the top by its handles, a tight knot I had to undo with my teeth. I could taste the water, grainy, metallic. Inside, a warm kitten smell. I lifted each one in turn, naming it.

'Tio. Red.'

'Stop,' David said. 'Put them back.'

'Boris.'

Their eyes were closed. I took a towel, stained with a skid mark, and tried to dry them off, hoping, though there was no reason to hope, that the movement might bring them back.

It was a few minutes before I realised I was crying which shocked me because what I felt most, now that I saw them, was relief. The kittens were dead and I didn't have to be responsible for them. I didn't have to worry about them, or feel afraid. I wondered whether that was what grief really felt like, the sort Mum felt when Nanna died, a grief that blew through you like a storm, but then left you. Cold, maybe even changed, but free.

It was easier to look at the bodies than look at David, his face, a wet ruin. He'd loved them. Now they were gone and a part of him had gone too.

18

We buried the kittens on the beach a few hours later, though we'd gone back to the shed first and sat looking at the slat. We were waiting, I suppose, hoping Blackie would return, but I'd known she wouldn't. Not ever.

I believed she'd known the fate of her kittens, maybe even before it'd happened. I thought about it a lot as we walked to the beach. But how could she be sure they were dead? How did she know she hadn't abandoned them, that they weren't still waiting for her? It felt like the most important thing to understand of what had happened, but there was no reason, or none a human could understand. Just like the gulls that fell silent before a storm. She'd known, that's all.

I finished digging the hole and sat back on my heels. 'Do you think it's deep enough?'

David sat with his back to me, chewing on a grass stalk. He'd shown no interest in choosing the place where we would bury them and in the end I had decided. I chose the spot where I'd kissed Alice and thought of her mouth and her hair as I scooped out the sand with my hands.

'Do you think I should leave them in the bag?'

I knew I ought to take them out, but I was afraid of touching them again. They were going stiff and the water around them stank.

'David?'

'Just get on with it.'

I stared at the hole I'd made, deep enough so that foxes wouldn't get them. I wanted it to be better than it was, just dumping them in the ground wasn't enough, but I didn't know what else to do. In the end I picked a clump of sea thrift and shred its pink petals into the base of the grave, then I took the kittens out of the bag and lay them side by side. Their fur was wet and Red, who I put in the middle, had his mouth open. Tiny teeth.

I scooped sand over them, patted it down with my hands and then sat, knees pulled up to my chest. David rolled the grass stalk in his mouth. He was looking out at the sea which was bulging against the lie of the land, building to a big incoming tide. I ran a tongue over my lips and tasted salt.

'Thanks,' he said.

'What for?'

He shrugged and I nodded. It was all he needed to say. I'd been able to do what he hadn't. I wiped my face with my sleeve and went to sit beside him. For a long time we didn't say anything.

'Were you scared?' he said, finally.

'What?'

'When you tried to stop him?'

'Didn't do any good.'

'Yeah, but at least you stood up to him.' He spat out the grass stalk. 'I wasn't chicken, all right? I'm not scared of him, it's just . . .'

'It doesn't matter.'

'I mean . . . I know . . . Oh FUCK!'

'It's OK. Neither of us could've stopped him.' His face half turned from me and I could only see his profile. 'Look, how about we go somewhere?'

'Where?'

'I dunno. Get a bus to Alnwick, there's this place Mum was on about. Bird-of-prey centre or something. We could—'

'Nah.'

'What then?'

He shrugged.

'Anything's better than sitting here. I've got some money, I was saving up for a bike, but I reckon we could do something with it, there's a go-kart place—'

He turned to me. 'How much money?'

'Forty-seven pounds and fifty-three pence.'

He thought for a moment. 'We could go hunting. Set up a camp. Do it properly.'

'Overnight?'

'Yeah, longer probably. Go to Harwood. Not mess around with rabbits though. We'll get a deer.'

I laughed. 'A *deer*?'

'There's deer in Harwood.'

'You can't hunt them.'

'Why not?'

'They're protected or something.'

'Bullshit.' He raised his hands to make a gun shape and pulled the trigger. 'It'll be ace, we can plan the route, decide the best places, map out wherever the water is, we could even build a hide.'

'You really reckon you could take a deer?'

'You think there aren't people paid to kill them? We'd be doing them a favour. Who'd know anyway?'

'The forestry people.'

'So we see someone we leg it.'

'Mum'd never let me go.'

'So don't tell her.'

'Just take off? No way, she'd go nuts.'

He drove his feet into the sand. 'I'll go on me own then.'

There wasn't a chance Mum would let me go, but as we sat there, the idea settling in my mind, I knew nothing would stop me. I'd just have to talk her into it.

All the next day and into the evening I waited for the right moment to talk to her. David was serious about going on his own and was planning to leave the following morning, with or without me. I was tense, frustrated, watching a video with Mum and

Olly, but I could barely focus on the TV screen. All I could think about was what David would be doing, preparing supplies, planning the route.

When the film finally finished I went to the kitchen and made myself a sandwich.

Mum came in and switched on the kettle. 'What's the matter? Are you still hungry?'

I wasn't really. I put the bread back in the bin.

'I thought we could all go out tomorrow night. Patrick's booked a table at Daniel's.'

'I can't.'

'Why?'

I took a can of Coke from the fridge, lifting the ring pull up with my nail and snapping it back until she couldn't stand it any more and took it off me. 'What's wrong, Leo?'

'Nothing.'

'Olly told me you pushed him yesterday.'

He'd seen us leaving David's and had raced back in the house to put on his shoes, running out to meet us a few moments later. I'd yelled at him because I didn't want him to see the bag with the dead kittens in. I'd shoved him hard in the chest, made him cry. I was angry, for him always being around, always sticking in his nose in. He didn't understand and I couldn't tell him, that was all.

'I didn't mean to.'

'Why did you?'

'He's always hanging about.'

'That's no excuse for pushing him. Of course he wants to play with you. He's your brother.'

'I know.'

'Things just haven't worked out with your dad. It doesn't mean you can take it out on Olly.'

'I'll tell him I'm sorry.' A pause. 'I don't care about Dad.'

'I know that isn't true.'

It was the moment. I blurted it out. 'Can I go camping?'

'What?'

'It'd just be for a couple of nights.'

'Do you mean on the lawn?'

I stared out of the patio doors. The moon was large and full.

'You *can* be angry with your dad, you know. He made a promise and he broke it.'

'It doesn't matter.'

'He's still your dad. You've every right—'

'Stop it! You want us to go, that's all. If me and Olly were in France you could be alone with Patrick. It's fine, but I don't WANT to go.'

'You'd rather go camping.'

'Yes.'

She came to stand beside me and folded her arms. I thought I'd blown it.

'You know, we used to talk about things. I don't understand what you have against Pat. It's not like he's taking anyone's place.'

I bit my lip. This was no time to rub her up the wrong way.

'How am I supposed to understand what's going on with you unless you talk?'

'Nothing's going on. You treat me like a kid, that's all.'

'No, I don't.'

'*Have him* if that's what you want. You don't need my permission.'

'I wasn't aware I was asking for it.'

I took back my can from where she'd put it on the table and opened it.

'He's very fond of you, and Olly.'

'Yeah.'

'He is.'

She put a hand on my arm. 'If you really want to go camping . . . With David?'

'Can I?'

'Don't think I don't realise how difficult it's been for you, having to look after Olly . . .'

'It'd only be a couple of nights.'

An intake of breath. 'I want to know where you'll be and you have to take my mobile.'

'Thanks, Mum.'

'Where?'

'Just the woods. Harwood Forest.'

She rolled her eyes.

'We'll have a map.'

She nodded. 'Then I better make some food for you to take with you.'

I threw my arms around her. 'Thanks, Mum.'

She planted a kiss on my head. 'Just promise me you'll be careful.'

I raced up to my room, my head filled with all the things I had to do to prepare. I started to make a list, but abandoned it, suddenly remembering I hadn't even told David I could go. I went outside, found a few hard clumps of earth to throw up at his window. When he appeared I gave him a thumbs-up sign and his face spread into an answering grin.

Next I went to the loft. It'd been a room once, but now it was full of junk and smelt of dust and mice. The light didn't work so I felt around for the torch I knew Mum kept by the ladders. Boxes everywhere, filled with family photos, some with videotapes, even an old camera that looked antique. Exercise machines, a rower and this thing that was supposed to make your stomach flat. I looked around for my sleeping bag, found it wedged behind a stack of books. I wrestled it free and took it back to my room.

I waited for Mum and Olly to go to bed before loading up my rucksack, but it was several times before I got it just right, laying out all the things on the bed, packing them, repacking them.

When I'd finished I looked around my room. A trophy I won in a chemistry contest at school, a blow-up globe balanced on the top of the microscope Dad had bought me last Christmas. The whole room, everything, seemed to be getting smaller, like a too-tight skin. I sat with the rucksack on my lap, wanting things to change, to burst open somehow. I couldn't wait for morning.

19

It was the hottest day yet, cloudless and still. I'd taken off my T-shirt and spread it across my head and shoulders to stop myself burning, but it just made me hotter and soon my sweat gathered in milky drops at the end of my nose.

We walked up the narrow lane behind the village, past Goolam Farm and the caravan site. We'd barely got going, but the steep climb made it feel like miles. Even when we reached the top we were only rewarded with one breath of cool air.

'Throw me your bottle,' David said.

'I'm out.'

'Shit.'

We sat on the grass verge to rest. To our right there was a huge field of barley, golden, dry as sticks.

A combine was nagging up the centre, leaving a cloud of dust in its wake. I climbed the five-bar gate and ran my fingers through my hair to bring some coolness to my forehead. Half the field was done and the combine was turning up a new line, shedding ears, cutting, grinding, leaving behind it a new landscape of stalks. Ahead the erect barley quivered with the darting and twisting of animals trapped inside. I couldn't see them, but I imagined them, rabbits, a stoat, a hare, voles, shrews, all thrown together in the shrinking cover.

In the distance I could see our cottages and beyond them, glazed in heat, the sea.

'Isn't that Olly?' David said.

'Where?'

'Down the lane.'

I looked to where he pointed and saw Olly coming round a bend on the lane, small, trudging steps. 'Shit.'

I jumped down from the gate and went to meet him. As I got closer I realised he was carrying the rucksack he used for school. It was covered in stickers. Mickey. Daffy. Pluto. He came to a stop, panting.

'What are you doing here?'

'Mum said I could come.' His glasses had slipped down his nose. He pushed them up with his index finger.

'No, she didn't.'

'I want to come.'

'You can't. You're not invited.'

'Please, I won't be a pain.'

'Not much you won't.' I went back to where I'd

dumped my rucksack and felt around in the side pocket for Mum's mobile.

'Don't! I'll be really quiet.'

I punched the number into the phone, made a mistake and had to start again. 'Why do you always have to mess things up for me?'

He started to snivel, not proper crying, but he wasn't going to give up easy. He'd got to know there was no way I'd let him come with us. He reached out to grab the phone from me, but I shoved him in the chest and he stumbled backwards, shedding his rucksack and landing with a thud on his bum.

David knelt beside him. 'Don't cry.'

'It's all right,' I said. 'I'll ring Mum, she'll come and get him.'

'Come on, Olly,' David said. 'It's all right.'

'He's just putting it on for attention.'

Olly buried his face in the crook of his arm. 'I want to come!'

Mum was frantic on the phone. I described where we were and she said she'd be along in five minutes. I hoped she wouldn't change her mind about the whole thing. She sounded pretty upset. I waited on the other side of the lane until I saw the car.

'He can't come,' I said, as she got out and walked towards us. 'Tell him.'

'I know. Come on, Olly.'

Olly didn't budge.

'In the car.'

'I don't want to.'

'You can't, Olly,' I said. 'You're too young. Go home.'

'All right, Leo. No need to rub it in. Why don't you boys go now? I'll take him home.'

David ruffled Olly's hair and stood up. I was scared Mum'd see the rifle, but he'd left it over by the gate. She grabbed Olly's wrist and said something, but her words were drowned, proper crying now, a full-blown fit. We walked a few steps before I looked back, saw her dragging him to the car.

I felt sorry for him, but there was no way he could come. The rabbiting was one thing, but this was a serious hunting trip. I'd thought about the deer, killing it, skinning it, and the blood, so much of it, dark and thick, covering our faces as we took cuts from the meat. And later, inside the small tent, David's pale face an inch or two from mine, his smells. It was easier to think about the deer.

We'd drunk all the water we'd been able to carry. Now we'd have nothing for ages. I suggested calling in at Goolam Farm to ask the farmer if we could fill up at a tap, but David was impatient to get going.

'There'll be a stream or something,' he said. 'Come on.'

We walked side by side, only dropping to single file when we saw a car on the road ahead. Once a tractor went past, spitting grit onto my bare legs. The heat was crushing, hot enough to make tar bubbles on the road.

Now and then we took off our rucksacks to let the air get to the skin underneath. David swung his back and forth as he walked, a red band over each shoulder where the straps had rubbed. The knobbles on his spine glistened, a half-moon of sweat on the upper curve of each one.

At a stile that led into a farmer's field, he stopped to look at the map. He had to be in charge of navigation, he said, because I didn't know how to read the contours of the land.

'We can cut across this field,' he said. 'Lose the rest of the road bit.'

'OK.'

I was relieved to get off the road though the field was harder to walk across, the earth dry and set in hard ridges. A crow, slick and shiny, landed some twenty yards ahead. It had its eye on something, but as I got closer I realised it was just a bit of broken glass, glinting.

'How big do you reckon the forest is?' I asked.

'Five miles long on the map, maybe three across the centre.'

'There used to be a lake in it, you know. Pretty big. And a village in the trees, like this ancient village from the Stone Age or something.'

'Yeah?'

'We did this thing on it at school. One day everyone left, nobody knows why really, but there was a couple of families who refused to go. They died when the lake dried up. The trees took over anyway, covered the village.'

'They didn't die.'

'What?'

'A lake's nothing. There'd be water everywhere, underground if you know where to look. Inside

222

plant roots. They won't have died cos they had no water.'

'Then what happened to them?'

'Dunno.'

'Ran out of food?'

'In a forest? Get real.'

I remembered the sketches I'd drawn of the villagers who'd stayed behind. Scrawny, thin faces. I'd got an A.

David looked again at the map, kneeling down with it open on his lap. He pointed at a small patch of blue, encircled by the forest. 'That's probably what's left of your lake. That's where we're heading anyway.'

I imagined ducking my head under the water. 'How long will it take us to get there?'

'Not sure. Come on. I think I can see a short cut.'

His short cut involved walking down a dirt track with potholes and deep rivets. The grass at the verges was thick and long, noisy with grasshoppers. As we passed they stopped their clicking, starting up again as soon as our shadows lifted off them. At the end of the track was Gillies Tip. I'd been there with Dad once, ages ago, when we needed somewhere to dump our old settee.

'We should go round,' I said, when we reached the fence.

'That means going back up the field and another mile down the road. You really want to do that?'

I shrugged. The fence was wire with gates joined with a chain as thick as my wrist. I read the sign hooked over the padlock. NO TRESPASSING.

'There's no one here.' He looked through one of the holes in the wire. 'Look, the place is deserted.'

'We'll never get over the fence. It's too high.'

David threw his rucksack over, stepping back and launching it. It landed with a thud. We'd have to get over now. He started to climb, slipping down because the holes weren't big enough to get his toes in. Undeterred, he tried again, running at it and nearly reaching the top with the jump. For a moment he clung there like Spider-Man, but then somehow he was on the other side.

'Now you,' he said.

He'd made it look easy.

I chucked him my sack and clambered up, dropping down several times before I reached the top and could swing a leg over. As I braced myself to jump down, I slipped and snagged my shorts, ripping a hole in the nylon lining.

David laughed. 'Any closer and you'd have sliced your dick in half.'

I checked nothing was showing.

'Look at this place,' he said. 'It's huge.'

Gillies Tip took in everything, probably a whole load of stuff they couldn't get rid of, but I guess what they didn't sell they burned, for there was a big black circle of earth in one corner. We walked up one of the aisles. A row of sofas sat facing each other like a dentist's waiting room, a line of chairs next to them, every type, stools, dining chairs, wicker chairs. Then a row of tables, one which looked like the desks we had in the science lab. A teddy bear sat on top, one eye intact, the other dangling from brown thread.

'Hey,' David said, brushing against my shoulder, 'I reckon if we keep walking straight we'll get to the fence on the other side.'

The main part of the yard was devoted to cars, a mountain of rusting carcasses piled on top of each other. Some of the stacks were as tall as a house and the cars leant as though they might topple over at any second. I edged around one, gumless, no tyres or seats, gaping holes instead of headlights.

'Shit! Get down!' David grabbed my wrist and pulled me down behind the car.

I listened, heard a formless shout. The car still had an engine, rotten, full of holes where the rust had burned through. No glass any more, but the wind-screen wipers were attached, erect, pointing in the direction of whatever it was we were hiding from.

'Who is it?' I whispered.

'Dunno.'

People. More than one. I tried to make out their words, but only heard a clatter of metal, then a laugh.

David crawled to the edge of the wreck and peered round the side.

'Is it the owner?' I asked.

'Nah. Kids. Nicking stuff.'

I pressed my face to a hole, breathing rusting metal, tasting its corrosion, but I couldn't see anything, just a patch of dry earth.

David looked back at me, mouth split in a grin. 'We'll get them. Ready?'

'What?'

Before I'd worked out what he meant he was on his feet, shoulders squared, fists clenched at his sides. I stood up, had to follow him, but the sight of what we faced hit me like a brick. There were two of them, men, not kids. Eighteen, nineteen years old maybe. They were by a pile of car radios.

'Hey!' David said. 'Who the fuck are you?'

At first, startled, they dropped the radios they were holding and looked like they were going to leg it, but then they realised we were kids. They looked at each other, sauntered in our direction. One of them, square-headed and fat around the belly, clenched his right hand. They wanted to fight.

'David?'

I had to go on. We couldn't fight them, no way, but he wasn't backing off.

'You nicking them radios?' he said.

The other guy, skinny, but taller, laughed. 'Fuck off.'

'You what?'

'You the owner's son or summat?'

'Mebbe.'

'Yeah, the fuck you are.'

The fat one laughed, the creamy-white skin of his belly poking out from underneath the hem of his vest. He had a turkey popper of a belly button with wiry black hair sprouting in tufts around it. I opened my mouth to speak, but I was too scared. We were just kids and they'd have us. We should've legged it right then, but David crouched down and unzipped his rucksack.

The fat one swaggered closer. 'You want a fist in the face, young 'un?'

Skinny walked forward to back him up, but David was still on the ground.

'What you doing?' I said. 'Let's get out of here.'

My heart whacked. They were nearly on us, but David still wasn't moving. Then, suddenly, he jumped up and ran past me, his mouth open in a screaming instruction to get the fuck out of there, laughing at the same time. We climbed a wall of cars, our feet skittering over the roofs, but when we reached the fence on the other side of the yard we skidded to a halt. Nettles, tall as a man, right the way along.

'Aw, shit.' I said. 'Climb!'

I looked over my shoulder, the men were closing, great strides, yelling. Fatty had a metal pole in his right hand. I'd got one leg over the top of the fence when I realised David wasn't following. He stood facing them.

'Come on!' I yelled.

The men slid to a stop. Still David stood. He raised his arms. I couldn't work out why the men had stopped, why David wasn't getting his head kicked in, then I saw it. He had the Glock.

'What do you think of this, huh?' he said.

'Where'd you find that? Get it for Christmas?'

'It's real.'

'Aye, course.'

'It's a Glock pistol and it'll blow your bollocks off.'

'No way that's real.' Fatty took a step forward, scratching his belly. 'Why don't you give me it, eh?'

'Yeah, like I'm gunna do that.'

'What would a fuckwit like you have with a real gun?'

'You're mashed in the head, you know that?' David cocked the gun. 'Can't you tell? It's fucking real, all right.'

'Leave them, David. Let's just go, OK?'

'David,' the skinny one said. 'That your name? David what?'

I shouldn't have used it. But who would they tell? They were thieves. They weren't supposed to be there either.

'Go on, then.' David waved the gun from one to the other. 'Take a swing. See what happens.'

'We were only looking around. Not looking for trouble.'

'Everything here's fucked, junk, get it? Worthless. Like you two.'

'Go home, lad. Take your toy with you.'

'Lad? I'm not your lad.' David pointed the gun at the ground and shot.

The men jumped back. Bricking it proper.

'Shit!' I yelled. 'David!'

'Have a go, I dare yer!'

The men looked at each other, but didn't move.

David lowered the gun. For a second I thought that was it and we'd get the hell out of there, but no sooner had the gun reached his leg than he raised it again and pointed it directly at Fatty's head. He counted down from five.

'. . . four . . . three . . .'

'Shit, David. *Please.*'

'. . . two . . . one. Bang.' David laughed. 'Go play with your dick, fat man.'

And then it was over. The men turned and went back the way they'd come, not running exactly, but they weren't wasting any time. David climbed up the fence, handed me his rucksack, and swung over to the other side where he collapsed into the nettles. He rubbed his arms and swore.

When we'd picked our way through to a clearing he turned round to look at me. I might've said a lot, told him what a prat he'd been. Why had he brought the Glock, when he knew, he'd told me, his dad got it out and cleaned it? What the fuck were we going to do if he noticed it was missing?

I thought it anyway, but I couldn't get the words out and, in the end, looking at him, grinning, full of hell or something, I just laughed. I'd never forget it, the dead cars, the smell of the metal rotting, and the Glock, the dust flying as the bullet hit the ground. I knew then something bad was going to happen, a strange feeling that came from nowhere and settled in the back of my mind. And yet even as we walked on, my heart thrumming in my chest, one foot, then the other, on and on, I wasn't afraid.

20

We continued walking, mostly in silence, choosing to follow the road rather than enter Harwood via Hoppers Wood. We thought it'd be quicker that way, not to have to trudge through undergrowth, but after an hour walking on hot tar, I'd have traded speed for shade.

Several times I had wanted to stop and rest, but David pushed on, maintaining the pace even when we reached a steep hill. It was late afternoon by the time we took our first steps inside the forest. Under the trees it was cool, and in the thick, almost dark.

David stopped, resting his foot on a fallen tree trunk, and opened the compass. He'd looked at it every so often since we left, though I saw no need for it, at least not until we were deep inside. I took full advantage of the break, dropping my rucksack and sitting beside him on the tree. Midges had feasted on my arms and my skin was raw where I'd scratched and slapped them off.

The forest floor was a damp carpet of pine needles and leaves. At the outer edges they were bleached, but further in, where the canopy was thick, they were dark and shiny.

He snapped the lid shut. 'We'll find somewhere to camp and head for the lake in the morning.'

There was a path, but not well trodden, suggesting only the occasional walker, or perhaps even an animal track. Gradually, the deeper we went in, what few shrubs and trees that had rooted themselves in the ground petered out and were replaced with tall, thin pine trees. Low down, where they'd been starved of light, their grey trunks were bare, spiked with only the occasional dry branch.

David wandered around, taking several steps to the right before changing his mind and going straight on. I didn't mind if he made all the decisions. He'd camped before and would know the best place to pitch a tent. We passed several areas I thought would be flat enough, but I was happy to follow and listen as he explained what would happen once he'd chosen the site.

The ground softened and felt warm. With each step my feet sank and made a sucking noise as I withdrew. David had found a stick and matched each stride he took with a stab at the earth. Finally, he slowed and then stopped. 'This'll do.'

It was a clearing, not as large as some we'd passed earlier. I stood, looking down, breathing hard. Shiny beetles crawled over the leaf foliage and a woodlouse, so grey as to be almost invisible, scurried in the direction of my foot.

'I'll do the tent because I know how to put it up,' he said. 'You can collect wood for the fire.'

I hoped he'd let me build the fire and light it too because it was one of the most important jobs. I'd seen him prepare fires before and I knew how best to arrange the wood so that it would last.

I left David to erect the tent and looked around for wood, moving further and further away from him until I could only just see him through the trees. I liked watching him when he wasn't aware of it, the concentration on his face as he got on with whatever he was doing. For several minutes he stood, the tent spread out on the ground in front of him.

I moved on, but had only gone a few feet when I stopped again. Fungus was growing out of the side of a trunk, layered and skin-coloured. I touched it, surprised to find it firm. Rainwater had puddled on its back. I dipped my finger in to taste. Warm and oddly sweet.

Wood. I looked about, picking up the driest branches and snapping the long ones over my knee. When I'd gathered as much as I could carry I took it back and got on with building the fire.

'You're doing it wrong.' He'd been banging in one of the tent pegs, but stopped to light a cigarette and walked over. 'There has to be a gap underneath so the air can get in.'

'I know.'

'And you'll have to get some stones to put around it or the whole forest'll go up.'

I started again and was still searching for stones when David called me over to hold up one of the tent poles while he bashed it in.

'Tie that off,' he said.

I bent down to secure the peg, but my knot was too loose so he took over, showing me how to do a bowline. It was tricky and my first attempt resulted in a loop that was too big; the next one was better and he let me do the last one myself. When we'd finished we stood back. The tent was even smaller than I'd imagined, and narrow, but a proper two-man tent he said.

Once we'd dragged a big stone across to use as a table, we set out the cooking utensils, hooking them onto a twig we propped between two stones, then we were done. If we hadn't been so hungry we'd have probably stood and admired our work for a bit longer. The site looked good, how we'd arranged things, but we had hot dogs to eat and the light was fading.

'We should have found somewhere near water really,' David said. 'I'll have to use the brine in the tin to heat them up.'

'OK.'

He chucked me his penknife to open the can of hot dogs. I'd seen a knife like it before in a shop in

Haresham, a large Swiss Army knife with corkscrews and nail files and screwdrivers all neatly packed into a two-inch-thick handle. I opened the can, tipped the hot dogs into the pan and then looked properly at the knife. It had a polished red glass inlay and at the base a small gold plate engraved with the initials G.C.

'This your dad's?'

'Lads from his regiment give him it when he left. You going to light that fire or not?'

He threw me his Zippo and I took the piece of dry bark I'd found especially for the job and lit the sticks at the centre, lowering my head as I'd seen David do to blow on the flame. It flickered for a moment and I thought I'd overdone it, but then it livened and spread.

'Let it get hot before you put anything bigger on or you'll smother it.'

'I've got it.'

I blew again, but smoke got into my eyes and I sat back, blinking hard.

David laughed. 'You're such a dickhead.'

'It's going, isn't it?'

And it was, a blaze of light that ate into the shadows around us and jetted a flurry of sparks high into the air. I could see patches of yellow-grey sky through the tops of the trees, the dark shapes of birds flitting from one branch to another, and then, suddenly, in just a few minutes, I couldn't see them any more.

We moved closer to the fire and ate, picking each hot dog out of the pan in turn, juggling it when it burned our fingers. Once we'd had our fill we lay back and stared at the sky. I needed to pee, but I was too tired and lazy to move.

'You think we've got enough wood?' I asked.

'Yeah, I reckon.'

I couldn't wait. 'I need to go, you know. You bring a torch?'

'Go?'

'You know . . .'

'Scared something'll bite you on the arse?'

He bared his teeth at me, growling as I stood up and turned away from him to unzip my flies.

'Don't go there, you dirty bastard.'

'You should've brought a torch.' I tried to go, but my bladder had seized up. 'Talk or something.'

He started to whistle, not a tune at all at first, but then it turned into *The Great Escape*. I joined in, even when I'd finished peeing.

'I must've seen it ten times maybe,' I said. 'That bit when they tell the blind man he can't go with them and he has to stay, but you know he's going to go.'

'Yeah, and at the end when the planes come over the top of the camp and blow everything up.'

His face looked weirdly twisted in the firelight, two deep sockets for his eyes and a huge gaping mouth. He handed me a small bottle of brandy from his rucksack.

'I thought it'd be better than cans, lighter to carry. It'll keep us warm.'

It wasn't cold. We mightn't have needed the fire at all if it wasn't for the light. I took a swig, coughing as it burned the back of my throat.

'Puts hairs on your chest that. Go on, have another.'

He didn't have any hair on the middle of his chest either, but then he'd plenty around his nipples and thick, dark underarm hair.

After a while the brandy started to taste good, not even sharp, or at least I didn't cough every time I took a swig. We lay back with our heads on the rucksacks, feet pointed at the fire, and handed the bottle back and forth.

'Don't you feel strange?' I said.

'How d'you mean?'

'You know, this place. We could be anywhere. I mean, look up there, all those stars. And down here, so much dark. Like being upside down.'

'You scared?'

'No!'

'Drunk though.'

I swallowed, mouth wet. Drunk felt good.

'Hang on a sec.' David pulled his rucksack out from behind his head and took out the Glock.

My stomach tightened, fear or excitement, I didn't know which. 'You could've hit them, you know, like a ricochet.'

'I didn't.'

'But you could've. You'd be in deep shit then.'

'They deserved it. Dickheads.'

'What if your dad finds out it's missing? He'll go—'

'You worry too much.' He grinned, his chipped tooth glinting with spit, and took aim at my head.

'Don't fool around.'

For a moment he kept aiming it at me, then raised it at the sky and fired, a flash and a bang that sliced the air and vibrated on my eardrums. Birds, thousands of them, took to the air, clattering branches, screeching, flapping, then, quickly, it was quiet, as though the forest had emptied of everything, but us.

I wasn't going to show I was scared. 'What did you do that for?'

'Got some kick on it!' He was laughing, triumphant. 'Don't tell me you don't want to fire it. I know you do. Back at the yard, I saw your face.'

'I don't.'

'Sure you do.'

'Someone'll hear.'

'Who? Nobody for miles around.'

He put the gun in my hands, wrestling with me to hold it.

'Careful.'

'Safety's on, dumb arse. Go on. Fire it. It's a rush.'

He showed me how to take the safety catch off and then I pointed it into the trees. I closed my eyes, briefly, opened them again, and squeezed the trigger. The kick bolted through my fingers and up my forearm.

'Shit! I think you shot an owl.' He laughed. 'Did you hear it? I heard something.'

I made him take it back.

'Something hit the deck, I swear.'

'Put it away, now. Please.'

'There's loads of—'

'I *mean* it. I don't know why you even brought it.'

237

He sighed and put it back in his rucksack.

My heart was thumping, blood racing around my body making me feel hot and cold at once. The gun had come alive in my hands and that had shocked me.

'Don't twist your knickers. I just thought it'd be a laugh.'

I lay back down. And then we drank, counted the stars until they blurred and we could no longer make out one constellation from another. Hours seemed to pass. Occasionally one of us would make a jibe or reach out and poke the fire, but mostly we talked, a million subjects, arguing, putting each other right on whatever we felt we knew the most about.

A sudden flash illuminated the trees, followed, after a hot, thick silence, by a rumble.

'That was thunder.' I waited. Another flash, another bang.

David's lips were moving, counting seconds. 'Nah, it's miles off.'

All at once rain fell, big, fat drops sizzling on the hot logs. We scrabbled inside the tent, laughing, grabbing our rucksacks and whatever else lay about, pulling it all in behind us like a badger pulling fresh bedding into its set. The rain smacked off leaves and branches, funnelled down the sloping roof of the tent walls and gushed into a waterfall off the zip on the door.

We lay and listened. The canvas was only a few inches from my face. I could smell the damp and hear the rain pattering, fingertip-tapping sounds, and then slower, heavy thuds. I looked at David, his breath held. I could just see the whites of his eyes and, as he turned to face me, the pale gloom of his cheeks. He unzipped the door and we peered outside. The fire was dead, a coil of black smoke rising, but no flames.

'Shit,' David said.

'It's all right. We'll just stay in here.'

My voice sounded different, sharper, but though I could smell the pine, the air was still muggy and warm. David stepped outside and probed the fire, but it was well gone. The wood stack I'd gathered was wet too.

'Bugger.' He came back inside the tent and lit a cigarette, wafting the smoke out through the door. He'd changed, but I didn't know how.

'You know, you shouldn't have taken the gun. Your dad—'

'So what? If he finds out not you who'll get it, is it?'

'Why's he so angry with you all the time?'

'Can't say I've asked him.'

'Maybe you should.'

'That's just how it is with him, don't show any feelings, don't let anyone see a weakness. Play football, do weights—'

'Thought you liked doing weights.'

He settled back against his rucksack.

'My dad took me to a boxing club in Haresham once,' I said. 'He bought me the gloves and everything. He even finished work early so he could take me and pick me up. I went a couple of times, but then I stopped.'

'Why?'

I shrugged. 'I made him think I'd gone. For two months we went, he'd drop me off and I'd make like I was going inside and then I'd go for a walk or something. Once I went to the pictures.'

'Why not just say you didn't want to do it?'

'I did want to, thought I did. Anyway, he found out, turned up early to collect me one time and went in to watch.' I stared at the dead fire. 'He left not long after that.'

I caught the glint of his eyes as he turned to me.

'What, and you think he buggered off because you couldn't box?'

'No.' I took a moment to steady my voice, twisting my fingers under the belt buckle on my jeans. 'I dunno, maybe.'

'That's just stupid.'

'Even when he and Mum were arguing all the time, it's like he was looking for a reason not to go. Only nobody could give him one.'

'So fuck him. His choice.'

'He was just trying to *help*. You don't know what he's like. He wanted to make things better. It wasn't his fault he couldn't.' I looked up so as to try and lose David's stare, but knew he was looking right at me. 'People think I'm a freak.'

'Like who?'

'Everybody.'

'Jaz and his sidekick? They're wankers. Don't be stupid.'

'It's not stupid to want people to like you.'

'Yeah, it is.'

'So why do you do weights then?'

He was still for a moment, silent, then he flexed the muscles on his arms, lifting them in a bodybuilder pose and clenching his fists an inch from my face. 'Cos I look fucking great, that's why!'

'Prat.'

'Yeah.' He pummelled my chest. 'But at least I'm not a fucking freak!'

I begged him off, laughing. We settled then, lying back in the tent with just our feet outside, an occasional drop of warm rainwater hitting my toes and trickling down the spaces in between.

'Are you cold?' I asked.

When I got no answer, I lifted my head to look at him. His eyes were closed. I nudged his shoulder with mine and he opened one eye.

'Come on,' I said. 'We better get inside our sleeping bags.'

'Too hot.'

'It won't be by morning.'

The tent smelt of damp clothes and our own cheesy smell. David arched his back to take off his jeans, scrabbling to get them off his ankles. I tried to get undressed at the same time, but we bumped elbows in the small space. I waited until he was in his sleeping bag.

'Hurry up,' he mumbled.

He watched, one eye fixed on me. I wriggled out of my jeans and then raised my legs to take off my socks. When I was down to my pants I got inside my sleeping bag and turned away from him.

He fell asleep quickly, shallow breaths deepening to a snore and then grunting close to the back of my neck. I was too hyped up to sleep. I felt him stir, drawing up his legs so that his knees rested in the small of my back. His foot twitched and kicked me on the thigh. I tossed and turned, then rolled over to face him, mesmerised for a time by his sleeping face, inhaling his warm, peppery breath. Outside, the forest muttered on, rustles, water dripping, the yelp of an animal answered with a bark from somewhere else.

At last, my eyes heavy, I drifted off to sleep.

Cold woke me. Out of the blur of a dream I groped my way back into my surroundings. Sounds, at first, a rustle of grass, birdsong, insect noises close to my head. It was morning, dawn giving the inside of the tent a soft, gold glow.

I shivered. My sleeping bag had come undone in the night. I tugged it to try and pull it across me, but it was trapped under David's leg. He groaned, putting his arm across mine and then reaching up the centre of my chest. Fingernails, stained with dirt, bitten down, dried blood where he'd ripped out a cuticle. He must've moved closer while I slept. I shifted, felt hot skin.

'David?'

My brain seemed to swell inside my head. I took a gulp of air from the thin gap at the bottom of the tent. I was hard, the tip of my cock nodding against my belly. David's hand moved across my stomach to the hem of my boxer shorts where it paused. I was still drunk, dreaming maybe. But then no, not dreaming. I felt his cock, a throb at the base of my back.

A decision. Go on or stop. Then, wetness, his tongue flicking between my shoulder blades.

'*David?*'

He pulled me back to him so that I could feel his hard-on. His breathing was heavy and deep, but awake, yes, awake. He took me in his hand and pulled back the foreskin. As he brushed the tip of my cock with his thumb I cried out, gulped several breaths and held them all. His touch was soft, then harder, tighter, quicker, rougher . . . My lips stretched into a scream, but no sound came. I dug my nails into his forearm, slapped and pulled the skin, but he wouldn't stop.

And then. And then.

After I'd shot, seconds of nothing but fast breathing, then he took his hand away and pressed it against my arsehole, wetting it with my stuff, and blindly nudged against the wall of flesh. Then, inside. I was too stunned to struggle. I cried out again, a stab of pain, deep in my gut.

I told him to stop, was sure I must've done, only it wasn't my voice I heard, but his, a stuttering of shits and fucks as he thrust deeper in me. All the time, he snatched and pinched the skin on my hips, until, with a heave that almost rolled me onto my face, it was over.

I lay there. Quiet. He swallowed. I brought my arm up over my head and breathed mouthfuls of fresh sweat and the salty smell of him. We lay for a long time, silent, his arm still over my waist, the skin goose-pimpled up to his elbow.

Nothing had happened. We were asleep, the two of us. Inside a dark dream. Sleeping. I closed my eyes.

When I woke again I was alone. I rolled over and swallowed, my tongue stuck to the roof of my mouth. In the glow of the tent my naked body looked strange, the tops of my thighs mottled a bluish pink though I wasn't cold. At first I thought I'd dreamt it, but then I felt a crusted snail's trail of spunk tightening on the back of my thigh. I worked my lips to get some spit going, but the effort brought a fresh swell of nausea into my mouth. I knew this time I'd be sick and crawled out of the door of the tent just in time, vomiting on a bare patch of earth close to the entrance.

When I looked up I saw David sitting on the stone we'd used as a table, staring at the black logs that had been our fire. I wiped my mouth, embarrassed, and crawled back inside the tent to dress. When I came out again I walked past him, couldn't meet his eyes. I looked at his hands, the brown-stained index finger tapping the ash from his cigarette.

'There's a can of Fanta in my rucksack,' he said. 'It'll be warm, but—'

'Give me a one.'

'What?'

'A cigarette.'

He didn't argue, lit a cigarette and handed it to me. I took a puff, feeling the cold band of his saliva on the filter.

We didn't speak again. Not as we sat, some distance apart, smoking the cigarettes, or later, when David stood up to pack the rucksacks and dismantle the tent. I left him to do it all, occasionally glancing up at him, but mostly staring at the fire, its black wet ash and the furrowed bark of logs untouched by flames.

When we were ready to leave I shouldered my rucksack and let him walk on ahead. I was damp and cold from the morning mist that hung like low cloud midway up the long trunks of the trees. On and on, only the soles of my trainers squeaking on the grass and, far off, the soft ksch-ksch of waves folding over each other onto the beach.

David had moved some way in front, but was still in sight. He didn't seem to be progressing at all though when I slowed and waited a second or two, he was definitely further on. I followed, not wanting to be alone in the forest, not wanting to be close to him either. A blackbird flew up out of the undergrowth in front of him, wings flapping, sounding its high-pitched alarm. He beckoned me to come nearer, touching my arm lightly when I reached him.

'Look,' he said.

A fox. We stood still so as not to frighten it though it had already seen us and stared back at us, ears pricked. It didn't seem to be afraid and observed us curiously, one paw raised from the ground, its thick brush gently twitching. Then, almost casually, it trotted off, body low to the ground, and disappeared into the trees.

We stood for a moment, looking after it, David's hand still touching my forearm. After a few seconds he turned to me and smiled. I smiled back and, together, we walked on.

21

By midday the ground had dried up and as we walked, hands hooked under the straps of our rucksacks, we kicked up tiny dust clouds. Hours passed in silence. I could see the bulge the Glock made in his rucksack, the outline of the muzzle pressing against the canvas. I couldn't understand why he wasn't more worried about his dad finding out it was missing.

'If your dad finds out the Glock is gone he'll go mental.'

David groaned and swung an arm at me.

'You shouldn't have taken it, that's all.'

'So fuck, all right?' He stopped, turned to face me. 'What did you think we were going to do, chuck stones at the deer?'

I shrugged.

'You thought the air rifle'd take it out, I bet.'

'No.'

'Yeah, you did.' He shook his head and walked on again.

I overtook him and ran ahead, laughing, my rucksack banging off my back. He snatched at my T-shirt, but I was quicker. He caught up with me though and landed a swat to my right ear.

We kept going then for a while, making the odd jibe, laughing at nothing, stripping grass seeds from their stalks and chucking them over each other. It was too hot to do anything really other than trudge on. As dusk approached, the flies got thick and buzzed around our heads, feasting on the sweat on our faces. I caught a bluebottle in my fist, felt it struggle and then opened my palm. For a second it just sat there, cleaning its crumpled wings, before I blew it back into the air.

After a while the path broadened to a track. I assumed it was used by the Forestry Commission because it was wide enough for a 4x4. I looked for David. Unusually, he'd fallen behind. He was standing, head lowered.

'What's up?'

He didn't answer. At first, I thought he'd seen something or maybe got stung. I went back to him. A drop of milky-coloured sweat fell from his nose, only as I reached him I could see it wasn't sweat. His shoulders were shaking and his fists were clenched. Not just the odd sniffle either, but violent sobs that sounded like they'd been knotted inside him for years.

I was about to reach out, put a hand on his shoulder or something, but the truth was I didn't know what to do. I hadn't seen anyone cry like that before, not even Olly cried like that.

'Hey.' My voice sounded feeble. 'What's wrong?'

When his sobs had quietened a little I dragged him down at the elbow and we sat together on the grass. I got him a cigarette from the packet I knew he kept in the side pocket of his sack and lit it for him.

He took a drag, sniffed, coughed. 'He just fucking killed them.'

The kittens. I hadn't thought about them for a while, but now I saw the row of their limp bodies in their sandy grave.

'Look, he did it cos he's screwed up.'

'No, it was to learn me.'

I didn't know what to say.

'Only you know what I learnt, Leo? I learnt to hate the fucking bastard.'

He took a long drag from the cigarette.

'I should've stopped him,' I said.

'You mean I should.'

'You've got to forget about it.'

'How can I? He's me dad. Shit, I'll probably turn out just like him.'

'No way.'

'In the junkyard with that fat bloke, all I wanted to do was pull the trigger, blow his fucking face off.'

It flashed into my mind, David with his arm raised, the look on Fatty's face as he'd backed away. I believed David had wanted to kill him, hadn't realised it then, but I knew it now. Sometimes David got a look in his eyes. Like when he was diving off the rock at Emmanuel Point, or when I'd shot the rabbit.

'You're nothing like him.' A silver thread of saliva dangled from the corner of his mouth. I put my arm across his shoulders. 'Don't think about him, OK? It's just you and me now.'

He slid me a grin and wiped a hand across his mouth. 'Tell me something.'

'What?'

'I dunno. Talk about that shit you find in those pools you're always looking in.'

'The rock pools?' I had to think a while. My heart was steadily thumping, the blood pulsing in my ears along with the hiss and whine of insects around us. 'OK. There are spiders that live in the sea, you know that?'

'Spiders?'

I told him about the sea spider that doesn't have a body big enough to hold its stomach so it spreads it out along its legs. That reminded me of the sea squirt, I couldn't remember why exactly, I just kept talking and I guess I spouted it all out, everything I knew about nothing that mattered.

'Sea-squirt tadpoles have spines. Scientists reckon they're what humans looked like 550 million years ago.'

He laughed and rolled his knuckles over my skull. I took it to mean that he wished he'd never asked, or that he felt better.

I felt good too, although the muscles in my legs

were tired, the skin brick red at the knees where they'd taken the brute force of the sun. Having stopped walking, I was aware of everything; the smell of David; the thin film of grime on his face smeared with tears; the blister on my right heel that had popped a while back and now stung. We got up and continued along side by side.

Suddenly he caught my arm. 'Check it out.'

We'd reached a rise in the contour of the land that allowed us to look back over the forest we'd walked through. A blanket of treetops stretched out before us against the slowly fading blue of the sky. It was getting darker, a gloomy grey gold, but further in, off the track, it was the sort of black you only found in forests. Thick. Solid.

David looked at the map to try and work out where we were, but it was only possible to make a rough guess. We pushed on, cooled by a breeze that dried the sweat and sent shivers down our arms and legs. David had marked the lake with an 'X' on the map, but among the trees, it was impossible to tell how far we'd walked or how much further there was to go.

The air was tasteless, the forest floor littered with arid bark and, every so often, the thin skeleton of a rodent. There was no path as such, but the pine needles were easy to walk across, nice even, and I liked the sounds the trees made, hissing, the splintering of a twig as some animal or bird clipped a branch.

Suddenly, David stopped in his tracks. 'Do you hear that?'

I listened.

'Water. There must be a stream here somewhere.'

'It's the trees,' I said.

He walked on, convinced he was right. I didn't want to raise my hopes. My head ached from thirst, but then I could hear it too, a faint trickle. It might still have been a mile off the way sounds travelled through the forest. Here, in the depths, even our voices had a different quality, like talking in a cathedral.

'It is,' David said. 'I'd bet.'

He found a clearing and swung the rucksack off his back. While David set up camp I headed off to find the stream. There seemed to be a monotonous whine of insects, or perhaps it was in my head, I couldn't be sure, but I kept having to stop and listen for the trickling again. Never far from it, but then never getting closer either.

When I turned round to look back, all the trees looked alike and I felt a moment's panic. If I lost David I'd never get out again. I sat down with my back against the trunk of a tree, closed my eyes, and tried to think. It was stupid to panic, all I had to do was call out and David would come. Then I heard water trickling immediately behind me. When I opened my eyes and turned my head my heart catapulted into my throat. A deer stood only a few yards away from me. No, not a deer. A stag.

I held my breath. He lowered his head and drank from the stream. The water reflected in his eyes. Huge eyes, dark and liquid. Great bloodied rags hung from his antlers. My mind whirled, repelled by the sight, but then I remembered they would be his velvets.

His nostrils flared at the air around him. He must've been able to smell me, but he didn't run. He licked around his mouth with a long cow tongue and snorted. Suddenly, his eyes were on mine. We locked in a stare. All that power. Something else, too, that made me afraid, as though at any moment he might charge me, hooves thundering, breath streaming from his nostrils, antlers shedding blood and skin. But he just stood there, beautiful, and terrifying. Then, a few seconds later, cool as anything, he turned and vanished into the thick of the forest.

I sat for an age, mesmerised, looking at the patch of ground where he'd stood. I knew I'd keep him for myself. Here we were, in the forest that was his, to kill him, but I knew we wouldn't.

I filled the bottles at the stream and found my way back to David. He was propped up against his ruck-sack, cigarette dangling from his right hand. The smoke rose from the tip in an almost perfect straight line. No breeze.

'I got water.' The sound of my voice jarred in my ears.

I chucked him one of the bottles and watched him drink, a trickle of water running down his chin, over his chest and into the dark blond hair below his belly button. Now that I was back with him, it was burning in me to tell him about the stag, but something held me back. Like Alice, I thought, the girl on the beach; I hadn't told him about her either.

The moment passed and we started telling jokes, awful jokes, but we laughed at them anyway as we stripped the ground clear for the tent.

Later, when we'd each eaten a tin of corned beef and I'd had a couple of puffs from his after-dinner cigarette, we lay back and watched the last light fade from the sky.

'What's Middlesbrough like?' I asked.

'All right. Canny. We lived in this nice terrace, could see the Boro ground from the kitchen roof. We used to sunbathe up there sometimes.'

'You and your mum?'

'She was a right one for the sun.'

It was the first time he'd mentioned his mum since the fair. 'What's she like?'

'Pretty. She had blonde hair, really long. Sometimes she just let it hang loose. She cut it all off one day, looked shit.'

'What she do that for?'

'Dad had buggered off. I got home from school and there she was with the scissors, hacking away.' He shrugged. 'They'd had a big scrap and she had a right shiner on her face, I suppose she was just upset. She'd freak out like that sometimes. She'd be all right for a while, stop drinking, or least knock it on the head a bit. Fine till he came back. Bottle of vodka under his arm and a bunch of daisies he'd nicked from some garden. It'd be cool for a while. I'd go to school, she'd be fucking on with the house, you know, making it nice, then they'd start on another bender.' He paused, his eyes fixed on some point on the ground. 'When she was in hospital . . . she was yellow, you know. The colour of piss. Even her eyes. Know what the bastard did? Slipped some vodka into her orange juice. Nearly fucking killed her. I stood and watched him do it, couldn't tell the nurse, he'd have gone fucking nuts, though I wanted to.'

'Shit.'

'Couple of months later, I came back from this school trip, adventure thing in Wales. No sign of Dad. Soon as I opened the front door I knew it. This stink, and a bluebottle buzzing around. Dozy, you know how they get this time of year.'

I swallowed hard.

'She always had some soppy shit playing on the stereo, but it was quiet. I went upstairs.' He picked up a twig and stripped the bark from it. 'Reckon she'd been like that three days, half on the bed, half off, her face all covered in sick.'

I knew I had to say something, but my mind blanked. After a bit, I said: 'Where was your dad?'

'They found him in a lap-dancing club, that wasted they had to lock him up to sleep it off.' He threw the twig away. 'Crazy thing is sometimes it was good, you know. They wouldn't fight and I'd go from being able to do what the hell I wanted, skip school, to the both of them being on my case 24/7. Only that's what I wanted, her do my lunch for school, him come home and fuck her brains out, anything, just as long as it wasn't a screaming match.' He forced a smile. 'You dunno how lucky you are.'

'Yeah.'

'No, Leo, you are. I know you miss your dad, but you've got things pretty normal.'

My life was normal, but then in the context of what he'd just told me, anything would be.

'Deep shit,' David said, filling the silence for both of us.

We didn't bother going inside the tent. It was warm enough to sleep outside and the sky was clear. Without saying anything, I unzipped our sleeping bags and laid them out side by side on the ground.

David fell asleep quickly, curled into me. The fire cast a soft glow over half of his face, the other in shadow. I watched him for a long time, trying to imagine the images that passed beneath his flickering lids, once or twice running my index finger over his lips, lightly, to soften them. He stirred, but didn't wake. After a while I pulled my knees up to my chin, wriggled to get comfortable, and dozed off to sleep.

I woke to the sight of David rolling up his sleeping bag. I looked at my watch, but it had stopped, hands frozen at midnight. David gathered together the empty water bottles.

'I'll fill them,' I said.

'OK. I just want to look at the map.'

I peed behind a tree. I'd been desperate, had woken several times in the night with the burning of a full bladder, but I'd wanted to wait until light. I reckoned it was still early, for the sun made shafts of horizontal light that only reached halfway up the tree trunks.

A bird squawked and fluttered above my head. I looked up, saw it was an owl, feathers puffed out, greyish brown, the colour of bark.

When I returned David was sitting on a stone, hunched over the map. His face and neck were smeared with ash and grime. A wasp dipped around his head and he swatted it away.

'I reckon we'll get there this morning,' he said.

'Yeah?'

I followed his finger across the map, but it meant nothing to me. A damselfly skittered on the air, its red needle body see-sawing forward and back as it flew.

Before setting off we washed at the stream. I was relieved to be rid of the stickiness on my skin, but even with rubbing hard it clung to me like sap. I stood over the tracks the stag had made. David chucked handfuls of water up to his armpits and over the back of his neck. He looked almost metallic, the morning sun gleaming on his skin, water bouncing off his shoulders in silver shards. I squatted down and filled the bottles, shyly staring at my hands, white starfish under the water.

'Ready?' He threw my rucksack and his, one over each shoulder, while I dried myself on my T-shirt. 'It's a couple of miles this way, I reckon.'

We had to walk facing the sun. It was already hot and we waded through a soup of midges. We trudged on for maybe another two miles, picking our way through seemingly impossible thickets of bracken that scraped and pricked our legs. Finally, we stumbled out onto a path.

Just as I noticed the tyre tracks, David ran ahead a few steps and hollered.

'You gotta see this!' he said. 'You won't believe it.'

I jogged to catch up and saw, planted in the middle of the track, a 4x4. It was an old Defender. We raced over to it.

'It's still got keys,' David said, diving into the driving seat. He tried the engine, but it turned over clicks.

'Forestry Commission,' I said, wiping the dirt off the logo painted on the side.

One tyre was completely flat at the front and inside, on the back shelf, there was a scattering of twigs and leaves. Feathers too, a nest.

'What do you think it's doing here?' I said.

'Dunno. Must've broke down. Mebbe they thought it wasn't worth the hassle of getting it out the forest.'

I stepped around it, reluctant to join David. It reminded me of the dead cars at the yard, though it was worse for the things inside; a sweet wrapper; a piece of paper with handwriting on. We'd grown used to having the forest for ourselves. Now, suddenly, there were signs of others.

'Come on,' I said.

We kept going, following the road until it came to a bridge screened off with yellow duct tape. Ahead of us, only a few yards from where David stood, was a deep ravine. We peered over the edge. Huge boulders at the bottom, sharp jutting rock all the way down, seeded with saplings.

The bridge had a metal frame and wooden slats made of sleepers. Wide enough for a car, for the 4x4, but you'd have to be nuts to drive over and chance the whole bloody lot coming down. Probably no one had been across it in years. No way of climbing down into the ravine and up the other side.

'How far do you reckon it is?' I said.

'Thirty feet.'

David took a step onto the first slat, still staying close enough to solid ground so that if needed to he could pull back. When the slat took his weight he edged forward further, leant against the metal railing and dropped a gob of spit into the ravine.

He looked back at me. 'We'll have to go across it. There's no other way.'

'Or go round. I doubt the ravine runs right through the forest.'

'Could be miles.'

He held his arms out and took a giant step forward, a leap of faith, then screamed. When he turned back to look at me he was laughing.

'You're a shit,' I said. 'Don't do that!'

'It's all right, solid as anything.'

'So why it's shaking?'

'It's not shaking, you are. Howay, you poof!'

'I'll follow you when you're at the other side. It mightn't take two.'

'Yeah, you want to see if it collapses, you mean.' He took another few steps, stopped. 'Fuck, it's like that bridge in *Indiana Jones and the Temple of Doom*.'

'That was made of rope. Keep going.'

He got to the other side and took a bow. No way I'd get across as fast as him. Once I was away from the side all I wanted to do was leg it over before I got chance to think, but I moved steadily. When I was halfway David started to stamp on the sleepers. The whole bridge made a terrifying crack.

'Stop it! Hey!'

'Who-hooo! Careful, you better hurry.'

'David, I mean it.' I gripped onto the edges of the bridge with both hands, felt my knees start to buckle. 'Pack it in, all right?'

He swayed from left to right, shifting his weight. The bridge shook, groaned another terrible noise that sounded like metal grating on metal. I got an eyeful of the ravine below.

'You got skiddies?' David jeered. 'I bet you have.'

The only way to make it was to shut my eyes and run to the other side. I fell to my knees and scrambled across the slats on all fours, flashes of rock underneath me. When I reached David I threw all my weight against him and punched his stomach.

'Bastard!'

We rolled around, fists flying. He threw a punch that hit me on the collarbone, jabbed another into my groin. I hit him back.

'Don't do that, don't ever do that!'

Pretty soon we were exhausted. It was hard enough walking in the heat never mind anything else. I lay flat on my back, panting.

'Fucking hell, Leo, can't you take a joke?'

'It wasn't funny. I could've fallen and then you'd be by yourself in here, wouldn't you?'

'So?'

'So you were pretty scared last night, blubbing away in your sleep.'

He stared at me. I felt bad for saying it because he hadn't been blubbing at all.

'Look, squits, OK?' I said.

'Yeah.' He looked ahead and for a moment I thought he wasn't going to forget it at all, then he stood up, kicked my foot and sidestepped before I could get to him. 'For now.'

The lake was smaller than I imagined it would be, looked more like a big pond, lily pads and a whole section of it scummed green, thick as hair. An emperor dragonfly hovered over the surface and dipped its gleaming sapphire abdomen into the water.

It was perfect, shielded on all sides by trees, tiny insects glinting like gold filaments in the air. There was a cabin too, not big enough to live in, and not Stone Age because it was made of concrete and had slats instead of windows. A bird hide maybe for there were a few different ones to those I'd seen in the forest. They scooted across the water now, black, fast, and hid in the reeds.

We dropped our rucksacks in unison, stripping off our clothes and charging into the water. Creamy cool. Perfect. We flicked and spat, lay drifting on our backs for ages, occasionally tossing great clumps of green algae at each other.

'Mint,' David said.

A pond skater scooted past my head. 'You think it's where that village was then?'

'Nah.' He righted himself and swam to the edge where he hauled himself out, shaking the water off his hands.

I lay for a while on my back and imagined flooded houses underneath me, still intact. I shivered and got out to follow David. He'd gone to explore the hide.

'I thought it'd be bigger,' I said.

It didn't even have a roof. We lay down inside it, dried in the sun and when it became too hot, we stretched one of the sleeping bags over the walls to make a shelter, using rocks to keep it in place. It was better then, cooler in the shade and we slept deep and heavy through most of the rest of the afternoon.

When I woke it was a while before I realised where I was. I could smell the pond water on my skin and then I heard soft plopping sounds of fish rising and the buzz and hum of the insects hunting across its surface.

I looked up. The sun was low above the trees, burning straight into my eyes. David had taken down the sleeping bag and was now standing on a rock he'd found to bring him up to the height of the top of the wall. He was still, the Glock in his right hand, deer-stalking.

I picked myself up, clattering about in case the stag was close. If I was noisy enough I might spook him.

'Shut it, will you? You're making a racket.'

'I'm starving.'

He sighed. 'OK. What have we got left?'

I rummaged around in his sack, found a Scotch egg, squashed and broken, a bar of chocolate. I halved them and put them into two piles. We scoffed them down and I was rooting around for a bottle of water in his bag when I saw a bundle of papers and stuff tied with an elastic band. I fingered through them, keeping an eye on the back of David's head in case he saw what I was doing. A bus ticket, a passport and the photograph of his mum I'd seen on the dresser in his bedroom.

It didn't dawn on me right away. I didn't get it at all in fact, just thought it was usually me who brought a load of unnecessary stuff and he'd been pretty stupid to weigh down his sack with anything we didn't need. Then, like a blast of wind in my face, it hit me. This wasn't a camping trip, well, it was for me, but not for him. He was running away.

I stood up and thrust them into his face. 'Why didn't you tell me?'

'What?'

'You're not going back, are you?'

He pressed his lips together and stared out at the pond. I couldn't believe it. I wanted to grab him hard and punch him. 'Why?'

'You really need to ask?'

I chucked the bundle at his rucksack. 'What did you even bring me for, if that was your plan?'

'I wanted you to come.' He sat with his back against the wall, facing me. 'I was going to tell you. I didn't want to ruin this, I knew it'd be great.'

'What happens now?'

'You go back.'

'Well then, it's not great, is it? It's shite.' My mind

raced. 'You take his fucking gun? You just disappear? He'll call the police, they'll—'

'I left him a note. He won't give a shit, all right?'

'He will about the gun.'

He flinched. I could see that had hurt him, but I couldn't stop. 'What did the note say?'

'Just that I'd gone camping. He said I could.' A flash of impatience. 'I dunno, it wasn't exactly an essay.'

'Well, thanks, David. Thanks for nothing. So you were just going to leave me in the middle of the forest, not say a word, eh? Just go?'

'No.'

'Then what? Write me a note too?'

'Oh, howay, Leo, get off me case. I didn't tell you because you'd be like this.' He shook his head. 'You don't understand.'

'No, I don't.'

'Would *you* want to stay with him?'

I clenched my fists. I couldn't let him leave, but neither could I blame for him wanting to go. I sat back against the wall beside him, picked up his lighter and started flicking it.

'You'll knack the flint.'

'I'll come with you.'

'Don't be stupid.'

'Why's it stupid?'

He didn't answer.

'We could go somewhere together, get jobs—'

He shook his head.

I put the lighter down. 'Where will you go?'

'Middlesbrough. Stay with my aunt, for a bit anyway.

She's got a pretty mean boyfriend so don't suppose I'll stay there long.'

'Then where?'

'There's this proz I know. She lets me kip on her floor sometimes.'

'A *prostitute*?'

'Yeah, she's all right.'

I looked away.

'Least she's got a job, her kids never want for owt. You should see the little lad's bedroom. She's got it decked out like an aquarium, fish on the walls, and over his bed she's got these stars on the ceiling, light up in the dark.' He sniffed, embarrassed. 'You'd wet yourself for it.'

I felt I didn't know him.

'Look.' He sighed, crossing his arms over his chest. 'You'll do canny, Leo. Maybe we can still write or you could—'

'You're leaving, just because of him?'

He lit a cigarette and blew out the first stream of smoke into a cloud of midges.

'I don't want you to go.'

A car on the main road. I hadn't realised we were close to a road. Its headlights swam though the forest, illuminating the tree trunks then disappearing like someone had taken a flash photograph.

'Look,' David said, 'no point talking about it. I've made up my mind. End of.'

He wandered out of the hide and started to collect wood for the fire. I went in the opposite direction. I needed to think. The trees swayed softly. I turned up my face to the last rays of the sun. It was the best night of the summer. And the worst.

When I got back to the hide David had already lit the fire. He'd got the mini radio out too and set it on top of the wall. Now he was sitting on his rucksack sucking on the side of his hand.

'What's up?'

'Just a splinter,' he said, through his fingers.

I looked at it. The skin on his thumb was yellow from where he'd squeezed out the blood. At the centre there was a spelk.

'I'll get it out.'

He held out his hand which I pulled into my lap, shuffling closer to the fire for light. I tried to draw the spelk with my fingernails, but it was too deep.

'Are you sure there's something there?'

'Yeah, it knacks.'

I stuck it in my mouth and sucked. His thumb tasted of salt and the forest, smoke and wood.

'Ow, shit, Leo, bloody hell, you'll have me thumb off.'

'Do you want me to get it out or not?'

I pulled back for another look. When I started sucking again he laughed. 'You're like a bloody vampire!'

The fire made shadows on his chest. In the trees a bird screeched. Almost at the same time I felt the spelk on my tongue and spat it out. 'There you go.'

He looked at where it had been and squeezed out a drop of blood. I picked up his hand and I guess he thought I was going to take another look at it, but I put it between my legs instead.

'*Leo.*'

I shifted a little, embarrassed, excited. 'Makes me kind of horny, sucking your finger. I bet it did you too.'

'Get lost.'

'You know it did.'

I dived for him and he fell over backwards, laughing. I rolled on top of him, my ankle kicking the fire. A shower of sparks rose up over our heads.

'Geroff!' He pushed me back and sat astride me, wrestling with my arms until he got them under his knees and I couldn't move. He always got me pinned in no time. I looked up at him. His lips were wet, a gleam of saliva I wanted to touch.

'Take off your pants,' he said.

I wasn't sure. We weren't asleep now. This was real. He let me go and, steadily, I pulled down my pants, freeing my cock while he shuffled to the side of me. I could feel his breath, waves of it through the tiny hairs on my stomach, hot then cold.

At the first touch of his tongue I thought I'd spunk up straight away so I tried to think about something else. There was an advert playing on the radio, a jingle I'd heard a million times. All I could think was, I didn't want to shoot into his mouth, but he worked his way up and down, to the bottom and then back to the top. Every so often his lips made a squelchy wet noise, air popping out of the side of his mouth. I put my fist in my mouth, my other hand pulling at his hair to get him off, but he flung an arm out and caught me on the nose.

'Aw, fuck . . .' I shot into his mouth, my backside jerking up and down. Even then I was trying to push him off me, but he held my hips until I was done.

As soon as he let me go I tucked my cock between my legs and shuffled back to the wall. 'What did you make me do that for?'

'It was nice, wasn't it?'

'You should've told me what you were doing.' I reached for my pants, but he snatched them away, laughing, and chucked them out the hide. 'Hey!'

'Awwwww . . . fuck!' he said, imitating me.

I laughed, uncertain. 'What did it taste like?'

'Like the sea.'

I remembered the times I'd gone swimming and got a mouthful. It'd tasted rotten and made me spit. 'Can you still taste it now?'

'Yeah.'

He stretched his arms out above his head, occasionally bringing one hand back to his mouth to smoke.

'Do me,' he said.

'I don't know how.'

He lifted his arse up, kicked off his boxers and chucked them in the same direction as my pants. My mouth fell open and I laughed, high on the thrill, naked now, both of us by the fire. I stood up and danced a circle.

He pinched a hot stick out the fire and chucked it at me which made me hop up and down. 'Do me, you spaz.'

I knelt down, the concrete hard on my knees, so

I pulled one of the sleeping bags underneath me to rest on. I was still laughing, breaths snagged in my throat. I looked at him and then took one deep breath to calm down.

His dick seemed at entirely the wrong angle to put in my mouth, but then I remembered how David had used his hand to guide it. I did the same, folding his cock into my palm.

'Do it, will you?' he said. 'You're making me crazy.'

When I put it in my mouth he sputtered out a laugh like I'd tickled him and I pulled back, unsure.

'Don't stop.'

My lips snagged on his foreskin until I got some saliva worked up and then it was smoother, easier. I looked down the length of his cock, saw the outer edges of my lips, the skin glistening where my mouth had been.

He breathed out sharply. 'Jeez!'

I must've been doing it right to make him crazy like that. I kept going, faster, scared and excited by the moment when he'd shoot. He kicked his heels, banging them off the floor of the hide, and then his back arched and he cried out.

I suppose it was that, the noise David made, the radio belting out some tune I can't remember the name of, the bass beat thumping like my heart, that's why we didn't hear. Neither of us heard anything, but it was David who saw him first.

22

I felt David's body go rigid underneath me. Stupidly, I carried on, thinking he was getting close. It was only when he grabbed my ear and I felt his fingernail stab the skin, that I pulled back. Even then I thought maybe I'd snagged him, but he pushed me away and skidded to the back of the hide, covering his cock with his hands.

I looked around, bewildered. David's dad stood at the entrance to the hide. For a second I didn't recognise him. The fire lit his face, a bronze mask. I stood up, trying to back into the corner, only I didn't get my weight on the back of my foot and fell, grazing my shoulder on the wall.

'Fucking dirty bastards.'

David's lips mouthed words, but he made no sound.

I stared at Mr Cauldwell. He was running his hands over his face, pulling at his mouth with his fingers, almost crying.

'*Dad.*'

I tried to speak, but only produced a croak. He glared at me, raising one hand as if he wanted to hit me, but kicked the fire instead, scattering burning twigs across the floor of the hide. A flash of sparks flew up into my face.

'My son. My son.'

The words were garbled with hate and shock. I tried to move further back, but there was nowhere to go. Mr Cauldwell's huge frame filled all of the entrance. There was no way I could get past him. I pushed myself against the wall and felt David's arm, beside me, a slick of cold sweat.

'Dad,' he said, again. 'Please.'

Mr Cauldwell launched at him, grabbing him by the ear and dragging him across the floor. I got a whiff of something strong, beer, mixed with sweat and aftershave. David tried to crawl, but he was skidding across the hide, yelped when he rolled over the burning embers of the fire. His dad hauled him to his feet and shoved him in the back, pushing him out of the hide. For a second they were illuminated by the flames, then they moved beyond the reach of the fire and disappeared into the darkness. I could hear David, screaming and yelling. I stood, paralysed, then heard David scream again and ran after them.

Mr Cauldwell's arm was hooked around David's throat and David was choking, sputtering out the odd word, his fingers clawing at the huge bicep, arms and legs flailing. I tried to yell at his dad to stop, but only a whisper came out. I couldn't move, useless, hands cupped around my balls, the cold earth sticky between my toes.

Still David couldn't get free. His dad pushed him away, kneed him in the back and then David was on the ground, shielding his head with his hands as the kicks moved closer to his face. He scrabbled to get away, but as he struggled to his knees he coughed out a gob of blood.

'Stop! You'll kill him!'

Mr Cauldwell turned. He seemed confused by the sight of me. He snatched at my head, but I ducked before he could get his fingers in my hair and then ran. Where? Where could I go? I went back to the hide and circled its small space. We were miles from home. How had he even got here? The road. Of course, the road. I thought of the car, the headlights that had made silhouettes of the tree trunks, but how had he known where to find us?

I pressed my hands over my ears to drown out David's cries. He was pleading now, his words coming out in a mutter mixed with yelps of pain. I pulled on clothes, some David's, some mine. Then, a moment. Everything slowed. I felt time click over itself. I saw the Glock, resting on the floor under the strap of David's rucksack. I snatched it up and ran back outside.

'Get off him!' I screamed.

At first he ignored me and carried on kicking. There was a trickle of blood coming out of David's ear, his body scored with cuts and printed with the tread mark of his dad's boots.

'Get away from him!'

He spun round, his teeth bared, shining with spit. He narrowed his eyes. 'That's my gun.'

'Yes, and it's loaded. Don't think I won't use it. I will.'

'You stole my fucking gun? Give it to me.'

'I'll shoot.'

'Fuck off home. This is between me and my lad.'

David was curled up, holding his feet, blood and snot and saliva dribbling from his nose and mouth. He was a making a dreadful sound, not tears, not even pleading any more, just strangled breaths snagging at the back of his throat.

I cocked the gun. I'd only ever seen David do it, never tried it myself. Mr Cauldwell took a step back.

'Now calm down, son. You give me that.'

For a second I felt a thrill. He was listening to me now. It could do that, the gun, this gun. It didn't matter that he was bigger and stronger. I pointed it at him, trying to keep the muzzle directed at one place on his body, but my arms shook from side to side. David could do nothing. It was down to me now. I had to get him away. His dad would kill him, he couldn't stop. I glanced at David, tried to edge towards him.

'What do you think you're going to do? Huh?'

'I'll use it.'

He believed me. I could see it. He knew I understood about the Glock. He believed I could work it.

'Give me the gun.'

David coughed.

'David? Are you all right?'

'Course he's all right.'

'He *hates* you.'

'You think you know about me and my lad? Give me the gun.'

He took a step towards me.

'DON'T MOVE!'

'Or what? You'll shoot me?' His tone had changed again. He'd decided I was bluffing. 'Scummy poof. I know your type. Private school—'

'Leo.' David reached for my foot.

'Does your mam know what you get up to? She soon will cos I'll fucking tell her. Fucking dirty—'

'Shut up!'

'Leo,' David said. His teeth were red. 'Leo.'

'GIVE ME THE GUN.'

It seemed to have got heavier. I was struggling to keep my arms up. David was tugging at my ankle. Blood had seeped into his right eye, puddling into the corner like a second pupil. 'Do it,' he said.

'Give me the gun!'

I raised it again.

'DO IT.'

I looked at David, back to his dad. I was confused. I couldn't listen, not with both of them talking at once. Seeing me falter, Mr Cauldwell took a chance and launched at me. I felt my arm shudder. A bang. The forest lifted.

David's dad stopped in his tracks. His eyes widened.

He was shocked I'd had the nerve to actually fire it. That had shown him. He never thought I'd shoot, but I had. I'd shown him. I closed my fist around the Glock. Now he'd leave us alone. He was scared now.

But then, he seemed to crumple. He swayed first and, in a movement that seemed to last ages, he dropped to his knees and fell forward. I thought maybe he was about to take another swipe at me and so I stepped back, but in seconds he was on the ground. Face down. Still. I stared at the stubbled head. One side was a different shape from the other. Black. Shining. Flesh and skin, something grey, and in among it all, silvery, white, the shattered line of bone.

Sounds came back, the clicks and screams of starlings lifting off the trees, a moorhen squawking across water, David's sobs. I looked down at him. His mouth was stretched wide as though he was screaming.

The gun grew heavy in my hands. I put it lightly on the ground next to my feet. The movement felt strange, like I hadn't moved for days. The starlings wheeled above our heads until, gradually, one by one, they began to settle.

I knew he was dead, but still I waited for him to move. There was a splatter of blood on my arm. Without warning I vomited into my hand, the force jerking my body forward. I wiped my mouth, circled the remaining spit in my mouth and swallowed. My Adam's apple felt large, like a bolt in my neck.

'Is he—'

Blood trickled into a pool at the side of his head. 'Yes. I think so.' My voice sounded strange, not me, an echo that came from the forest.

'He can't be.'

I walked closer. His eye stared up at the sky, not seeing it. Time crept forward, each second an echo of the gun. I'd no sense of whether minutes were passing, or hours.

'What have you done?' David said. 'Oh God. Shit.'

I knelt in front of him, took him by the arms. 'You told me to.'

'What?'

'You told me to. You said, "Do it."' He had, hadn't he? Yes, no, oh Jesus. 'He was going to kill you, David.'

I looked at the blood on my arms. Just a man. A man who drowned kittens in a bag. Tiny eels. Fist. A fist. I closed my eyes. So much blood.

'You hated him.' I raised an arm and fingered the cut above David's left eyebrow. It was deep, oozing blood into his eye, down his cheek into the corner of his mouth. 'Didn't you?'

He was shaking.

'You hated him.'

He closed his eyes, two fat tears rolling down his cheeks.

Please. Oh God. Do something. Something. I'd have to be strong, it was me now, not him. I'd have to look after him.

I sat on the ground next to him for a long time, shivering, and looked at a patch of earth free of blood and footprints. Blades of grass, a beetle crawling

through the stalks. When I lifted my head again the
light had changed, the moon higher, fuller.

'We need to move him,' I said, finally. 'We can't
leave him here.'

I looked again at the body. Yes, that's what it was.
Just a body. Limp. Like the fish. Like the rabbit. It
would be difficult to shift it though. Inconvenient.

'Hospital?' David whispered.

'No.' I heard the words before my mouth opened.
'We can't tell anyone. We'll go to prison.'

'I don't—'

'We have to hide it.'

I walked over to where the body lay, edging around
it as though it was some creature washed up from
off the sea. I thought, the tide will come and take it
away. Do something.

I pulled the ankles, but it was a dead weight, like
someone drunk. He smelt of drink. The body. I used
the word again, in my head, over and over. Not a
person. A body. I didn't know him. It wasn't anyone
I knew. I'd found him there and now I had to move
him, that was all.

The blood had seeped into the earth, soaking it
red. Astonishing I'd hit him in the head like that. Like
knocking a tin can off the top. I turned him over,
nudging him first with my foot, then knelt down and
shoved with both arms. He was cool to touch, the
skin clammy.

'David?'

He was sitting up now, his eyes fixed on some point
beyond the pond. He'd put one of his knuckles in

his mouth, capping it with saliva that dangled off his hand and swayed, shining.

'You've got to help. Put your hands next to mine and push. We have to move him into the trees. We can't leave him here.'

He looked at me.

'We've got to hide him.'

He stood up, wandered about, dragging his feet.

'David.'

He turned round, stared at me, lost, then staggered in the direction of the hide. No use.

'Look what you've done,' I said, looking down at the body.

I sat, slumping onto my side, my head level with the body's head. One eye, wide, red, stared back at me. I brought my knees up to my chin and lay still, I don't know how long, but I got used to looking at it. It changed, tiny shifts, shadows that moved over its face.

At last I stood up, no feelings inside me. I was cold, that was it, cold and clean, as though I'd just walked out of the sea.

I started to whistle. The tune was from some car insurance ad I'd heard a few hours ago on the radio. I listened for the radio now, still heard it, close to me on the breeze, then further away. Couldn't hear the words of whatever song was playing so I carried on with the ad, the same bit over and over until I'd run out of spit.

David came up behind me. 'Let's move him then.'

I turned round, startled. He had tear tracks on his

cheeks and his mouth was caked with dried blood. He looked different, something in his face I knew I'd seen before, but couldn't place where.

'OK,' I said.

And then we did it. Somehow. We used the tent to drag him, tying his ankles to the strings so he wouldn't slide off. We hauled him down the path between the trees, grunting, sweating. Stopped. Rested. Moved on. We were good at jobs, working out the practicalities of moving him and then the task itself. Deeper into the trees, deeper, on and on, until our arms ached and we collapsed on the ground, exhausted.

I had no idea how far we'd moved from the pond, but it felt like miles. I couldn't decide on the best place to leave him. I was sure I'd passed lots of places that would've been secluded enough, but something was always wrong, a parting in the undergrowth I thought might be a path, or the trees weren't close enough together. A bit further. Just a little bit further.

It was David who finally stopped, hands on his knees, panting. He couldn't go on. I looked around. There was a thicket of bracken. If we put him at the centre then it would be OK, wouldn't it? It would have to be.

My mind flitted from one problem to the next. Not just this one. Not just where we'd put him. It would be light soon and we would have to take every-thing out of the hide, then find the car. And then what?

I tried to focus. I'd concentrate on getting the body

into the right place first, then I could think of all the other things. There were details that had to be got right. It helped to think in detail. A zoom lens. I was safe as long as I was in detail. Things had to be done, that was all, and perfectly, no mistakes. It calmed me. I was best at thinking things through. I nodded at David and together we lifted the body again, shuffling into the sea of bracken.

The stalks snapped and flattened. Everywhere we'd walked there'd be traces and I knew I'd have to put that right somehow, but I couldn't do it all, the footprints, the blood, the paths we'd made through the forest. The body kept making a mess, an arm that flung out and got snagged on a twig, the blood that gathered in a pool on the tent canvas. It irritated me. Even dead he was creating problems I'd have to solve. I hated his weight too, the awkwardness of having to shift his great bulk, and his beer and fart smell which filled my nostrils and clung to the back of my throat.

When we reached the centre of the bracken, I glanced at David. I could just make out the white of one eye, the other black with blood. He hadn't spoken all the time we'd been moving the body, just did as I said, resting when I said we could, moving on again when I said it was time. I wanted to say something to him, but there was no time.

We heaved the body forward the last few feet and then let it drop to the ground. I edged around it, gasping. It seemed big, such a big thing to hide. I wanted to cover him, but I just stared at the wide expanse of its back. No, covering was a mistake.

I knelt down. People had to believe he'd shot himself. Suicide. Or perhaps the forest would keep him and he'd never be found. Think.

Car keys.

I felt his trouser pockets for a bulge; the cloth was tight and I had to burrow in. He had a wallet, some coins and a small bunch of keys. I recognised one of them as a car key, the others would be for the house. I took the wallet and the keys and shoved them into the pockets of my shorts.

'We have to go back and get the gun,' I said.

We should've brought it with the body. I felt a moment's panic. I hadn't thought about that. Stupid. Now we'd have to go back and get it, make the trip twice. I hadn't been thinking and was furious with myself. David merely nodded, staring blankly at some invisible point in front of him. As I walked past him I brushed his arm and it seemed to bring him back and together we returned to the pond. No words, only our breaths, out of sync and then settling into a single rhythm. Even then I had to think. We had to find the right way to the pond, couldn't waste time taking the wrong route. It was me who would have to do it right, I couldn't get us lost, I couldn't mess things up. Morning was still a few hours away, but there was a lot to do. We needed the dark.

A gap in the trees ahead and I saw the moon flash on the surface of the pond. My pace quickened to a jog and once I'd got the gun, I went to the hide. The fire had almost died, but I stamped on the few hot embers and picked up our rucksacks.

When I got back outside David was standing at the edge of the pond where it had happened, his arms crossed over his chest as though holding himself, staring at the water.

'David?'

'I was thinking about the houses, the Stone Age people.'

I touched his arm and he looked at me, startled, as though he hadn't expected it to be me standing there. 'Come on.'

'Do you think, do you—'

'They left,' I said. 'Like you said.'

We walked back to the body, quickly now, picking our way through the undergrowth, stumbling on the tracks we'd already made and then finding the island of bracken. As we got closer, David hung back.

I wiped the gun on my T-shirt and pressed it into the body's right hand, cold sausage fingers. I kept looking at the hand, the hand and the gun, because I didn't want to see the head. When it was done I stood up and made my way back through the bracken.

Around us the forest drank in deep breaths from the night. At the pond we washed in silence. I looked at my hands under the water, tiny pink pricks where brambles had bitten.

We would have to say that his dad had run off. He'd left David before. People disappeared, never came back. As long as they never found him we would be safe. And it was a good place. I'd chosen a good place.

We walked on through the forest to the road. It was closer than I imagined it to be and as I took the first few steps onto tarmac, my heart thudded. Apart from the 4x4, the road was the first sign of life, of other people. We stood staring at Mr Cauldwell's car. He'd parked on the verge. No other cars. A quiet road and at this time of night, I told myself, no one could've seen it. What if they had? Perhaps they'd think it belonged to a fisherman, or been abandoned like the 4x4. It was run down enough, rusted, one panel a different colour from the others, almost looked as bad as the cars we'd seen at the yard.

'You'll have to drive,' I said. 'Can you?'

David didn't answer, just moved towards the driver's door and got in. I went round to the other side and slid into the passenger seat. The interior smelt of his dad, his cigarettes and aftershave, oil from his work clothes. I looked at the back seat, a jacket and a base-ball cap. I handed them to David and told him to put them on.

Soon we were moving along the road, David leaning forward in the seat. He did everything smoothly, did it well. I imagined it was what he must've looked like when his dad had taught him, eyes narrowed, determined to do it right.

After a while we reached the village. A few street lamps, but no one moving about. I decided we shouldn't pull up outside the cottages and risk waking Mum or Olly so we left the car in North Beach car park and walked home.

We let ourselves in through the utility-room door of David's cottage, but once we were in the kitchen I was lost for what to do next. David rested on the edge of the table. I pulled out a chair and sat in front of him. A tap dripped onto a plate, tap–tapping. I closed my eyes, saw the second before Mr Cauldwell fell onto his face, that surprise. When I opened my eyes again I saw a crumpled beer can.

'You'll have to drive to Middlesbrough,' I said.

'I'll decorate my room. A different colour on the walls. White, the floor too.'

'You can't stay here, David.'

I couldn't look at him. I stood up and paced the floor, trying to think things through. Back to Middlesbrough. He couldn't stay. I worked through the details, but they got jumbled in my head and I had to start again. There wasn't time. It was getting light. I needed to think.

'You have to drive the car to Middlesbrough. Forget about it all. All right?'

'He'll be all right there, won't he?'

I took a breath. 'Yes. It's a good place. Did you hear what I said?'

His eyes flicked to me.

'He was always taking off, right? That's what happened.'

I would have to believe it. We'd both have to believe that his dad had left, no reason, no explanation, because that's what he did. He was that kind of man. People did that, they went places where no one would find them and got themselves new lives.

'Only this time he doesn't come back. Tell your auntie you were afraid, that when he didn't come home you didn't want to be by yourself.'

284

'I want to stay here.'

'You can't.'

'Where will you be?'

'We don't have time to talk about it. We have to do this now.'

I thought of the body under the moon, the blood spreading out over the leaves of the bracken.

'Have you got some money?'

The question made no sense to him.

'David. Look at me. Do you have money?'

'No.'

I took the money I had saved for the bike out of my rucksack and closed his fists around the notes. My mouth was dry, tongue rough.

'You can't come back,' I said. 'No matter what happens. You can't come back here.'

I gave him the car keys.

'You can never talk about it either. He just left one night and you don't know where he went. He left you.'

'Leo?'

'Nobody will blame you for taking the car because you can say you were frightened about being on your own.'

'I'll write.'

I blinked. 'You have to forget you even knew me.'

And I would have to forget him. I put his rucksack on his lap, shoved it against his chest when he didn't move. 'Come on.'

We walked back to the car in silence. When we reached it he hesitated, turning to look at me in the pale light. 'I'm scared.'

'I know.'

He put his arms around my neck and drew me into an embrace, but before I could hold him back he'd pulled away and got in the car. There were things I wanted to say, but I couldn't think what they were. He looked at me through the window, then faced forward and slowly moved off. And I stood, the first layers of dawn strengthening, growing, second by second, and watched him leave.

23

David and I had slipped into a strange existence, eating breakfast in cafés in the middle of the afternoon, drinking, sometimes all night. I made half-hearted attempts to attend lectures, but knew, really, it was over. My tutor had rung, leaving a message on the answer machine asking me to go in for a chat. When had that been? Two days ago? Longer? All I remembered was David playing it back, a spliff dangling from the corner of his mouth he imitated the lecturer's voice, laughing. Something had broken, a lamp, I couldn't remember. Just the laughing, at that, or something else, hysterical and then tears.

Now, late morning, I looked out of my bedroom window at the wood below. The sun had barely risen and as I stood the dull grey cloud released the first flakes of snow, so soft and slow they seemed suspended. I tried to follow one as it spiralled through the branches, but lost it in the haze of all the others.

David had gone out early and once or twice while I'd been lying in bed I thought I'd heard him return. It'd got like that more these last few days, I would be sure I'd heard him when he wasn't in the flat, the sound of him moving around, or sometimes not even that, a silence that felt as though I was walking into a room he'd just left.

When finally I heard the door it was accompanied by his voice, calling. I shuffled into my slippers and went through to the living room. He was shaking off the snow from his scarf, but it still clung to his hair and eyelashes.

'You look like shit,' he said.

He looked different, something about the way he moved. Sharper, more together. 'We need to talk.'

'What about?'

He rested on the edge of the armchair, the ends of his scarf knotted around his fists.

I felt a chill run through me. 'They know who it is, don't they?'

'Yes.' He waited for me to sit down. 'My aunt rang my mobile. The police have been in touch with her.'

'I don't understand.'

'Dad had put her down as next of kin. They want her to go to Seaton, but I said I'd go.'

Instinctively I wanted a drink, but felt unable to move from where I sat. It felt as though I'd practised this moment a thousand times, all the nights I'd lain on my back in bed and stared into the darkness, imagining how it would be when, finally, the waiting was over. But the waiting hadn't prepared me for the fear.

'When?' I asked.

'Tomorrow.'

I looked at him. His face was expressionless. He got up and I expected him to get a drink, but he merely hung his coat up and then sat down again, rubbing his hands.

'There's some wine left,' I said.

'No. I need a clear head.'

He seemed, if anything, calm. I wasn't sure how to take it. He'd never refused a drink before. Perhaps the drinking had been his way of dealing with the waiting and it was easier for him now things had come to a head. I wondered whether everything about his life since Seaton had been preparing him for this, but it couldn't be that simple.

'How do they know it's—'

'The gun. He had a licence. Once they had a name they went to his medical records. That's how they got my aunt's address.'

I'd always thought he'd kept the gun illegally. Ridiculous it hadn't occurred to me he might have had a licence, but then, as time passed, the way I'd thought about the gun had changed. It had become less important, though I didn't understand why.

I pressed my fingers into my eyes and then pulled them down over my face. 'What else did they tell you? Exactly.'

'Nothing.'

'They must've said something.'

'Just broke the news. It was Aunt Jackie they talked to.'

A film of sweat had gathered on my top lip. I wiped it away and moved over to the bookcase where there were photographs of Kathryn, Mum and Olly. I stared at the photograph of Kathryn and me in Ibiza. I'd spoke to her only once, late at night, drunk, couldn't remember what I'd said. I turned away and sat down beside David.

'I've got to go,' he said. 'But they've got no reason to link you with Dad's death.' For a few seconds our hands were inches apart, his knuckles white from where he still held the scarf. 'I'm not asking—'

'We're in it together.' I tried a laugh. 'Do you know, I'm almost relieved?'

He seemed to change then, casting the scarf over the back of the chair and fishing out a rollie from his cigarette tin. He tore off the sprouting tobacco from the end and chucked it into the fireplace before running his tongue lightly around the filter. 'Sooner it's over the better.'

'Yes.'

'I thought we could drive up tonight.' He looked at me through the smoke. 'Spend the night in Seaton before . . .'

He trailed off, but I understood. I wanted to go back too, now more than ever. I'd always known we'd return together. Or I could stay where I was. In theory, it was a possibility not to go at all. David was right; unless he told them they'd have no reason to connect his father's death with me. It'd occurred to David too, he'd had to acknowledge it.

I watched him roll the ember of his cigarette against the side of the ashtray.

'What was it like for you?' I said. 'Afterwards, I mean.'

He shrugged. 'The first few days were a bit of a blur. I remember the drive to Middlesbrough very well. Funny, I was sharp as anything, head buzzing, you know?'

'You must've looked pretty messed up.'

'Three cracked ribs.'

'What did your aunt say about that?'

'Told her I'd got into a fight on the estate where me and Dad had been staying. She didn't know any better, didn't even know where we'd been living.' He closed his eyes, bringing his cigarette up to his mouth to take a long drag. 'She wasn't daft, reckon she knew it was my dad. Took me ages to work out why she never said anything, but I figured she was just glad to see the back of him.'

My thinking was getting clearer all the time. I was reminded of something Mum said after Nan went into hospital. She'd been sitting at the kitchen table, tearing a paper towel she'd used as a hanky into tiny pieces. *Each of us lives one step away from total clarity.* I'd been drifting, now I wasn't.

'What about you?' he asked.

I rested my head against the back of the sofa and tried to put order into the those first few days. They'd been nothing like David's.

'Things just kind of settled, without me doing anything. I kept thinking I'd have to say something, explain where you were, where he was, but I didn't have to. People, Mum, they made up their minds, some rent was owed, they reckoned you and Dad had done a runner. It didn't take a lot and nobody looked at me for the answer. Maybe because I was just a kid, I don't know.'

'God.'

'It wasn't all like that,' I added. 'The landlord found your dad's bank cards and stuff, passport. I heard him telling Mum about it, but I went round and got them, got rid of them. He kicked off when he went back, said someone had stolen them, but nobody could prove anything. Garrison was old, I reckon Mum thought he'd imagined seeing them.'

'Lucky.'

'Was it?' I stared at him, suddenly impatient. 'There were plenty of times I wanted to be the one that left. Not to have to stay there—'

'Right, Leo, because I had it easy. Easy living with Auntie Jackie and her fuckwit of a boyfriend, then on me own, roughing it, sleeping on floors—'

'Sorry. Did you move in with the prostitute?'

He looked surprised.

'You told me about her. The stickers on the ceiling that lit up in the dark?'

'Fucking hell, you've got some memory.'

I shrugged.

'Yeah, she was cool. Stayed there a while, just till I could get in the army.'

I swallowed. It was the first time we'd really talked about the years in between, but though we'd barely touched on it, I suddenly felt unable to go on. There was *what* had happened to each of us in the days, months and years following, but there was more to it than that. That night had changed us and I'd thought I needed to understand how, that by talking to him, somehow I'd have a better grasp on things, but we could spend the rest of the night talking and be no closer to making sense of it.

Perhaps it was as simple as the two of us being chained together. We were both aware of how one could fuck things up for the other. I needed to be free of it. I saw that now, and freeing myself of the past would be the only way to free myself of David.

24

We'd barely got five miles up the A1 when the snow changed to sleet, long rods that shone in the headlights. At times it got so heavy I struggled to see the road ahead and drove crouched over the wheel. Seconds of blindness from the spray off a lorry obscured the windscreen. Once David offered to take over the driving, but I refused. I was glad to have something to concentrate on.

By the time we arrived in Seaton the sleet had hardened to hail, small, white beads that hopped like fleas across the tarmac. The shower lasted only a few minutes though, softening again to sleet as I pulled up in North Beach car park. I switched off the engine. The tide was out, revealing a mile or more of hard, dark sand, but it had begun to turn and tongues of water, roughened by the wind, reached out towards the land.

The golf course was much the same, the clubhouse still there, though less grand than I remembered and still with the same oversized flag hanging limply on its mast. But what else remained? Of this place? Of that time? Certain things I knew. I remembered everything about that summer, even how I'd felt about it, but I couldn't remember how I'd explained them to myself. Alice and those dolls. What was that about? And David.

David who'd run away from home, but told his father where he was going, who'd taken the Glock, his father's most prized possession. He'd wanted to be found. I realised I'd never understood or even tried to understand how the events of that summer had appeared to David. Perhaps I hadn't tried to find answers at the time because I was a child and a child doesn't need that kind of explanation.

We set off in the direction of the tideline. The sea was rough, murky where it warred with the sand on the beach. A chip carton cantered past me and was swallowed by the mouth of a wave. I watched the foam spread out to my feet, a seething uneasy arc repeated all along the beach.

'I thought coming back would feel different,' David said.

'How?'

'I only remember being happy here.'

It oughtn't to have been true and yet I could see he meant it. I shivered, turning away from him to look back at the village. To the west were the farmer's fields where we'd once walked. Beyond them, a dark ridge on the horizon, swept by drifting columns of sleet, was Harwood Forest.

David thrust his hands deep into his pockets. 'We should think of finding somewhere to stay.'

After driving around for twenty minutes we settled on the Wheatsheaf, a small pub on the outskirts of Seaton. At least we'd be able to get a meal and a drink without having to go back out.

A group of locals, sitting by a burning fire, turned to look at us as we walked in. The landlady, a stout blonde with large breasts cradled in a cream silk blouse, had been talking to them, but when she saw us she walked over, smiling broadly.

'I've only got a twin,' she said. 'Nice room though, sea view.'

We followed her up a steep, narrow staircase in a cloud of her heavy scent. By the time we'd reached the top she was gasping, hardly able to get the words out. 'Just one night?'

'Yes.'

'Uh-huh. This one at the front's pretty quiet. You won't be bothered.'

She looked to David, then back to me, before unlocking the door to the room and showing us inside. I felt a flush of heat burn under my collar.

Two single beds, barely a space to stand up between them. Tea rings on the bedside tables and candlewick bedspreads right out of the seventies. David edged past the landlady, swung his bag onto the bed nearest

the window and gave the mattress a firm squeeze
with the knuckles of his hands.

'Good bed.'

The landlady looked at me, one eyebrow raised,
and handed me the key. 'Breakfast's seven till nine.'

'Thanks.' I waited until I heard her footsteps on
the staircase. 'That was a bit much.'

'She'll have seen it all, even in Seaton.'

'I doubt it.'

I put my holdall on the other bed. At least it would
be cheaper than two separate rooms. I checked the
bathroom, no bath, just a shower and a pink curtain
fringed with mould.

David stood by the window, flicking ash from a
cigarette out of a small gap. The smell of briny sea
air and smoke was so redolent of the past it made
me feel sick. I'd expected coming back to be overwhelming, but it wasn't the place, it was David in
the place. There were things I needed to say, but for
a long time we were silent, stepping around each
other in the room, unpacking the few things we'd
brought with us.

'Want to get a pint?' David said.

'Yeah, but first . . . What's the plan?'

He went to the door. 'I wasn't aware we needed
one.'

I'd tried to talk to him about it earlier, but he'd
shied away from it. 'They're bound to have questions.'

'No point guessing what they'll be.' He turned
back to the door. 'I'll get you one in.'

'David? We can't talk downstairs.'

'What's there to talk about? You're thinking too much.'

'So we just walk in? No story?'

'Got any better ideas?'

'We could tell them the truth.'

He laughed. 'A bit late for that, don't you think?'

'We were kids. You know, that's the thing that really fucks me off. If we'd have gone to the police then they might've seen it as self-defence.'

'But we didn't and we're not kids now.'

I paced up and down, but there was no room to move and I felt dizzy. 'Well . . . I'll do what I have to do.'

'The fuck you will. You think I'll let you blow the lid on everything just because you've lost your bollocks?'

I steadied myself on the chest of drawers. 'All that's over, David. You don't tell me what to do any more.'

'Fuck off, Leo. You're all confessions and bullshit. We wouldn't even be here if it wasn't for some bloody keep-fit doctor taking his dog for a walk.'

'We have to face up to what we did.' I added, almost to myself, 'I do.'

'Because it's all about you, isn't it? Do the right thing?' He snorted. 'You think you're going to get a round of applause for taking it on the chin?'

'I wouldn't be doing it for anyone else.'

'You're not doing it at all.' I could feel him behind me, close enough to hear his breath. 'I was there, too.

Remember? Look, they haven't even asked to see you. I could go on my own.'

'No.'

'You think you'll get your life back? It's never going to be like that.'

'You didn't do it though. I did.'

'No, I just let my father rot in the woods.'

Silence.

'You buckle, you implicate both of us,' he said.

'I'll say you weren't there.'

'Sure, you just woke up one morning and decided to kill me dad, did you?' He threw his hands up. 'This is shite. Nobody believes it's murder.'

'Just ask around the bar, David. There won't be a person there who doesn't think—'

'Of course! They want to believe something exciting happened in their shitty little town. Not that some poor sod couldn't hack it and blew his brains out.'

'You talk like you actually believe it was suicide.'

'I have to.'

'But it's not what happened. I shot him and *you* told me to do it.'

He shook his head in disbelief.

'You know you did.'

He stared at me. 'I said, "Do it."' He was telling you to give him the gun.'

'Don't you fucking dare!' I jabbed him in the chest. 'You know what you meant.'

'I meant give him the gun. Oh, fuck, Leo, what does it matter what anybody meant. He's dead.'

'It *matters*.'

'The point is nobody saw anything. You don't have to throw your life away.'

'What life?'

He walked to his bed and searched for his cigarettes. 'Look, he killed himself. That's it, that's all there is. Happens all the time.'

'But it didn't happen to him.'

'You don't remember things exactly as they were. Nobody does.' He lay back against the pillows, lit a cigarette and placed his free hand behind his head. 'You add things, take others away.'

'Not about that.'

'Really? Are you sure?'

I closed my eyes. For a long time he didn't say anything else, then he got up and walked to the window, putting his arms out to the frame. 'Let it go, Leo.'

'I can't.'

I sat on the chair beside the door. Seeing me rub my eyes he came over, one hand outstretched to my shoulder, but I shrank from him.

'It's all right,' he said.

In the tiny space he seemed huge though; in part, that was what had drawn me to him all those years ago. I remembered now how I'd felt on those nights in Seaton, before I knew him, when I'd gone out to the headland after dark and stared at the sky above the sea. The blackness had gone on forever and I'd been filled with excitement, the future rich with possibilities.

'I need to be free of it,' I said. 'Of you.'

He flinched, but didn't look at me, then he said: 'If you tell them everything now, you'll never be free. There'll be a trial, Leo. For Christ's sake, it'd go on for months and then . . .' He trailed off. 'Look, rest for a bit. We're going round in circles anyway.'

He wriggled down on his bed, turning away from me and pulling the pillow under his chin. After a minute or two I lay back on my own bed, knew there was no way I'd sleep, yet moments later I felt myself drifting off.

I dreamt I was running. Somewhere I knew, though I couldn't put a name to it, some area of the beach that seemed to repeat itself like a film looped over. Salt stung my eyes and the sound of crashing waves filled my head. Then, suddenly, I wasn't running any more. David was there, high up on the roof of the pillbox, his face a blur, but I got the smell of him, the sun and sea on his skin and underneath, fainter, the smell of his sweat that both excited and repelled me.

Forward then. Or back. We were naked, facing each other on the sand. I could hear my breaths, shallow, deeper as I reached out to touch the circle of hair around his nipple. I was opening my arms, delighted by the weight of his body against mine. I stroked the furrow of muscle down his back.

Then, a laugh, though in my dream David's face held the same expression, not laughing. I opened my eyes, blinked. David was staring back. The room. Potpourri. Cigarette smoke on his breath.

'What are you *doing*?'

'What you want.'

I shoved him hard in the chest, trampling back the bed sheets to get up. I staggered to my feet, feeling sick, looking for the door.

'Leo?' He'd moved over to my bed and now lay, head up on one hand. 'Shit, Leo, it's what you want.'

'Haven't you had enough of me already?'

'Leo—'

'I will tell them the truth,' I stuttered, trying to get the words out, but I'd no breath left. 'I don't care any more.'

I didn't give him a chance to reply. I was desperate to be out of there. Anywhere. I slammed the door behind me and ran down the staircase, pushing my way past a couple in the hall. Outside the cold night wind hit me squarely in the chest, but I kept going, breaking into a jog as I moved through the village and reached the green. I heard David's laugh echoing in my mind, saw Alice by a tree, naked dolls spread in a circle around her.

Finally, heaving breaths, I stopped at the road that led down to the harbour. Ahead of me, nothing. Nothing but sea and wind and darkness.

25

The night moved over me slowly. I lay still, eyes fixed on the ceiling. Gradually, light began to push through the curtains and shapes of furniture emerged. I couldn't tell whether David had managed to get off, but when I pulled back the duvet and stood up he rolled over to face me.

'I didn't hear you come back in,' he said.

'It was late.'

I went to the bathroom and splashed my face with water. My reflection was startling, sunken eyes, two-day-old stubble. The strain had fed on me, eating away invisibly, but now it was there for everyone to see. Last night I'd had the conviction I wanted to tell the truth. But why? Because it would free me of the past in a way nothing else could? Or because I believed it would free me of David?

Though what he'd said last night had struck me. A trial would tie us together for months to come. I didn't want that. I couldn't even stand being in the room with him now. Several times as I lain awake I'd thought of ringing Mum, or Olly, but I was afraid of what they might hear in my voice. Whatever I did now would impact on them.

And then there was David.

Part of me wanted revenge for what he'd done to my life. If I'd never met him none of it would've happened, but, most of all, I resented him for denying his part. By saying he'd told me to give the gun to his father, he'd acquitted himself of all responsibility and it just wasn't true.

I shaved and dressed in the bathroom, every so often having to grip the basin and hold myself still. When I was ready I went outside to wait for David in the car park. A pale winter sun was slowly burning off the mist, but a large section of the hawthorn hedge that separated the grounds from the neighbouring field was still in shade, a heavy frost whitening its branches.

When David eventually appeared at my side, he looked different, a flicker of nerves perhaps, but immediately it vanished. We didn't have to be at the police station for another hour, but with nothing else to do and neither of us wanting breakfast, we got in the car and set off.

After a few miles David asked me to pull over at

the side of the road. I carried on to a lay-by and parked. For a moment he was silent, then turned to face me. 'I need to know what you intend to do.'

'I don't know.'

'That's not good enough.'

'I'm sorry, I really don't know.'

'You're going to land me in the shit, that it?'

'No.'

'Then what?'

When I didn't answer he laughed. 'God, you've really made a good job of fucking up my life.'

'*Your* life?' I shook my head. 'It's easier for you.'

'Because I didn't pull the trigger? I wouldn't be making such a fucking drama out of it if I had. What do you want, Leo? Confessing won't change a thing.'

'It'll change everything.' I turned away to watch the passing cars.

'At least wait until you've heard what they've got to say. Listen to them, Leo, for Christ's sake.' He took a breath. 'Can't you do that?'

I didn't answer.

'We don't even know what they think.'

I thought. 'All right.'

'And let me do the talking. They'll expect that. He was my dad after all.'

We continued along the road, arriving early as I expected we would, but it took ages to park. For once I was glad of the problem. We might've talked, smoothed over what he'd say, but he was silent and I no longer wanted to press him. Whatever happened now I was resigned.

The police station was a small building set back from the main road. David led the way inside, pushing through the double doors at the entrance. At the main desk there was a stocky, bearded policeman turning over the pages of a logbook.

'Can I help you?'

'David Cauldwell. I've got an appointment with DI Harbridge.'

He wrote David's name on a notepad and nodded at me.

'This is a friend. Leo Fisch.'

'Wait here.'

I circled the waiting room. On the floor there was a large red stain which I immediately took for blood, but then I realised it was paint. I sat and stared at it. A few minutes later a door opened and a short, balding man appeared. Harbridge, I assumed. He wore brown trousers and a beige shirt, the buttons pulling over his paunch.

He shook hands, first with David, then with me. 'If you'd like to come this way.'

His face was difficult to read, but the handshake had been reassuring. He used a card to open the door to the rest of the station and then led us into a small room halfway up the main corridor. Once we were inside he gestured for us to sit down.

The only window in the room was barred. Otherwise, it looked nothing like the interview rooms I'd seen on television. A cactus sat on the windowsill, its thick, green leaves flabby from overwatering. Three easy chairs were positioned around a small coffee table.

I sat down, sweating under my clothes. David was on my right. Harbridge opposite. He offered us tea and I was about to refuse, but David agreed.

'Yes. All right,' I said. 'Thank you.'

He nodded at someone. I turned to see who it was, but the door closed.

'Thank you for coming, Mr Cauldwell.'

'This is Mr Fisch,' David said. 'He's an old family friend. Do you mind if he sits in?'

'Not at all.'

My back was rigid against the chair. I shifted, crossed my legs.

'I'm sorry for your loss,' Harbridge went on. 'As I explained to your aunt on the phone we have now made a formal identification.'

'Yes,' David said.

'We have a few details we'd like to check with you though.' He looked at a folder on his lap. 'I'm afraid we don't have complete remains, despite an exhaustive search.'

'How did you identify him?'

'From the gun. Do you remember your father owning a gun?'

'Yes, of course. He was shot?'

'Forensic examination determined he died as a result of a bullet from his gun, a Glock 9 mm pistol. We believe it was self-inflicted.'

'Suicide?'

'I'm afraid so, yes.'

'I see. You're sure?'

'As near as we can be. We consulted his medical

records; he'd been to his doctor several times complaining of depression and his notes suggested he was a high suicide risk.' He paused, looking up from the folder at David. 'Were you aware of any of this?'

'I was sixteen.' David tried a smile. 'You know what teenagers are like. I think I was too self-centred to have noticed anything much.'

Harbridge leant back in his chair. 'Nobody reported him missing.'

'He'd done it before, was always taking off when I was growing up. For a long time I just thought he'd got a job somewhere else.' A slow nod, eyes fixed on the table. 'He always talked about going on the rigs. After my mother died he . . . struggled.'

His words sounded rehearsed, but then I suppose they'd had to be. He would've had to explain the absence of his father more than once. I couldn't look at him any longer, but I heard him take a breath and then nothing, not another for what seemed like a long time.

'I'm sorry,' Harbridge said. 'This must all be quite a shock.'

I glanced at him then. He'd put his head in his hands, but I couldn't tell if he was crying, or hiding his relief.

'I knew the doctor had given him some pills, but I didn't know what they were for.'

'They were antidepressants,' Harbridge said.

David raised his shoulders, held them for a second. 'He didn't believe in taking a load of stuff.'

'He was referred for counselling too, but there's no

record he ever attended. Is there anyone else you'd like us to contact?'

David shook his head. 'I just can't believe he killed himself. You're *sure* it's suicide?'

'There's nothing to suggest anything else. As I said the medical notes point to him being a high risk. They'll have to be an inquest of course, but then you'll be able to make arrangements for his burial.'

'Thank you, yes.'

'I've dealt with a lot of missing-person cases. Not here, Manchester. As I understand, it helps people to know what happened, even if it's bad news.'

He was getting together his notes as he spoke. He stood up, his chair scraping across the floor. The interview seemed to be over and I hadn't said a word.

We walked to the car and drove in silence back to Seaton, my hands shaking on the wheel. I gripped it tightly to steady them, aware of David staring at my profile. When we reached the coast road he asked me to stop. For a full minute he sat in silence, just breathing, then got out of the car and walked, head down, hands driven deep into his pockets, towards the beach.

I followed. I felt sick. I hadn't said it. I hadn't told them the truth. Perhaps I'd never meant to.

'Did you know all that?' I said. 'About him seeing the doctor?'

'I knew about the pills.'

My head stung with adrenalin. 'When you asked him, Harbridge, when you asked him whether it was really suicide, I thought that was it, you were going to tell them. You. Shit.'

A wash of deep blue stretched out along the horizon. David stared up and down the beach, took a breath. 'I need a drink.'

We found a pub and sank the first couple of pints quickly. David sat quietly for a long time, huddled over the fire, spreading out his hands over the blaze. He kept rubbing them, a dry papery sound. I remembered thinking it was exactly the same sound the wind made blowing through a reed bed.

The place was almost empty. A bored-looking teenager stood behind the bar, drying glasses while he watched football on the big screen.

Again and again we'd gone over the sparse details of the interview until we'd worn it threadbare. Then David had lapsed into silence, drinking steadily, drinking to get drunk. Towards early evening the pub started to fill up, and finding the noise and laughter intolerable, I took us outside. I bought a bottle of Jack Daniel's from the local Spar and we sat in the car overlooking the bay.

He sat, feet up on the dashboard, a cigarette dangling from his fingers and the ash growing long. We'd been in the bar longer than I thought and it was dark now. A sharp winter wind shivered through the marram and the moon was high and small, apologetic.

It wasn't supposed to be like this. We'd got away with it. I'd got away with it. Part of me wanted to go back and tell them they were wrong, but, I realised, only a small part. I had my life back, changed, unchanged. I cracked down the window and the sound of the waves came in, insistent, indifferent.

'We didn't even need to convince them,' I said. 'They didn't suspect a thing.'

'No.'

'That's wrong. It's . . .'

'Done.'

He'd been scared. In the police station I'd noticed a sheen of sweat across his forehead and I'd felt satisfied when I'd seen it, but now I was ashamed. The Jack Daniel's lay heavily over the gassy lager. I managed to open the door and stagger towards the pillbox. One hand resting on its outer wall, I vomited.

I heard David behind me. 'Are you all right?'

'Fine.'

He touched my shoulder. I was shivering.

'Come back to the car.'

'No, I might be sick again.'

We started to walk along the beach, up and down. After a few minutes I stopped and tossed my head back to take a deep breath.

'Any better?' David asked.

'Why did you tell him where we were going to be?'

He looked puzzled.

'Your father.'

He kicked the sand with the heel of his boot. 'He was me dad, for fuck's sake. I wanted to know he cared. And he did care.'

'Cared enough to kick your head in.'

'He cared. He wouldn't have been as angry as that if he hadn't.'

I had to keep pressing him. I needed him to make the right response. 'You didn't think that at the time, David. He'd have killed you, if I hadn't—'

'No, he wouldn't.'

'Yes, but you didn't think that at the time or you wouldn't have told me to do it.'

'We've been through this once already.' He sighed. 'I've told you. I meant give him the gun.'

'You can't say that.'

'Can't I? It's the truth.'

I broke away from him and walked ahead. Could he have meant that? There was no way of knowing the truth of it. In the end that was the tie that bound us together. He would always say that he meant the gun, and I would always think he'd asked me to save him.

I went inside the pillbox. Someone had smashed a bottle close to the entrance and my feet crunched over the broken glass. The moonlight was bright enough to read the graffiti, might've been the same graffiti, I thought, kids don't change. I walked further in. I had to crouch now, where once I'd stood erect. Behind me I heard David. He ducked his head and came inside.

'What do you want me to say, Leo?'

The wind whistled around the walls, sealing us in. I turned to face him, putting a hand up to his face. His breath was warm against my palm. Tentatively, I started to kiss him, but he didn't respond and I pulled back angrily, almost losing my balance. He grabbed both my arms and thrust himself against me. A spasm of rage he'd taken control again, hemming me in. Viciously, I took hold of his belt and spun him round to face the wall. A blurting noise escaped his mouth as air pushed out of his chest, but mixed in with that I heard laughter. I saw the glint of one eye, turned on me.

'Come on then,' he said.

He unfastened his belt and I pulled his jeans down over his arse. I freed my cock, not bothering to make things easier for him, and thrust it into him. His arse was tight and dry. David spat into the palm of his hand and reached behind him, smoothing spit over the crown. The feel of his cold fingers and warm spit was so incredible that for a second I thought I'd come into his hand, but then he let go of me and braced himself against the wall.

I drove into him, felt the slick of spit slide in around the sides of his arsehole. He moaned, an alarming sound in the small, hollow space. I clenched my teeth, wanting to hurt him, but with each thrust the tight ring of skin slackened. I looked down, mesmerised by the sight of my cock sawing in and out, my belt and buckle flapping against his soft, white cheeks. His hand came round again and squeezed mine and I began to move faster, bucking and thrusting until finally, with a wrenching cry, I came.

A salty tear ran into the corner of my mouth. I pushed him gently away, zipped myself up and went outside to sit on one of the tank traps. The cold damp of the concrete seeped through to my legs. Behind me I could hear David, the broken grass creaking under his feet. He perched on one of the tank traps further up and lit a cigarette, sparks snatched up by the breeze. Ahead of us, waves creamed over on the beach. I was spent, felt nothing.

He cleared his throat. 'I loved him, you know.'

'Who?'

'My dad.'

'I know.' All these years it had suited me not to know it, yet of course it was true. 'And I killed him.'

I waited, but when he didn't reply I closed my eyes, seeing us lying on the beach as boys, getting up and walking away, the imprint of our bodies left behind in the damp sand. His, sharp and clear, the shape of him, mine, fading. Nothing. No sign I'd been there at all.

'What will you do now?' he said, after a long pause.

'Go home. Pack in my degree, I expect. Dunno.'

'Kathryn?'

I circled the spit in my mouth, a bitter taste of vomit and whisky. 'She doesn't know who I am.'

A sound that might've been a laugh. 'Well, that makes two of you.'

Our eyes met. It was true, of course. Had been true.

David pushed himself off the tank trap and flicked away his cigarette. The moon came out from behind a cloud, sending ripples of silver light up and down the stalks of the marram grass. I shivered. It was so beautiful it took my breath away, but it was cold and time to move on. I stood up and followed David back to the car.